Pawpaw
Patch

Pawpaw Patch

A NOVEL

Janice Daugharty

HarperPerennial
A *Division* of HarperCollins*Publishers*

A hardcover edition of this book was published in 1996 by HarperCollins Publishers.

HarperCollins books may be purchased for educational, business, or sales promotional use. For information please write: Special Markets Department, HarperCollins Publishers, Inc., 10 East 53rd Street, New York, NY 10022.

First HarperPerennial edition published 1997.

The Library of Congress has catalogued the hardcover edition as follows:

Daugharty, Janice
    Pawpaw patch : a novel / Janice Daugharty.
      p. cm.
    1. City and town life—Georgia—Fiction. 2. Women in business—Georgia—Fiction. 3. Beauty operators—Georgia—Fiction. 4. Creoles—Georgia—Fiction. 5. Racism—Georgia—Fiction. I. Title.
    PS3554.A844P38 1996
    813' .54—dc20   95-53305

ISBN 0-06-092798-4 (pbk.)

97 98 99 00 01 ❖/RRD 10 9 8 7 6 5 4 3 2 1

My love to Larry Ashmead for loving this book

Confusion now hath made his masterpiece!

SHAKESPEARE

Acknowledgments

Thanks to Jayne Anne Phillips, Jason Kaufman, and Sue Combs for their inspiration. Also to my children, Laura, Bill, Angie, Mike, Frank, and Stacey; and my grandchildren, Polly, Betsy, and Laney. And of course, Seward.

part

one

chapter one

Chanell had just one thing in mind when she hitched a ride to Atlanta with that fool Archie Wall: getting out of Cornerville for a day. Maybe have him drop her by Lenox Square Mall while he went on to the capitol to take care of his law business. She'd eat at that French place her ex-sister-in-law, Bell, was always talking about.

Chanell shoved a tape in the VCR and toggled the timer to twelve o'clock, so she wouldn't miss *The Young and the Restless*. Fridays, the soaps always hooked you, to keep you coming back on Monday. Some woman might find out her husband is going with her best friend or that her poor mama had left her, a bundle on her rich mama's doorsteps. All beautiful, brave, and famished women, the way Chanell's overfed customers would like to look, and one reason Chanell had moved the slender portable from the house to the front-porch beauty shop. From twelve till three, weekdays, Chanell's customers would pin their eyes on the TV screen, placed catercorner on the counter next to the shampoo bowl, rather than peer into the gilt-framed mirror above the driers on the adjacent wall. When Chanell was done, when they turned, they would behold themselves in the likenesses of their idols. Also, they had quit clotting into the beauty shop later in the evenings. Also, Chanell loved to gab with them about the soaps while the stories droned to the tune of hissing hairspray and gusting driers.

Still, in the evenings, they thronged to Chanell's house, to drink iced tea with Chanell, to laugh with Chanell—nobody could make them laugh like Chanell, nobody kept up with the latest like Chanell—sassy, independent, and voluptuous, what her ex and his buddies called "stacked."

Yesterday, she'd turned forty, and last night some of her customers had surprised her with a birthday party—a regular blowout—complete with cake and bouquets of balloons and the kind of party hats kids wear. When her divorce from T.P. had been made official, last March, they'd thrown a party then too, with blown-up condoms. Now, she felt guilty for not telling them she was going to Atlanta with Archie Wall. One thing she'd learned as a small-town beautician: her customers expected her to be open about everything she did, minor or major. She didn't know why she hadn't told them, only that she'd like to do something private and daring before she died, and going to Atlanta was about as private and daring as she dared.

She leaned in to the mirror to check her eyes, shadowed to bring out the brown. Lots of women were having their lids tattooed, but Chanell didn't need to, and her customers were always saying how lucky she was. Well, pretty faded the same as ugly, she'd decided, but she still had a few years left. Really, she was always amazed at how swarthy the face in the mirror appeared, compared to the tawny high-school face pictured in her mind. Still, she looked more thirty-five than forty with the light at her back. Of course, black hair was bad to show up gray, but if she dyed it, the black would turn burnt burgundy or soot. If she could come up with the right formula for a natural-looking black tint, she'd be set for life. She was working on it.

On her way out, she shut the shop door, and she hadn't stepped off the concrete stoop before one of her neighbors popped around the corner of the cream stucco bungalow.

"Hey, Miss Neida," Chanell said. "How you doing this morning?" She shouldered the strap of her stuffed bag and stepped away to let the old lady know she was leaving.

"You going somewhere?" Cradling a boxed Toni and a bundle of roasting ears, Miss Neida tripped suspiciously around the spat red plastic of popped balloons. All fat appeared to have settled in her spool-shaped body. Her arms and legs were pegs.

And then Chanell remembered she'd promised to perm her next-door neighbor's hair that morning. "Miss Neida, I'm sorry. I plumb forgot," Chanell said. "I'm going to Atlanta today."

"Etlanna?" said Miss Neida.

"Yes 'um." Now the news was out.

The mossy-haired old lady stood waiting for Chanell to explain about the trip, and probably about all the hoopla last night. Then she placed the bundle of corn on the edge of the stoop and rambled sullenly across the knitted grass boundary of her own yard, toward her house: the ancient two-story brick jail jutting from the bluff of Troublesome Creek, where bullous vines snaked from the sweetgums toward the carved-out yard.

"I'll catch you tomorrow then," Miss Neida called.

"Miss Neida," Chanell said, "I'll for sure put in that Toni first thing in the morning." Miss Neida always paid Chanell in whatever was up in the garden. Chanell hated corn, and as a matter of fact considered ketchup the closest thing to her favorite vegetable.

Miss Neida flapped one hand at her side, hanging her head to show she was hurt. "Go on," she said. "I don't want to be no bother."

Hoeing in the vegetable garden behind the renovated jail, Miss Neida's husband Jim stopped and squinted at Chanell. He wore blue denim overalls without a shirt, his mounded white shoulders pinking the shade of the faded flannel he would slip on when fall came. He stood straight and tall, with a quick rise from chest to crotch, like an elephant's belly.

Chanell's peacock, George, strutted behind the old man, iridescent blue and green tail feathers sweeping the corn rows like the tulle train of a wedding gown.

"How you, this morning, Mr. Jim?" Chanell said, and set out walking before he could answer. "If George goes to scratching in your garden," she said, "just run him home."

Good neighbors, though a bit nosy, who by rights could complain about the turnstile tumult of Chanell's cottage and the screeching wails of her peacock, both puncturing the peace of the gravel loop set back from the main crossing in Cornerville.

On *Knots Landing* such a drive-around would be called a cul de sac, but in Cornerville the houses were plain frame, most built in the fifties, with nothing to set them off. Except for Chanell's, Miss Neida's, and Miss Pansy's. Chanell's off-white stucco cottage was dwarfed by overgrown azaleas and reaching magnolias and Miss Neida's columnar, Spanish-style jail; Miss Pansy's winged white house, set in the center of the crescent like a decorated cake, was all angles and gables, with a wonderland widow's walk elled along the south side, to the front, facing Chanell's house. A field of magenta phlox electrified the lot between Chanell's place and the post office, on one corner, and the Baptist Church, on the other, fronting Highway 94.

Chanell started across the highway, toward Archie Wall's high-floored white house, but had to wait for a Walmart semi jerking eastward from the sole traffic light in Cornerville, gears shifting and engine scolding, on the long, straight stretch to the start of the Okefenokee.

Archie Wall's primer-gray pickup was parked in the dirt drive between his house and his one-room brick bank, spot-shaded by an island of great marching liveoaks given generous leeway when the road around the courtyard had been paved. On the splintering veneer door of the bank a cardboard sign read OPEN EVERY OTHER DAY, which meant if you weren't a regular customer you had no way of knowing that every other day meant Tuesdays, Thursdays, and Saturdays, and that Archie Wall was teller, loan officer, and president of the bank that served little purpose save making change. He also owned the brittle-gray, two-story hotel, on the other side of the bank. The only stack-floored building in Swanoochee County—other than Miss Neida's jailhouse—also giving way to time, to too few people and the federal government's small-town reconstruction with red brick in the seventies. Archie Wall's row of property was sandwiched between blocks of frame houses and the backside of the courthouse square with its newish, one-cell jail.

Chanell watched him step through the front door to the long, empty porch with a manila folder of papers under one arm. He turned to lock the door, then tested the rattley knob.

As he started off the porch, he spied her lacing between the oaks out front and stopped on the concrete doorsteps.

"Morning, Archie Wall," she said, swinging her shoulder bag.

"So you're really going, huh?" He looked like a cartoon character drawn from circles, with his round balding head and belly and stubby arms and legs that lent as much girth to his stature as elongation.

"I said I was going." She stopped. "Did you think I wouldn't?"

"I just thought . . ."

"It is all right, ain't it?" she said. "I mean, yesterday when I cut your hair . . ." Chanell kept his feathery gray hair trimmed close around the ears. That's how she had learned he was going to Atlanta, and how she happened to hitch a ride. Yesterday, she'd trimmed his hair for free, him haggling over three dollars, and her hemhawing—"never mind"—till he gave in and said she could go with him to Atlanta in exchange for the haircut. Okay, so she had flirted! But it didn't count: Archie Wall was not her type, and anyway, you never could tell if flirting had any effect on the bachelor lawyer. Flirting won her way with most men, but half the time she still felt as if she'd lost. The way to Archie Wall's heart was through his wallet.

"I just thought you might of changed your mind," he said and started down the doorsteps. "Give me a minute, will you?" He headed along the narrow dirt drive to the back of the peeling white house. "I gotta load up some cucumbers first."

Chanell got in the truck and propped one arm in the window. Eight-thirty in the morning and already hot, the kind of heat that seemed textured of the locusts' hum in the touching oaks. She sat there, waiting, wondering. Had Archie Wall been trying to slip off without her? Was he afraid to be alone with her? Maybe he thought she was making a play for him. Cucumbers! Why cucumbers? Probably he was taking them to some of those Atlanta lawyers. The kind of corny thing he'd do. Everybody said he was so smart he was dumb. Not a dab of common sense. But he would work for free—the only lawyer in Swanoochee County. They all claimed they'd pay him when they could. Never did; or most didn't. They seemed to think of his lawyering as something you couldn't lay hands on, not tangible like land or a new pair of shoes. Not Chanell. She believed in paying back, whether it be money or spite. It had been Archie Wall who'd finally managed to get rid of T.P.; said if T.P. continued to contest the divorce, he'd take him to the Supreme Court in Washington, D.C. T.P., big and bad in Cornerville, believed Archie Wall and didn't cotton to going before a judge as hard to picture as Mr. IRS. When T.P. finally did sign the papers, he drew an Indian teepee under his name. Chanell supposed that meant he was going on the warpath against Archie Wall. But since she'd divorced T.P., he hung around the house more than when they were married. One more reason she was going to Atlanta, to get away from T.P. and his buddies for a day, maybe hook up with some fellow who didn't have a red neck.

Directly, Archie Wall came shuffling along the weed-bound path with his round head bobbing under a warped felt hat. No manila folder under his right arm now, but a hamper basket of cucumbers bumping against his knees. He set the basket in the bed of the truck and opened the driver's door, little feet mincing on the gravel-laced dirt like a donkey's.

"Have one," he said, heaving onto the truck seat and poking her plump thigh with a long green cucumber.

*　　　*　　　*

"Ain't it hot?" Chanell said for something to say, awkward and out of sync since Archie Wall had poked her leg with the cucumber. What did it mean?

"It's hot all right." Archie Wall veered toward the emergency lane for a semi to pass, then drove on slowly up I-75. "Bet you wish you hadn't come."

"No," she said. "I'm fine, just fine."

A string of smart cars pulled in behind the semi and tooled north, sun striking the shiny paint and blazing on the highway. Everything ahead looked dead. Automobiles ghostly gliding across the humped white overpasses, traffic weaving languidly between lanes, billboards glazed with a hot plaster of sun. The heat on the pavement and dried grass shoulders shimmered like gas fumes.

"Macon, Georgia," Chanell read from the sign coming up, "ten miles."

Archie Wall took off his hat, placing it on the seat between them, and raked stiff fingers across his scalp.

Chanell wondered what that meant—was he warming up to make a pass?—then decided he was probably getting set to stop for lunch. "Bet you starving to death. Ain't you, Archie Wall?"

"Not yet." He put his hat on again and screwed it down on his bowl forehead. His face was bland as grits.

"Lord, I am!" She laughed and tilted her head into the hot wind batting through her window.

He seemed not to notice. Sat up, gazing through the windshield, spattered with lovebugs. The back of his blue polyester-blend shirt was wet with sweat, his tight round gut dented from the pressure of the steering wheel.

Alone with Archie Wall, Chanell didn't know what to do, what to say, and felt sure he couldn't help noticing her jouncing breasts, her hips that seemed to take up half the truck. She felt ripe and overblown, not at all her bold self, as though she positively oozed sex. But it was hard for her to stay quiet; Fridays were usually her busiest days at the beauty shop, where she talked with customers, advising them about their troubles.

"Guess you in a big hurry to get to Atlanta, huh?" she said, trying to keep the tone and train of talk used in the shop.

"Anxious to get there and get back," he mumbled.

A blue highway patrol car pulled up on the inside lane; the patrolman's eyes scanned the truck. Archie Wall tipped his hat, held his speed at forty-five, and watched as the patrolman sped away up the interstate.

At a little after one, Chanell felt like she was melting. She was itching all over from the woolly olive blanket spread on the truck seat. She imagined smelling the hairy fibers of the blanket, like cat hair, which tickled her nose and made it run. Also, the smell of the hot ripe cucumber, steeping with oil from the vents of the gutted truck dash, made her stomach gnaw. She needed to pee.

Twenty more miles to Atlanta, according to the sign coming up.

She sat forward to let her back dry and took a compact from her white, multipocketed shoulder bag. Got her lipstick out and made up her face. Her nose was sweating oil, her tan skin was streaked orange from the blend of powder and sweat. She finished her face and flapped her shirttail. Her new Guess jeans were stuck to her behind.

"Almost there." She sighed and jacked a knee on the seat between them, covering the cucumber. She moved her knee, trying to stave off thoughts of what the cucumber meant.

Archie Wall kept squinting up the sun-sparked highway as

if searching for a lost dime. He'd been looking smaller and smaller to Chanell since they got out of Macon, him and his primer-gray pickup. She couldn't imagine what he looked and acted like in front of those Atlanta bigshots. Nobody else in Swanoochee County made as many trips to Atlanta as Archie Wall, not even the district representative, whose hair she trimmed once a month. And nobody seemed to know what Archie Wall did when he got there; they all seemed to assume that lawyers, like representatives, just went to the state capital to confuse the already-confusing laws. But the county representative was well thought of. Not so with Archie Wall.

Chanell checked her digital watch to signal that she now had to eat and go to the restroom, and set it to chime in ten minutes. Just in case the first signal didn't take. They'd been on the road for six hours—a four-hour trip—and whether or not Archie Wall considered her to be making a play for him no longer seemed too significant.

Almost there. Fifteen miles to downtown Atlanta, and Chanell could see, in the city's unveiling ahead, gay billboards and jets tacking the ribbons of haze over the interstate, and tiers of pines, tops of highrise buildings gnawed by the smog, the gold dome of the capitol outshining the sun.

Two hundred and fifty miles of slow motoring up the fast interstate, and all of a sudden Archie Wall cut quick off the next exit, holding the truck fast along the sharp curve. No blinker, no nothing.

Chanell held to the door handle and braced both white Reeboks on the floorboard. God, he must need to go to the john bad! She shut her eyes, feeling the truck swerve, her neck drawing till her head touched the rear glass.

Did she imagine that Archie Wall was breathing harder? Like a man getting what T.P. would call "a piece."

Oh, Lord, what if he was stopping at a motel? Or what if he just pulled up to a gas station and she thought he was about to rape her and he wasn't and she made a fool of herself by acting like she thought he was? The whole scenario reeled off in her head like a bad movie: Archie Wall switching off the truck, folding his knee on the seat, arm flung casually across the back, with a smile she would take or mistake for leering. Her either getting out and huffing off—she backed herself up like a video in reverse—or just sitting there sniggering and gazing out while he picked up the long, smooth cucumber and . . .

She kept her eyes closed till she felt the pickup juttering to a stop. And when she opened them, the first thing she spied was a rectangular sign with red letters that read GEORGIA STATE FARMERS MARKET.

She sat forward. "Why're we stopping here, Archie Wall?"

"To sell these cucumbers," he said.

By three o'clock, Chanell started smelling a rat. They'd already driven along miles of sawdust aisles, between sun-ticking tin stalls of watermelons, cantaloupes, peas, potatoes, apples, and bananas; they'd sold Archie Wall's cucumbers for four dollars a bushel and were headed back along the traffic-thick service-station route, past Wendy's and Burger King, seeking the entrance to I-75. On the third trip past Wendy's, Chanell decided she'd had it. "Archie Wall, turn in right there." Before she could point left, he cut right, crossing the outside lane and setting off a concert of car horns, to the southbound ramp of I-75.

"Archie Wall, you gone get us killed!" she yelled, holding to the dash. "Besides, you going the wrong way."

He pumped the brake pedal—an eye-sized patch of metal

peeping through the black rubber—till the truck stopped. "Didn't that sign say south?" he asked. His blue eye dots darted in the rearview mirror.

"Yeah," she said, looking back at the tapered black Buick stopped behind them. The driver pressed down on his car horn, head rising like mercury on a thermometer.

"Go on, Archie Wall," she said. "We'll get on 75-south-bound and then get off at the next exit to turn around."

He popped the clutch, hit the gas, and merged with the traffic. His round cheeks were as red as a painted doll's. Keeping to the left lane, he peered ahead, while traffic cruised smartly around the puttering truck. A Negro man leveled his red sports convertible with the pickup and tooted his horn twice.

"Blow your nose," Chanell yelled across Archie Wall. "You'll get more out of it."

Hot wind whipping at her broomed ponytail, she sat back, fuming. Poor Archie Wall. "Okay, turn off on the exit coming up," she said.

She braced her feet again, but he went on. "You missed it," she yelled, then lowered her voice. "Don't worry, you can take the next one."

Usually, she would pat a man, woman, child, or dog when she spoke that way; so she reached out to touch Archie Wall's arm but drew back her hand. Though it seemed weeks since she'd imagined Archie Wall as lover, she still didn't want to give him ideas. She was too hot and miserable—really needing to pee now—to bother imagining how his arm would feel, what he would do. Besides, he didn't really seem human, not human in a way that everybody else she knew did, not needing a pat for pity or praise. The hairless, sunned skin on his forearm looked like any other man's, but she'd never thought of him as a man. Nobody ever talked him up to be a man. To Cornerville, he was nothing but a joke.

She sat up, watching him, familiar and pink against the smoggy haze ahead. On each side of the interstate, steel-and-concrete buildings and overpasses whirled counter to the bight of the sky, a dead gray locking in the heat. Every mile or so, a rust-brown railroad track would break the gray, a sharp taste on her dulled tongue. The sky above was a wrung blue.

Archie Wall drove on, not paying a dab of mind to the man in the Oldsmobile passing on the left. The man eased alongside, shot him a bird, and spirited into the haze like a dream demon.

"Here comes your exit, Archie Wall," Chanell said. "Put on your blinker."

He held his speed at forty-five, passing the next exit.

Well, well, well. Chanell still had her feet braced; she needed to pee bad. "Archie Wall, ain't you going to Atlanta?"

"Done been."

"Huh?"

"'Bout as close to Atlanta as I plan to get." He kind of glanced at her for the first time.

"You mean to say we ain't going to Atlanta?"

"Reckon you could put it that way."

She blotted the sweat from her face and neck, a trickle tickling down the valley of her large breasts, now chapped and raw from the wicking cups of her bra. Mad swapped places with pity in her head, a metallic spit misted from her tongue, and her face heated up like the sun after a cloud passed. All this time . . . all this time, while she'd expected to be on her way to Atlanta, he'd never had any intention of going. Damn him! She knew him now, and everybody had been right. He was a joke. She thought about the year she graduated from high school, parties and net prom dresses crowding out most memories of a younger Archie Wall, fresh out of law school, visiting the combined student body of upper and lower grades to fumble through one of his little talks on the law. In her hot head she saw him, dressed in a wide striped tie, same blue shirt—the same wide-collar style as the one he had on now. Not grease spotted then, but neat. Too neat. Chanell and her friends had thought he was so square. Joy Beth, seated beside Chanell in the musty school auditorium, gagged herself—"Dig that tie . . . gag-ag-ag!" Everybody had laughed; nobody took him serious. Now he stayed to himself, except for business.

At the next exit, Archie Wall pulled off the interstate at his same old speed, sun spearing them both in the eyes, and held the truck steady up the ramp curve. He got to the end and sat there looking, left to right. After a minute or two, he eased on out ahead of another pickup, and pulled over in front of a Jiffy Mart.

"I thought we might stop for a bite to eat, Betty Jean," he said, getting out. "Let you go to the little girl's room."

Nobody else called Chanell by her given name, and she'd have liked to forget that anybody remembered such a common tag. Otherwise, why would she have changed it to something French? Something with class. She felt like walloping Archie Wall with her shoulder bag. But after he'd ambled on into the store, she got out and trotted around the corner to the airtight restroom. It smelled of bloody Kotex and fake lemon deodorizer, so she tried to hold her breath and hurry.

When she got back, rounding the corner of the Jiffy Mart, she saw Archie Wall standing with one small foot propped on the truck bumper. He was eating Vienna sausage from a can with a plastic fork. A pack of saltine crackers on the hot hood lay next to an RC Cola. He was smiling.

She stopped and leaned against the brick wall of the Jiffy Mart, no longer hungry, no longer needing to pee, at relative peace now. The kind of peace that madness brings. He hadn't wanted her to come, she was sure of it now. She didn't know whether he'd deliberately driven so slow, suffering the heat gladly just to see her suffer, or whether he'd been driving as fast as his old truck would go. She didn't know whether he'd stopped this side of Atlanta to deprive her, or was afraid to drive in the city. But she did know she'd be lunching on Vienna sausage, instead of French crepes, with the stingiest lawyer in Georgia. And then it came over her like the Holy Ghost. She should really make a play for Archie Wall; she should tease him and torture him and make him beg her to marry him.

chapter two

Chanell didn't mean it—she really didn't. She never had any intention of making a play for Archie Wall. Her imagination, spurred by the heat, had simply kicked in. Problem was, sometimes what went into her mind came out of her mouth.

It was nearly nine o'clock when Archie Wall at last crossed the Alapaha bridge, back in Swanoochee County. Chanell's "new fiancé" was still poking along, making slow time toward the blinking red traffic light in Cornerville. She was already thirty minutes late for clogging practice. No time to change into her clogging outfit. Behind, the setting sun rayed around dark, mushrooming thunderheads, and ahead, lightning streaked the smudged sky over the red tower light at the courthouse, while thunder rolled eastward with the clouds and Archie Wall's truck.

"How 'bout running me by the gym, Archie Wall?" She fanned her shirttail. Her sweaty clothes had dried stiff; her armpits felt raw as a baby's butt.

He was chewing on a toothpick, peering out at the summer-shrunk river that funneled between rocky banks west of the cemetery. The air, batting through the open windows in waves of cool and warm, came alive with the scents of willow and leaf mold. Sudden lightning spiked in the night sky, ripping a seam through the white-sand cemetery on the left and flaring the wind-riven tupelos that marched against the current, a pewter gash through the pinewoods.

By the time they got to the crossing, the sky was dark, forcing the street lights on in the courtyard, their hooded glow showering lit rain to the dry grass and sidewalk. Great drops pecked at the windshield, sliding through the canker of dust. A green smell.

Chanell was about to crank up her window—keep from getting wet again—when she saw T.P. standing next to his high black pickup in front of the Delta store. Inside the truck, his buddies' faces stood out in the flickering lightning like snapshot negatives. T.P. had one long leg up inside the truck before he spotted her, then he jumped out, waving and hollering.

"Shit!" Chanell said, drawing away from the window. "Go on, Archie Wall."

He was just sitting there at the traffic light as if he had to stop. No traffic, nothing. He glanced over at T.P. heading for the truck, and woke up for the second time that day.

"Hey!" T.P. yelled, waving both arms.

Archie Wall stepped on the gas, and as they shot past the flat brick courthouse, Chanell looked back and saw T.P. leap into his truck and cut esses on the red-tinted road at the crossing. Out of control, the black truck swerved toward the courtyard, two-wheeling along the sidewalk, then crossed 94 to the tilted sidewalk in front of the post office. Leveling on the straightaway, behind Archie Wall, T.P. picked up speed. Centered on his truck cab, a row of yellow lights danced with the lightning, thunder blocking the scold of the truck's twin glass pack mufflers.

Archie Wall bit down on his toothpick; his eyes blared in the lit band of mirror. He squeezed the brakes and veered right, either stopping to reason with T.P. or hoping he'd pass.

"Don't stop right here, Archie Wall," she shouted. "He's drinking bad!" How could she tell? It was Friday night, and on Friday night T.P. would be running with his beer buddies.

Sitting high, with the toothpick dangling from bloodless lips, Archie Wall hit the gas, moving on between facing rows of frame houses toward the old school, where rain skipped across the fenced-in playground. Lightning pulsed over the wringing swings and the rocking whirlaway, like a scene depicting the end of time. Archie Wall eased off the gas, then mashed it, eyes framed in the brilliant mirror. T.P. hot on his tail; gym coming up. "You want me to just go on?" Archie Wall said.

"Might as well let me out at the gym." Chanell knew T.P. wouldn't give up, would follow them clear to Fargo, thirty miles of highway paved through the pinewoods, maybe run them off the road. She stuck the cucumber in her pocketbook and got ready to hop out and make a run for the open gym door, a frosted bead curtain hung in the blackness.

Archie Wall angled right across the sidewalk and slewed the truck into the mud yard before the gym, stopping beneath the giant wringing oak. Close as he could get to the door.

T.P. swerved alongside, splashing a shield of milky water from end to end of Archie Wall's truck. Turning his mute, bland face to the sudden swell of light, water and rushing sounds, like a sunlit wave in a flood, Archie Wall never flinched or blinked or said one word, just slow-turned to follow the progress of the glimmering black truck's gigantic black tires and wings of water to its stopping place at the front bumper of the primer-gray pickup. Archie Wall's face, his left arm, and his blue shirt were plastered with gray mud, like a trick of shadows. T.P. bailed out of his truck, his long, skinny legs like a buck deer's, and loped to Chanell's window. "Where the hell you been?" he yapped, grabbing the roof of the truck and shaking it.

"None of your beeswax." She tucked her pocketbook under her arm and tried to get out, but couldn't open the door for T.P. leaning against it. "Get out of my way." She rammed the door against his slim hips.

He shoved her back with the door and stuck his head inside, fouling the cab with his beery breath. "Hear tell you went to Etlanna." His keen tan face warped in the lightning, pearls of rain studding his clipped black beard. Nothing going on behind those eyes.

"Get out of the way so I can go in." Chanell pushed against the door again. "I got clogging practice."

"Uh huh, I hear you!" He gripped her shoulder, pinching the tender nerve between her neck and shoulder blade.

She slapped his hand. He pinched harder.

"You better look out who you messing with, you shit!" she squealed, trying to wriggle free.

Archie Wall started babbling about the law: restraining orders, divorce decrees, damage to property, mud, and mayhem. . . .

"No shit!" T.P. broke in, bearing down on Chanell's shoulder.

His sister, Bell, was standing in the gym door, short red dress flapping in the wind like her red mouth. Not a word breaking through the fuss of thunder, the fuss in the truck. Both hands on her thick waist, wide sash whipping, she stomped her black shoes and pointed a ringed finger at T.P.

He'd heard it all before. Joy Beth, Chanell's best friend since grade school, toddled up behind Bell and peeped through the rain and shook her head. Both were tall and stout, but next to Bell, Joy Beth looked short—like sisters dressed alike for Sunday school. Their heavy legs turned white in a burst of lightning that colored both madeup faces old. "Get in my truck." T.P. let go of Chanell's shoulder, backing up, and pointed to the idling pickup. His three buddies, sipping Bud, were staring out the side window as if watching the fights on TV.

Chanell got out, hoofing through the mud toward the high black truck, then dodged to the side and straight for the gym door. Bell, still hanging in the doorway, was stomping out a dance, a crowd of other cloggers gawking behind her. A blur of red skirts through the rain.

T.P. took two long strides through the merging mud puddles and hooked his fingers in Chanell's ponytail. "Get in the fucking truck!" he yelled.

Yanked around, with her back bent, she dug in her pocketbook and pulled out Archie Wall's long green cucumber. T.P. must have thought it was a gun, because he let go just as she stood and conked him on the crown. The cucumber splattered, seeds washing down his bony face with the rain and settling in his beard. Spinning, as she spun, he laughed and jerked her ponytail again.

"You sonofabitch!" Her scalp felt blistered, even in the cool rain. Her eyeballs felt scalded. Hairdos covered with their hands, Bell and Joy Beth dashed down the doorsteps, shouting at T.P. An electric claw of lightning reached from the sky to the oak, and they darted back to the door like wind on water. Rain hammered the tin top of the lofty white gym and crashed through the oak, puckering the puddles of brassy-scented gumbo.

On her knees now, so mad the mud looked red, Chanell felt the rain switch at her face; her pocketbook slid to the ground. She could see Archie Wall's truck, him sitting, mud-pied, behind the steering wheel, hollering too, something about the Supreme Court.

Bell yelled, "T.P., behave yourself!"

He still held fast to Chanell's ponytail, laughing. "You're not going in there, showing your ass."

"Says who?" Chanell beat at his shins, pounding mud into his butt-tight blue jeans.

"Says your husband," he hollered. "That's who."

"For your information," she yelled, "I don't belong to you anymore; I belong to Archie Wall. We're getting married."

T.P. let go and cackled with his hands on his hips. Still on her knees, Chanell watched as Archie Wall started his truck, backed up, and circled under the oak, then juttered onto the highway. "T.P., you get yourself to the house." Bell, who looked smaller wet, was at Chanell's side. "You hear me?"

Joy Beth, squinting through pointy wet mascaraed lashes, stooped and caught Chanell by one elbow. Bell took the other, helping her to her feet.

T.P. got in his truck, still cackling, and cruised in behind Archie Wall, who was as good as married now.

By Saturday morning, the news was out.

The sky was clear and leaching in the July heat, a shimmery brilliance spiking along the loop of tidy white houses with flowers blooming in kept yards—red geraniums and blue morning glories and color-worn perennial petunias—to the corner, fronting 94, where the red brick of the Baptist Church bounced soft sunrays. The Christ-blood red of the brick in sharp contrast to the white spire pointing accusingly at the tired blue sky.

Another scorcher, Chanell predicted. She turned on the window air-conditioner in the shop to get ready. Saturdays always brought a full day of doing hair, more today since she'd canceled all Friday appointments to go to Atlanta. Soon the two hair driers would be battling with the air-conditioner, but the shop would still be cooler than inside the four-room stucco cottage.

Chanell used to believe that Saturdays were so hectic because women in Cornerville wanted to look good for Sunday; but after a while, after weekdays got just as hectic, she caught on that Chanell's Beauty Shop was a gathering point, a meeting place for women to air their unholy vanities, to let their hair down for her to wash.

She looked out the side window and saw Miss Neida with her boxed Toni coming out the domed wooden door of the old jail and crossing the yard.

Chanell's peacock was pecking along the viny banks of Troublesome Creek, his blue-green tail feathers rattling to full strut. The eyes on his fanned feathers winked in the hot breeze that passed from the wet leaves of the sweetgums to the blind of bullous vines. All night, he had clawed the bench where he roosted on the front stoop, as restless from the storm as she was from the fight.

Miss Neida toed the fading bits of red party balloons and crept on toward the shop, stopping to brush her feet at the door.

"Come on in, Miss Neida," Chanell called and began rinsing the shampoo bowl with the spray attachment.

"How you, sugar?" Miss Neida's gray inset eyes settled on Chanell's face. She stepped inside and set the Toni next to the sink.

"I'm fine." Chanell's stomach gnawed from drinking too much coffee, but she wouldn't tell that. Made it a practice never to complain. Unlike some people. "How you this morning, Miss Neida?"

"Got that old hurting in my side." Miss Neida wedged into the shampoo chair.

Chanell jacked the floor lever to raise the seat. "I declare." She always cut such comments short to discourage her older customers from getting started on their ailments. "You cook them roasting ears last night?" asked Miss Neida.

"No 'um." Chanell cranked the other lever to lower Miss Neida's head to the shampoo bowl. "But I'll get to them tonight." She'd wait a few days for the corn to go bad, then dump it in the woods behind the house. Didn't feel so guilty about throwing stuff out after it went bad, about the big-eyed starving children on pamphlets she got in the mail.

Miss Neida's short, mossy hair was damp from fresh washing. Chanell squeezed pearly coils of shampoo from a tall plastic bottle and began scrubbing up a lather. She liked to do her own shampooing—Miss Neida knew that. Everybody said Chanell gave the best shampoo anywhere. The old lady's nickel eyes closed, the crinkled skin of her face folding around her tiny ears. Now and then she'd scrunch her eyes when Chanell got too rough.

"Tell me if this water's too hot." Chanell sprayed her hair, working one hand into the soft fluff of gray.

"No 'um, that's fine." Still, Miss Neida scrunched her face, eyes closed as if she was dozing.

Chanell wrapped Miss Neida's head in a towel and sat her up.

Miss Neida tugged the green-dotted cape close around her neck. "Don't want to catch cold."

"Yes 'um." Chanell pulled the standing bin of perm rods closer, picking for the smallest ones. Miss Neida's hair was so thin and fine that perms didn't take on big rods. Tonis didn't take half the time anyway—not the best perm on the market. Chanell's were. Try telling Miss Neida that. "You don't want your hair trimmed, do you?" Chanell was already winding one clinging strand before she decided to ask.

"Not if you don't have the time." Miss Neida glared at Chanell. "Don't want to put you to no extra bother. Just shave my neck."

Chanell took the clippers from the top drawer of the counter and plugged them in, running close along Miss Neida's trenched nape, over crusty moles and tucks. The soft z-z-z-z of the clippers filled the narrow shop scented with honeysuckle shampoo. Double squares of sun from the two east windows blazed the gilt mirror and the chrome rims of the driers, firing the white tiles of the floor and a lock of red hair under the magazine table by the door. The weak air-conditioner was proving to provide little more than another background racket. A lawnmower purred in the distance.

Miss Neida cleared her throat. "Hear tell you're getting married," she said.

"Ma'am?" Chanell switched off the clippers.

"I say, I heared you're getting married. That so?" Miss Neida stiffened. Chanell didn't answer; she couldn't. She was too shocked and too mad. And just to think she'd planned to trim the old gossip's hair. For free! She switched on the clippers again. How in the hell did news travel so fast around here?

She knew she should set the record straight, because to not answer meant it was so. But she wouldn't. Maybe she wanted to see how far the ridiculous rumor would go, how fast—she could always count on Cornerville's rumor mill for relief from the little-town doldrums. Or maybe it was pride; after all, she'd started the rumor on herself. Anyway, in the beauty business, one got used to rumors like the reek of ammonia. She passed Miss Neida a thin square pack of Toni tissues. "How 'bout handing these to me?" If the old biddy wanted a home perm, she'd get one. Miss Neida placed the pack on the lap of her blue print frock, peeled off a tissue, like a cigarette rolling paper, and held it over her right shoulder. "Well, I wish you luck."

Chanell parted her hair and clamped it off into six sections, then began winding a strand on a pink plastic rod. "Right away, I guess?" Miss Neida said.

That did it! "Yes 'um. This fall." Lord, Chanell wished she hadn't said that. And then she didn't care—Miss Neida had already branded her a bad apple anyway. Beat talking about roasting ears and the hurting in the old lady's side. Chanell's eyes traveled over the block of months on the 1991 calendar above the combout station, from July to October. "October," she said.

"I was in hopes you and T.P. might work things out." Miss Neida sighed, licked a finger, and passed another tissue back as Chanell snapped the band on a rod.

"Well, Miss Neida, you know how that goes," Chanell said. Who knew better than Miss Neida and Mr. Jim how Chanell and T.P. had fussed and fought? More now than ever.

"You hear 'bout Miss Pansy's brother putting her house up for sale?" Miss Neida nodded to the window behind her, where the winged white house across the road showed like a picture on an easel.

"Yes 'um. Sad, ain't it?" said Chanell, glad to change the subject.

"Sad ain't the word!" Miss Neida wiggled straight and passed another tissue. "Get down and people'll shore kick you."

"That's how it is around here, Miss Neida." Chanell's hand was resting on the sloped old shoulder, felt it go tight. "Is Miss Pansy still in the hospital, Miss Neida?"

"Out and in. In the rest home right now." She squirmed around to stare through the window. "I'd shore like to catch a ride to Valdosta with you one of these days . . ." Chanell lost her hold on a rod and had to rewind the strand. She felt sorry for Miss Neida, but not that sorry. Last time she'd driven the grouchy old lady into town, Chanell had wasted a tank of gas, driving store to store in one-hundred-degree heat, trying to save a dime on Blue Plate mayonnaise. Chanell changed the subject.

"Who you reckon'll buy her house? Big old place like that."

"Can't never tell," she said. "But I shore hope they ain't bad to fuss and fight."

Chanell knew she meant like her and T.P. Since they busted up, he hadn't missed two nights in a row coming over and starting something. Used to, he hung out at the beer joint on the Georgia-Florida line, coming home once or twice a week.

"What you reckon they asking for it?" Chanell held to a strand of hair and looked out at the shining white house on the mowed emerald island of grass.

"A pretty penny, I 'magine," Miss Neida said.

Chanell wound the last strand on the back section and took the clip loose over Miss Neida's left ear, then started winding at her temple. "Nobody I know of could afford to buy it."

Miss Neida squirmed; the strand slipped from between Chanell's fingers. "Nothing around here but poor old dirt farmers," Miss Neida said. "Excepting Archie Wall."

Chanell didn't know whether the old lady had said it for her benefit, but she decided to let it pass and maybe the rumor would too. But she felt the insinuation file itself in her mind with a snapping shuffle of other nonsense that could drop from her mouth at any time. She snipped the plastic tit from the perm-solution vial and began doping each hair-sheathed splint.

The ammonia reek burned high in her nostrils.

chapter three

By noon, Chanell had done five heads of hair. Still had a frost, a reverse frost, and a dye job to go, and two li'l ole church ladies wanting fifties-style wave sets.

The black wall phone by the door was steadily ringing around the storm of driers, Mr. Jim was shooing the peacock out of his corn patch, and Chanell was tramping from the shop to the yard, trying to keep peace with her neighbors. "Chunk something at him, Mr. Jim," Chanell yelled from the corner of the shop. "George, get to the house!" Mr. Jim, now leaning on his hoe handle in the wilting green blades of corn, went back to hoeing. George waddled toward the creek, his fanned feathers like irises blooming on the ferny slope.

Chanell hurried inside again and put Linda Gay, her last customer before lunch, under the drier. She called Lula Bell Hale over to the combout station and, eyeing the waxed-paper-wrapped sandwich set by Lula's pocketbook on the floor, began slipping the bobby pins from her thinning brown hair. Most Fridays, Lula Bell's standing eleven-o'clock appointments meant she was spending the day. Like a picnic at the park. Chanell couldn't figure if she brought her lunch because she often had to wait past noon for her hair to be done—should Chanell hire another beautician to help with the overload?—or because she considered the beauty shop an outing from the average-day routine of her house. Not on Saturday, Lula Bell. Not on your life, Chanell thought, and then felt she had been truly ungrateful for Lula Bell's willingness to wait, and sorry for the guileless woman whose washing days had probably been appointed Mondays and whose weeks seemed to begin or end with those Friday pin-curling celebrations, her ritual pinnacle. One waited on and another waiting with a crown of metal wave clamps, Chanell seated Lois Wilson on the throne of special treatment, and began pinching and lifting the spring-loaded clamps from her hair. The tall, angular woman had already talked down poor listless Lula Bell—tracing kin and tacking meanings to meaningless shoptalk—then tried to involve Linda Gay in a shouting match above the whooshing of the driers. Earlier, when Chanell had come back from one of her peacekeeping missions on George-the-peacock's behalf, she'd caught Linda Gay and Lois hissing behind their hands. Had they been talking about Chanell and Archie Wall, the rumor, or about some other unknowing soul at the mercy of their relaxed tongues?

Chanell finally talked Lois out the shop door and into her car, and leaving Linda Gay filing her nails under the drier, decided to go into the house for a ham sandwich and a glass of tea.

Her doll-house kitchen with its regular-sized white range and refrigerator felt as if the oven had been left on. She stood a minute in front of the open Frigidaire, got a glassful of ice and held it to her cheek. A musty odor breathed out as she scanned the sticky shelves. She needed to dump the squash and cucumber pickles in the rusty-topped Mason jars that Miss Neida and the other ladies had put up, but then she'd have to wash the syrupy jars and return them. She'd have to lie and say how much she loved the pickles, encouraging Miss Neida and them to give her more. And they'd never start paying in cash. She could buy a new refrigerator with what they owed her.

She took a plastic pack of processed ham slices from the meat keeper, wondering if it was too old to eat, but didn't check the expiration, because if it was out of date she'd have to eat potted meat. Or corn. The tumble of roasting ears lay drying in papery shucks next to the door.

Sitting at the square table with its foldout leaves folded under, staring out the open jalousie window framing the woods, she ate the sandwich, deciding that the ham tasted a bit sharp and slick, but not spoiled. Well, she'd know by three or four—it was one now—if she had ptomaine poisoning. She wouldn't get sick; she never did. She felt guilty about the wasting corn with a curly worm nesting in the brown floss. Remembering the starving children on the brochures, she was reminded that she needed to go to the post office while Linda Gay was getting dry. But Bell, a regular on Saturday, was coming for a frost job at two—her coarse hair took forever to come up. Besides, she'd want to talk while they waited for the bleach to strip the brown, like a clean canvas to be painted over. Joy Beth, next on Chanell's schedule, would want to talk too, and Chanell wanted to talk to her about spreading the rumor that she and Archie Wall would be getting married. It had to have been her, not Bell. Bell didn't gossip. Chanell wondered if she'd still be friends with Joy Beth and Linda Gay, whether they'd even speak, if not for her doing their hair. In the ninth grade—not that Chanell held it against them anymore; she hardly thought about it anymore—Joy Beth and Linda Gay had sent a hate letter to one of T.P.'s fiery old girl-friends, signing Chanell's name. Chanell, a new cheerleader with a crush on T.P., despite denying she'd written the letter, had to put up with the mad girl's threats and accusations for months, while Joy Beth and Linda Gay sniggered behind both girls' backs. Flanked by her tough buddies, the hard-eyed ex-girlfriend would corner Chanell in the school restroom and threaten to whip her ass, or make a scene at basketball games, calling her "whore" and "bitch." T.P., lanky and sweat-slick after a close basketball match, would swagger with Chanell across the confusion of court geometry with his head blown up bigger than the basketball.

Chanell heard a car drive up in front of the house, and in a couple of minutes Joy Beth and Linda Gay talking in the shop with the door open. Letting out what little cool air had man-aged to collect around the driers' heat. She swallowed the last bite of her sandwich, refilled her tea glass, and wiped bread crumbs from the mahogany tabletop with a paper towel.

On her way to the shop, she stopped in the living room to raise the two windows each side of the plain plank mantel. A hot breeze fluttered between the sheer white curtains with the whine of lawnmowers on the courthouse square. The ceilings were so low in the one-bedroom house that the air was sti-fling at head level. When she stepped out the screened door, to the front stoop, starting around the corner to the shop on the north end, she could hear the two women talking. The low, just-between-us tone stopped her. She stood in the cor-ner between doors, listening and watching her peacock strut-ting across the gravel road from Miss Pansy's sun-scorched lawn toward Chanell. Knowing he'd spied her and would soon be bristling about the stoop, begging food, she flattened herself against the wall and tried to wave him off. But dumb to motion, he kept coming, blue-green feathers sweeping the clipped grass off the stoop.

"I don't know what's come over her." Joy Beth, with her back to the door, was brushing out the teasing in her fine dark hair, crown down.

"Well, maybe she has to get married. You know?" Linda Gay had the drier hood lifted and was digging the collar of cotton from her neck and ears. Chanell could see her in the standing hand mirror, set between the shampoo and combout stations, her chalky face rimmed red.

"You reckon she's pregnant?" Joy Beth quit snatching the brush through her crinkly dry hair.

"But Archie Wall, of all people," said Linda Gay, stretching high in her same old blue gabardine skirt and matching jacket. "Who'd of thought it?"

"Well, you know Chanell—man hungry." Joy Beth began brushing her hair again, her mannish body jerking with each rake down.

George stood in the shop doorway now, facing Chanell. She reached back and slammed the screen door and stepped into the shop as if she'd just come out of the house. "Shoo! shoo!" she said to George. The old bird circled the stoop and paraded off the side, then shrieked like a woman.

"Whoops! She caught me," Joy Beth said to Linda Gay and cackled. "Brushing my hair wrong."

"It's your hair," Chanell said, standing next to the comb-out station. "If you don't care if it breaks, I don't. Linda Gay, you want to come over here?" Chanell sipped some tea, feeling the sweet liquid travel down her closing throat, and placed the glass on the counter beside the apothecary of combs set to disinfect in blue solution.

Linda Gay, shapeless in safe-blue gabardine, gathered the plastic cape on her shoulders and tiptoed over like somebody slipping into church late. Her face was as white as her ears were red. Joy Beth brushed slower, working from ends to crown. The purring of the air-conditioner got loud.

Chanell crossed to the door and slammed it, then went back to Linda Gay and started snatching brown plastic rollers from her hair. Her scalp, pink under scrolls of Moonglow-moussed hair, turned redder with each snatch. She flinched, but sat straight, kneading her hands. Then in a tight, cheery voice, she began telling about taking her journalism class to the Folks-Huxford genealogy library in Homerville to research the backgrounds of Swanoochee Countians for a book titled *The Talebearers*, which she'd masterminded and planned to make a tradition at the century-old school.

"I do know," she said, "it can take my bunch of twelfth graders the longest time to do a little research." She switched to cracker talk, like she'd do in what she considered uneducated company. "We hadn't no more'n set foot in Homerville, before they everlast one put in to go to the Burger King. Hee-hee, ah me." Joy Beth kept brushing, her teased hair flat and fried on the ends. She roved her eyes in the mirror over the shampoo bowl, from Chanell to Linda Gay, while Linda Gay yammered in her old academic, please-the-teacher voice, and Chanell snatched rollers. Chanell knew that Linda Gay was trying to tape over her voice in the earlier recording, to track over tracks that could lead to her capture. She hadn't been named "Most Diplomatic" in their senior yearbook for nothing. Well, it wouldn't work this time.

While Linda Gay chirruped on, Chanell stood casting about for something to strike back with, even knowing that when she was mad she risked saying or doing something stupid. She should bite her tongue and let it go, but her teeth felt too loose. She tried reasoning with herself by using yesterday's mess as an example. She looked behind her at Miss Pansy's white house through the window, inspired by the wonderland widow's walk, and inspiration overrode reason.

"Guess y'all heard Archie Wall's buying Miss Pansy's house, huh?" Chanell wasn't voted Best Actress in the twelfth grade for nothing either.

"You're kidding!" Joy Beth stopped brushing and looked at Chanell as though she couldn't decide whether her beautician was over being mad or not. Just hoped she was. What had been said was insignificant. Her close-set temples appeared closer with her stringy hair flat.

"That's what Archie Wall said." Chanell jerked a roller free on Linda Gay's temple. She sat stiff and self-satisfied but suspicious.

"Well, that old coot!" Joy Beth went back to brushing, flitting her blue eyes from Chanell to the house. "All these years of setting on his money, and now . . ."

Chanell saw Bell's new blue Buick gliding up the road and braking in front of the shop, where heat waves swarmed from the gravel like gnats. She got out, swinging her giant cordovan pocketbook. Chanell turned up the heat inside. "Archie Wall ain't as stingy as you might think." She felt braver with Bell there, a party to her picking. Bell, who was like a sister, the one she'd never had.

Bell stepped inside and closed the door, her clear green eyes seeking out one and then the other. She seemed to sense something in the air by the way she spoke, a clipped "How y'all doing?" Like stepping over peacock poop on the floor. A smile played around her once-fine mouth, now gathered like broadcloth with a neat whipstitch. She slung her weighted pocketbook to one of the drier chairs and leaned forward, running fingers through her Persian Gold hair. Listening beneath her webbing hair, she unclipped her heavy gold hoop earrings and dropped them in her green pants pocket. Chanell talked on. "Archie Wall's getting me all new clothes, too," she said. "Course, the way I'm putting on weight, I'm gone be needing 'um." She released the last two fingers full of Linda Gay's rollers in the bin, held her back, and stretched. Then she took the flat black brush and pulled it through Linda Gay's roller-molded mop.

By now, Bell was peeking through her screen of hair, trying to pick up where Chanell was going, trying to figure, it seemed, whether or not Chanell was serious. She took a magazine from the wicker rack under the north window and, thumbing pages, wandered to the door.

Linda Gay's weak gray eyes stayed on the Chanell in the gilt mirror, while Chanell brushed, yanking the woman's hair from her high forehead like a loose wig. Linda Gay liked her hair styled loose and natural—inconspicuous, she always said—so Chanell styled it in an old-timey bouffant, spraying it stiff with the latest lacquer, Hard-to-Hold Hairnet. She snatched off the cape and flapped it before Linda Gay's face.

Linda Gay got up, straightening her safe-blue skirt. Brushing hair from her padded shoulders, she turned to the drier chair for her overflowing black pocketbook, with her eyes still tacked on the mad woman's eyes in the mirror. She took a twenty-dollar bill from her blue cloth wallet with duplicated rows of green whales, wheeled in her serviceable suede loafers, and flattened the bill on the counter by the door.

"See you at church tomorrow, Linda Gay," said Joy Beth, leaning on the shampoo chair. Both she and Linda Gay sang in the Baptist choir. And Linda Gay, always the teacher, taught the teenagers in Sunday school.

Linda Gay lifted her boneless face, placed a hand on one of Joy Beth's, then sallied out through a rush of incoming hot air. Chanell knew what Joy Beth would be up to next; she would now switch to the color and shape of the strongest character around—Bell—and try to get back in with Chanell. She and Linda Gay went out of their way to be like Bell and to be liked by Bell. Everybody did. But Joy Beth's ingratiating was more general—she wanted to be like and to be liked by everybody. Now she was trying to get things back to normal by ignoring Chanell's being mad. It wouldn't work.

"Bell, you're next." Chanell shook the cape with a snap and held it up, shooing Joy Beth from the shampoo chair.

Joy Beth backed off and picked up the magazine Bell had placed on the drier chair.

"Now, I want y'all to go ahead and talk about me," said Chanell. "Right out in the open, right to my face." Chanell hit the lever on the chair and backdipped Bell's heavy gold hair in the basin. "Go ahead, talk!" She knew Bell hadn't talked about her, but included her to take the edge off the accusation.

"Chanell, I didn't go to talk about you behind your back," Joy Beth said, putting the magazine down. "Linda Gay just . . ."

"What about you, Bell?" Chanell sprayed Bell's hair, which shed water like duck feathers.

"I just got here."

"Which one of y'all called up half the county and told them I was marrying Archie Wall?"

"I was trying to straighten out what Linda Gay started," Joy Beth said. The tattoo work of fine blue veins stood on her pale face.

"I didn't call *nobody*." Bell stared up at Chanell, her green eyes like portals to her thoughts. Her broad tan face looked sharp with her hair slicked back.

"Well, it's not so, and y'all know it's not so—I told you last night," said Chanell. "I said that to get rid of T.P."

Joy Beth started toward the door. "I've gotta run to the house a minute and check on my pot roast. I'll be right back." Still smiling through tender pink lips, her pride, she was trying to leave things on good terms, more for Bell's sake than Chanell's. She wouldn't be back in a minute.

Chanell squeezed thick green curls of herbal shampoo on Bell's wet hair as Joy Beth tipped out, watching from the window till she got in the car.

"Can you believe that?" Chanell switched off the sprayer so Bell could hear her good.

Bell kept her eyes closed, listening. She snorted, laughing, small teeth shining in her skint face. "Get this shit out of my hair and get on with my frost job; I gotta get home and make some phone calls for Pete."

Chanell turned the sprayer on again. "Bell, I swear and be-damned if people in this place don't know when you pee."

"Well, next time keep your mouth shut." Still laughing, strangled with her head back, Bell took the corner of the towel and blotted her eyes where the spray was chipping away her green shadow.

"Looks like I would, don't it?" Chanell laughed too, feeling the tightness in her chest go slack. "T.P. just makes me so mad."

"His ass!"

When the sun went down that evening, the Troublesome Creek crescent got hotter, like an oven switched from broil to bake. Sandwiched heat, as if the sun now burning beneath the earth had spun white-hot stars in its arc across the charred sky. Only the cool sound of keening water from neighbors spraying their flowers provided relief—if you listened and didn't feel, if you measured cool by sound instead of feeling. If you kept still and didn't move. Tree frogs peeped from the vine swell of the shrunken black creek, mosquitoes whirred like simmering earth, and katydids shrieked as if the air itself was on fire. Somewhere a dog barked just to be barking.

All day, a breeze had lifted off the creek, and it now lay, leaving the sheer curtains limp on Chanell's living-room windows. Two quarter-sized patches on the balls of her feet were seared from standing—she'd not taken a break since lunch. Sick as she was of talk and heat, she ate a hot chicken pot pie in front of the TV set in the living room, half listening to a man with white hair combed across his bald head tell about the oldest skeleton ever found—a black woman, three hundred thousand years old—how all humans had descended from her. Chanell's mind kept flitting from face to face of her customers, especially Linda Gay's and Joy Beth's. The rumor was like the ham she'd eaten for lunch, the bad effects would show early or not at all. A little stomach upset, Linda Gay and Joy Beth. By nine o'clock, Chanell found herself dozing where she sat, with her neck wrenched back on the couch. Her thighs were glued to the green vinyl, and she had to peel her skin from the seat to get up and go take a shower. T.P. always showed up on Saturday nights, and she wished he would come on. She'd learned that he took her being dressed for bed as an invitation. Usually, she let him stay to keep from bothering the neighbors. Besides, she could do with a little loving now and then. Hadn't men always used women? The only way to get rid of T.P. was to make him feel married. Sunday mornings, he would get up and out before she got done making breakfast. Nothing lost but a little pride on Chanell's part. Maybe he wouldn't come tonight, she decided, stepping from the shower and leaving the spigot dripping on a carved streak of rust. Maybe he'd taken her at her word about marrying Archie Wall, just as everyone else seemed to. No, he'd be back, if for no other purpose but to make his buddies think he was the one who had broken off with her. She slipped on one of his frayed white T-shirts, even knowing how sloppy turned him on. But then, any way she dressed turned him on since they got divorced. Before, when they were married, he'd call her a slob if she wore flipflop sandals. A good excuse to slam out of the house.

Last October, she'd filed for divorce while he was off in the deer woods where he camped from October till January, the end of deer season. T.P. worked only in summer, either for the tobacco farmers or in the logging woods. Then he really worked, harder than anyone Chanell knew. Some summers he even went to Canada to work in tobacco, where his untaxed wages tripled what he could make in Swanoochee County. What he earned during summer he lived on during winter. But always before he'd had Chanell's money to fall back on. If he didn't have enough money for a truck payment, if he needed gas or beer, he'd come to Chanell. Once, she'd even loaned him money to buy a Valentine present for his girl-of-the-month. How did she find out? She found the jewelry-store bill of sale in his dirty jeans pocket while doing the wash: two diamond heart charms, $38.95 each. One for Chanell, the other for Miss February. He couldn't go to his sister Bell for money anymore—Pete, her husband, had put an end to that. His mama—Mama Sharon to Chanell—lived month to month on her social security but still gave her baby as much money as she could manage without starving. When Chanell and T.P. got married after high school, they had lived with Mama Sharon until Chanell could earn enough to buy the stucco cottage she now lived in. Without T.P.'s help. But it was Mama Sharon and Bell who had sent Chanell to beauty school—$2,000, all of which Chanell had repaid except for $150. She hoped to pay that back by Christmas, and then she wouldn't feel like such a user for taking their money to start a business, then kicking Mama Sharon's baby out of the house. When T.P. didn't show by twelve, Chanell went to bed. Too hot to cover up, but the mosquitoes were so bad she finally had to pull the sheet up to her chin. She considered getting up and closing the single window at the head of her bed, where the ripped screen admitted mosquitoes into the room, but she was too tired, too hot. A mosquito buzzing around her left ear made her shrink, the blood in her head pumping from waiting for it to light. The inside of her thighs were sticky with sweat, so she kept them spread, waiting for the mosquito, for T.P. By one o'clock, she was so hot and itchy that she got up and went to the bathroom for a wet cloth to place on her forehead. Sprawled on the lumpy cotton mattress again, she replayed the whole day to get her mind off the heat. Linda Gay and Joy Beth, the rumor. None of it seemed real.

By lying still with the sheet over her head, she finally felt her face begin to prickle, drowsiness creeping down, a sweet tingling from the inside out. Then she heard the glass pack mufflers of T.P.'s pickup as he turned in at the Baptist Church and squalled up the straightaway to the house. Stinging all over, she sat up, waiting till the truck toned down out front, headlights flashing through the living-room windows and across the foot of her bed.

He got out and slammed the door, radio broadcasting a fast country song. "Chanell," he hollered, coming quick across the stoop and banging on the screen door. It flapped, jarring the windows throughout the house.

Chanell got up and crept to the living room, lit only by the glow from Miss Pansy's moon-white security light. Watching him through the door window, she hung back in the strip of shadows along the wall.

"Hey, baby, lemme in." Blap, blap, blap.

Drunk as usual. "Go on, T.P., or I'll call the law."

He laughed, peeping through the door glass with hands each side of his face. "What good'd that do?"

He was right; last time the sheriff came, he said he didn't mess in family doings. "Lemme in, babe," T.P. said. "I ain't drunk; I wanna talk."

"We ain't got nothing else to talk about, T.P."

"Yeah, we do, babe. Lemme in." He shook the screen door till the latch prong flipped free from its eye, then opened the wooden door and stumbled inside.

Chanell heard a man laughing out front, then another, a loud hoot coming from the pickup. He'd brought his buddies.

"Babe, listen." T.P. crept closer, long legs slicing the rhomboids of light, head turning to search the shadows along the wall.

Chanell backed to the bedroom door, feeling for the baseball bat kept by the jamb. "Get the hell out of here, T.P., or I'll knock your brains out."

"Babe, you ain't got the heart to hurt me." He reached out, stepping into her cover of shadows, not five feet away.

"I'm telling you, T.P." She backed up.

"Sugar, you the best-looking gal in Swanoochee County." He stumbled into a chair, spinning it around.

"When you're drunk, I am, T.P." She clutched the bat, ready to swing. "How come you to bring your buddies?"

"Huh?" He fumbled the shadows like a kid playing pin-the-tail-on-the-donkey, his hand just missing her face.

"You think you can come here and get a little while they laugh at me out there?" She backed again, clear of the doorway, and he followed her into the bedroom.

"Listen, babe. You know me better'n that. You know I got all respects for you." He touched her face, drew back as though shocked, then stroked her breasts. "I ain't staying. I just got a minute."

She jerked away, feeling the ghost of his hand following. "I got an idee, T.P. Why don't you go get your buddies and I'll give them a piece too." She laughed.

"Don't talk thataway, Chanell. You a lady . . ."

"Get the hell out of here." She got a good grip on the bat, set to swing. She was at the foot of the bed now, her eyes fully tuned to the grainy gray dark. He came on.

"Listen, babe, I been thinking about you hooking up with old Archie Wall, and I think it's a good idee. I do!" He nodded. "Look, way I see it is you can get it going with him, you know, and then we'll knock him off, take his cash. See?"

Then he grabbed her, kissed her, a soppy soft kiss, whiskey sweet. "Get out of here, you sonofabitch." She swung the bat and he ducked, backing and laughing.

"Think about it, babe. Think about it. Think about what I got here in my britches, about old Archie Wall's . . ."

She was wrong, he wasn't drinking; he was smoking pot. She could smell it, like scorching pepper and wood.

She swung wild, following him, and finally clubbed his right shoulder with the bat. She could have struck him in the head, but she didn't want to kill him, and a lick to the head would make this whole business serious. She wanted things back the way they were when he would pull her ponytail and say stupid stuff. Them fighting just to be fighting. But not talk of killing. She knew he meant it, and that made the rumor more real.

chapter four

If Chanell had been looking for peace at church on Sunday morning, she'd have gotten a fooling. From the time she stepped into the varnished pine vestibule till the time she stepped out, everybody was eyeballing her.

Seated in the same third pew from the front where she always sat, she saved a place for Bell, who was singing in the choir— four rows of chairs packed into an alcove behind the cresentoid pulpit. All varnished yellow pine spiking sunlight in a burst of holy brilliance. On the altar table, below the podium, a bouquet of pink glads fanned above the engraving, DO YE THIS IN REMEMBRANCE OF ME. Bell had on a maroon robe with a white vee collar that made her look square-shouldered and important, like Bea Arthur on the TV show *Golden Girls*. That's the kind of look she had. Or like a man dressed up in women's clothes. Gold hoop earrings big as her bangle bracelets. Cupping one elbow, she held a maroon songbook high, each rapturous note delivered to the sun-gilded ceiling. A vibrant cajoling of same old songs.

Chanell, beautician and friend, considered Bell. The coarse dark hair sprouting on her mustache area and on her arms and legs. Maybe even her shriveling breasts. Too many male hormones, Chanell supposed, and though Bell never mentioned the hair, Chanell figured it bothered her. What Chanell hoped to do, after she got a jump on her bills, was order an electrolysis machine; then she would shock every single hair on Bell's massive arms and legs, if she wanted her to. How would Chanell bring up the subject of that kind of hair? How would she ever find the time? She thought about the small domed timer pictured in her beauty-supply catalog and how much time it would take to tweeze all the hairs, time Bell didn't have either. She kept the books for her husband's logging business, made out payroll every Friday, and drove his Negro hands to the doctor in Valdosta, forty miles there and back.

Scooting to get comfortable on the hard, slick pew, as the choir lit into "Lily of the Valley," Chanell tried to avoid nicking gazes with two of her customers across the aisle. If only Chanell hadn't gone with Archie Wall last Friday, if only she hadn't told T.P. she was marrying the old bachelor lawyer, if only she hadn't beefed up the tale in the beauty shop. She singled out Joy Beth and Linda Gay, paired in the second row of the choir, songbooks lifted bosom high, and tongues flapping, and the whole business kept running through her head. She could smell it, sharp-cheesy, above the sweetish stale breath of the church.

She took a hymnal from the rack on the pewback ahead and looked up "Jesus Saves." She'd missed the page number called out by the song director, Miss Pansy's brother. Chanell knew the song by heart, had been singing it all her life at this same church where her mama first took her. The first visit looming in her mind as a blue nylon net dress that smelled stiff, the same one that she'd ripped the ruffle off while playing at the old jail after church, and the magic of her mother's needle conjuring the dress whole again. She had to quit daydreaming, she had to quit beating herself for running her mouth, for being so weak with T.P. (He'd ended up staying half the night, her fighting with him about Archie Wall, him trying to get "a piece.") And then she felt guilty about poor Archie Wall, across the road there, ignorant of the whole affair. And it was hard to feel sorry for Archie Wall, because you got the feeling that he didn't have any feelings, just money. So everybody said. And where did they think he got it from if they never paid him? And the whole mess agitated in her mind like a washing machine off balance.

The kingly-bald song director called out another number. She missed that one too. But she sang out anyway, hearing Bell's high soprano roll over the varnished pine apse with its triptych of sun from the facing wall of windows. Bell had what was called a cultured voice, like some fancy lady singer on a TV Christmas special. What T.P. called put on, "old opera doings." Chanell loved Bell's voice. Not that she was all that crazy about music now. But Bell was.

Trying not to think about such in church, Chanell thought about how she used to love rock and roll, about the small suitcase-style record player she'd taken to Pound Parties around Cornerville, a full-fledged teenager at thirteen. In some ways prettier then, with smaller features, her sloe eyes fitting in with her smaller figure. Not so busty, but balanced, thighs threatening to explode to fat, though shapely and promising that she'd still look better longer than fair and fat Linda Gay—a cow—or even Joy Beth, who had been better-looking too before she got done growing.

Dwarfed in one of the thronelike altar chairs, the new preacher got up and strolled to the podium while the choir filed from the alcove to take their seats with the congregation. A slight young man with reddish hair and weak-blue eyes, he beamed, showing too-large teeth and a square, jutted jaw. A student, so the rumor went, fresh out of seminary. Nervously leveling a stack of white note cards on top of his brown leather Bible, he waited for the heel clicks on the polished floor to cease.

The choir was still leaving the alcove. Joy Beth, shuffling behind Bell, smiled at Chanell and teetered on toward the rear of the church. Usually she sat with Chanell and Bell, all three snickering like schoolgirls over nothing. Bell slid in next to Chanell, settling into the pew with a jangling of bracelets, a rasping of nylons. Her rose perfume mingled with the inky smell of the church program Chanell was using as a fan. The air-conditioner, a faint hum, barely cooled the air, the glittering sun on the shrubs through the windows a reminder that inside was still cooler than out. Chanell felt the heat gather in her face and radiate. Linda Gay was tipping from the choir loft, around the pulpit, and Chanell decided that if she followed Joy Beth to the back, it would be a sure sign that war was on, that they'd taken yesterday's rebuff to heart. Linda Gay sidled along the right aisle by the wall of windows, never glancing at Chanell and Bell as she passed.

Chanell didn't look. She knew they were sitting together. Smiling to cover their Sunday sins. She felt a sharp pang of dread, like a slap on the back. Right between the shoulder blades. She could feel their tongues, like knives, slicing through her coward's heart.

The new preacher started with how glad he was to serve the church in his turn, and what a great job Brother Sikes, before him, had done in Cornerville. Such a good, quiet place to live, he said in a flimsy treble. Bell snorted, elbowing

Chanell in the ribs. Then she scratched her shaved legs, nails rasping on nylons and bracelets jangling, and sat back, bracing herself for the lull between singing. While the preacher droned announcements, Chanell's mind drifted. She could hear Linda Gay and Joy Beth whispering, three pews behind. Why had she let herself get so carried away? Why couldn't she just once act like she didn't care? She could have walked into the beauty shop and pretended nothing had happened. She could have kept her mouth shut during the fight with T.P.

The preacher asked everybody to be in special prayer for Miss Pansy, who'd been sent to the nursing home, and for the other sick and shut-in members of the community. Then as he began preaching, some mild sermon to keep from stepping on toes and getting run off like the last—the church called it "transfer"—Bell wrote Chanell a note on the front of her church program with the tiny red pencil from the donation-card slot.

The faint arched scribble read: "Did T.P. show up last night?"

Chanell wrote back. "Yes, we had a big fight, he's decided marrying A.W. is a good idea. The money, you know. Says we can knock him off, etc."

Chanell handed her the skinny red pencil with the note. Bell read it, glanced sidelong at Chanell, then wrote: "His ass!"

Chanell poked Bell's stocking-cased leg under the maroon robe. An ugly snigger erupted from deep inside Bell's throat, where the melody of pretty songs usually made up.

Chanell opened the bulletin and read all of the prayer requests and the program for the night service. Next Sunday morning the new preacher would be preaching in Fargo—alternating Sundays between churches—and Cornerville Baptist Church would have only Sunday school. She felt the same childish thrill as when she'd had a day off from school. Her heart glowed in her chest. Why did she come to church if she felt that way? she wondered. Habit? Maybe because most of her customers came. Or because of Bell. Or did she hope at some point to get better? Maybe go to heaven on her perfect church attendance when she got old and died. The little girl Chanell popped to mind again, getting a column of foil stars by her name on the Sunday-school attendance record. She flipped the bulletin over and was shocked to spy the same name printed in the column of upcoming events.

"Engagement announcement," it read. "Chanell Foster and Archie Wall to be married in October. Date forthcoming."

Chanell's hands shook, her face burned. Mind fast-forwarding, she could read all kinds of possibilities in the placement of the announcement. She'd told T.P she was getting married, she'd mentioned October only to Miss Neida, Linda Gay typed the church programs, Joy Beth ran them off. Even Bell, who handed out the programs, could have been in on it. She tapped Bell on one relaxed knee and passed the program, watching her tan makeup mask for signs of Judas.

Bell cut her green eyes from the preacher to the bulletin, reading it, and turned, stretching them at Joy Beth and Linda Gay. Then she placed a bejeweled hand on Chanell's, squeezing as she wagged her head. Bell's tipped nose tipped a little higher. "Act like you didn't see it," she whispered. "The more you stir, the worse it stinks."

Chanell didn't think so. Once something was out, especially in writing, it was like a throwaway comment in the courtroom that couldn't be taken back.

Weak in the knees, Chanell started to go home after church, but as usual Bell put in for her to go to Mama Sharon's for dinner. Chanell and T.P. may have been through, in a manner of speaking, but Mama Sharon and Bell were still family.

Chanell's own mother had died of cancer when she was sixteen. Her daddy had remarried and moved away when the Swanoochee County division of Sampson Powder Company set up camp in another region. Tough and tense men, like Chanell's daddy, would rise at five in the morning, meet at the commissary by six, and load up in the white trucks with reddish-brown company logos. Out in the pinewoods, they would dig and load tree stumps till twelve noon, then hurriedly eat last night's leftovers from black satchel lunchboxes, and trudge back to the giant yellow tractors and trucks, working on till six, at which time they'd return to their camp families. That's what Chanell gleaned, from living in the camp and watching the other daddies, about the tedium of her own daddy's days. Not from what he said, but from what she saw. Once he did tell her that the fat hearts of aged tree stumps—trees either cut for timber or turpentined to death—were ground for gunpowder and dynamite. He never told it as if it was important—not with pride in what he did—but matter of factly, like a man would tell why he went away to war. Swanoochee County was still noted for its vast pine and hardwood forests, so Chanell never quite understood the company's move, her daddy's move, never understood her daddy's not asking if she'd like to go with him. She was out of high school by then and planning to marry T.P., spending three-fourths of her time at Mama Sharon's. She wouldn't have gone with her daddy anyway; maybe he had understood. Chanell doubted that was the reason. Really, after her mama died, her daddy had quit being a daddy, quit with family, period. He'd grown suddenly awkward and aloof in the hollow, death-free house with no buffer between him and his only daughter. As though the threat of death had trapped them inside, his feeble spirit for fatherly duties was aired with the house's medicine smells.

The disbanded camp, where Chanell was born and raised, had become the second quarters for Negroes in Cornerville, now pilfered and wild with vines, scrub oaks, and palms. Palms planted by the company now scattered in dusty-green volunteer stands, stunted to palmetto size. Across ten acres of sandy, weed-choked ground, carved out of woods, the remaining whitish frame houses with Sampson-red trim still defined the precise rows of twelve family dwellings, parallel to Highway 129. Chanell remembered the camp houses in rows, though many of them had been moved and remodeled throughout the county—repainted in unsuccessful disguises of popular colors—and the camp now appeared laid out in diamonds. On the walk home, after unloading from the school bus at the commissary, she used to count off the houses—fourth house, tenth row—to find the right one. More secure than perplexed by the same-ness, though often afraid she might step inside the wrong house and be embarrassed. Now, though the house rows had been disturbed, she could still pick out her old house, the only one on the tenth row to survive the move. Like the houses, the old Sampson commissary, hub of the camp, had been relocated for a county recreation center, down the paved road facing the gym and across from Mama Sharon's.

To keep the sun off her new blue Buick, Bell parked under Mama Sharon's shade oak at the end of the road. Four house-bound roads east of Chanell's place, with the same creek augering through black gums and bays to the Alapaha River on the western boundary of Cornerville. Bell and Pete's double-wide trailer sat at the start of Mama Sharon's road, and in the middle, Mama Sharon's Church of God across from the low white recreation center, which hardly resembled the high-floored Samson commissary on its lift of wood pillars. From where Bell and Chanell sat, cocooned in the car's cool newness, they could see Pete slumped in one of the rockers on Mama Sharon's unpainted porch. Work boots crossed and propped on a porch post, cap bill low over his eyes. Sullen in his forced Sunday leisure and not about to look up at Bell in her Buick bought with his sweat. His pride, buying Buicks, only the biggest and finest—he hated Jap cars, hated Japs—though he'd be hard put to say why. Though he'd be hard put to say why he sat here Sunday after Sunday, banked in by womanly houseplants and shackled to a porch post, when he should be in the woods working. Sundays! "I still say, forget it," said Bell to Chanell, switching off the engine and snatching the ring of keys from the ignition. Bracelets jangled and nylons rustled as she got out.

Chanell got out on the other side, thawing in the heat of the festering sun. "I can't forget it, Bell," she said, following Bell up the path of the dirt yard to the porch. "Not and it in the church bulletin."

The unpainted front porch was lined with tubs and pots of houseplants, sprigs rooting in tin cans on brittle plank shelves beneath fluted tin eaves. Scraggly crepe myrtles hid the dogtrot house from the road, and spotted about on the bare gray dirt tobacco sticks, teepee-style, staked every plant one could imagine, from orange trees to persimmons to aged rosebushes gone to thistle. What little yard there was, between the house next door, on the left, and the woods, on the right, was crammed with outbuildings: a screened rabbit hutch on rotting stilts, a tin-topped sweet-potato bank, and a sinking log shed walled with rusty hanging tools. Mama Sharon had even kept her outhouse out back, though she no longer used it. Her diamond-wire chicken yard, in the crook of woods behind the house, was home to fluffy white hens and one rooster that crowed any time he took a notion.

"How you, Pete?" Chanell said.

Pete tipped his cap bill, then laid his hand on the drowsing white cat next to his chair. "Chanell," he said and closed his dark, troubled eyes. The lines of his lean tan face were like tucks in leather. A successful logger, he worked hard for his money, money turned over to Bell, who shopped as hard as he worked.

The white cat stood and arched its back, wrapping its long body around the porch post and then Bell's leg. She kicked it away, tipping on spike heels across the porch to the screened door; the cat yowled, but trailed her with its periscoping tail scutted.

Not unusual, Pete and Bell not speaking to one another. Not that they were mad, they just had nothing to say, usually, unless they were talking business. Occasionally, she might call him "shitass" and laugh, and he might call her "bitch" and laugh. When they didn't laugh you knew they meant it.

In the dank living room, with its army-issue cot, ruptured vinyl couch, and musky padded chairs, Chanell could smell steamed okra, fried chicken, and sweet black tea wafting from the kitchen beyond the dogtrot, or middle porch. As usual she was hungry, a thick gnawing in her belly. Love of eating was something she had in common with her customers, a sort of sport. Like body builders lifting weights to build muscle, they focused on food and put on fat, then dieted grudgingly.

Bell set her great Aigner bag on a small, wobbly table along the wainscoted wall between doors. "I know Mama's 'bout to burn up half the time," she said. "Looks like she'd open up them windows or get a air-conditioner, one." Heat-runneled mullions were locked down each side of the mantel, where a white crocheted doily draped from the center. A mahogany-trimmed clock squatted on the scarf with dozens of gift figurines crowded end to end. An orange-tinted picture of Chanell and T.P., taken right after they got married, seemed to belong in the time warp of dust and shadows, the cold soot air of the closed room.

"Sister," Mama Sharon hooted from the kitchen, "that you?"

Bell laughed and stepped through the door to the bowed dogtrot, where a watershelf along the left side held a dull aluminum bucket and a white enamel pan. "Same evertime you see her," said Bell.

The very quality Chanell loved in Mama Sharon, her sameness. And not just the sameness of manners and heart; Chanell loved that Mama Sharon looked the same as when she first saw her. Not changing to be changing like everybody else. Something solid in that. Something sure in the fact that Mama Sharon had never seen fit to change from fat to thin—she never mentioned it—or cut her mane of brown hair. As she had gone gray, the brown had blended to tan, a unique color, smooth and straight as fine sewing thread. When Chanell was in beauty school, living with Mama Sharon, she used to brush her mother-in-law's hair one hundred strokes each night, gliding the boar-bristle brush from crown to waist. Not for practice, as she practiced teasing Bell's hair, which smelled like the nylon locks of the practice mannequins. Mama Sharon's hair smelled like the inside of an old paper-lined trunk.

Bell stopped off at the watershelf to wash her hands, to get rid of germs from shaking at church, as she always said. One courtesy she'd like to do away with, shaking hands. The sweet-soap smell mingled with Mama Sharon's lard-fried chicken and steeping tea, all masking the ripe-mud odor of the watershelf runoff, where flame-red periwinkles foiled the dead dirt yard.

Chanell followed the creaking-board dogtrot to the high-ceilinged kitchen with its swarming waves of heat. Mama Sharon, standing at the white stove with her back to the door, wore her hair up in a bun and had on a no-brand purple frock that whispered as she stirred in the oversized pots. Chanell crept over and, hugging the air around Mama Sharon's head, cupped her hands over the shorter woman's glasses. "Guess who?"

"Chanell Foster," Mama Sharon said right off, not even turning. Her voice was liquid and clipped. Feeling her hair lift, Chanell peeped around Mama Sharon at the cast-iron skillet of slimy okra and a blue-speckled pot of creamed corn. A large bone-white platter of fried chicken wings and drumsticks warmed on the center panel of the white range.

"How you today, Mama Sharon?" Chanell said.

Mama Sharon's round head shook; she clanked the wooden spoon on the rim of the corn pot.

Chanell backed up, watching Mama Sharon's padded shoulders shake. "You okay, Mama Sharon?"

Bell stepped inside the kitchen door and took a fly flappet from a nail on the facing.

"I been better," Mama Sharon said.

Bell stared at Chanell, her molded-clay face oily from the heat. "What's ailing you, Mama?" she asked.

"A little case of the can't-help-its, you might say." Mama Sharon sniffled, fishing her handkerchief from the bosom of her purple frock.

"Somebody hurt your feelings at church?" Chanell placed her hands on Mama Sharon's quaking shoulders.

"T.P. in jail again?" Bell swatted a fly on the pine harvest table, where salt and pepper shakers were grouped with a jar of red pickled peppers and a bottle of cane syrup.

"Sister, don't talk like that about your brother." Mama

Sharon stirred the speckled butterbeans shimmering with a skim of grease, then sidestepped away from Chanell.

"He's about due one of his capers." Bell swatted another fly.

"For your information, young lady," Mama Sharon sniffled, "your brother was in church this morning."

"In church?" Chanell said.

"In church." Mama Sharon turned and socked Chanell cold with her gray bubble eyes. "Where you and Bell oughta been."

"We just got out of church, Mama." Bell cranked two blue ice trays from the frosted-over compartment of the squat refrigerator.

"I meant *real church*." Mama Sharon was still eyeing Chanell, the tip of her long nose red as Rudolph's.

Bell had quit going to the Pentecostal Church with Mama Sharon after she got married, and Mama Sharon often accused her of making the switch because the Church of God, the only *real church*, was too strict for her only daughter. As a Baptist, Bell could smoke and dance and cuss out T.P. Bell claimed to have switched from saved to lost only so that she could cut her hair. Mama Sharon ducked head to shoulder and wiped a tear from her cheek.

"Mama Sharon," Chanell said, "what in the world's wrong?" Chanell hugged her, smelling snuff and rust. Mama Sharon had always been predictably sensitive, often evasive, but never cold.

"I wouldn't of thought it," she said.

Oh, Chanell thought, the tightness in her head letting down. She laughed. "Mama Sharon, you must of heard I'm getting married to Archie Wall. Right?"

"I wouldn't be so proud-acting if I was you." She shook her head. "Ain't nothing to be proud of."

"I'm not, Mama Sharon." Chanell meant she wasn't getting married, but sounded as though she meant she wasn't proud.

"Well, I wouldn't be if I was you." Mama Sharon, already smiling, already over it, either way, threatened to paddle Chanell with the corn-coated spoon.

"Mama, it's a lie!" Bell popped the ice from the trays into a clanking metal pan atop the white metal sink-and-cabinet unit. It was all getting funny now; Channel wondered what had happened at the Methodist Church this morning. "What did they do, Mama Sharon, put the announcement in the Church of God program?"

Mama Sharon dabbed at her eyes under her wire-rimmed glasses. "T.P. asked a special altar prayer for his marriage this morning. Said he'd been trying to patch things up with you, then along come Archie Wall . . ."

After dinner, they sat on the front porch: Mama Sharon wedged sidelong into the porch swing with her bad leg laid out across the wood slats. One heavy elastic stocking was rolled on the calf, where a vein strutted to the instep of her blocky black shoe. In her purple dress and crownlike bun, she looked like a poor queen. The easy screak of the swing chains kept time with the crickets in the woods at her back, with the Sunday sun ticking on the raftered tin.

Bell sat in a kitchen chair between Pete, dozing in a rocker, and Mama Sharon, bad-mouthing Archie Wall from the porch swing, while Chanell recombed her hair for church that night. It seemed that Archie Wall, having been brought up that morning at church, had stuck in Mama Sharon's overblown head and was now a mere topic for passing time. When a car or truck would pull up at the recreation center, two weed fields down and across the road, Mama Sharon would cut into what she was telling to comment on the latest concerning whoever happened by: news was that Joe Cribs was leaving

Paula for somebody; Mama Sharon wasn't saying who because she knew how to keep her mouth shut and like the Bible said, "Judge not lest ye be judged," but she did wonder how in the world two men could have things to do with one another, especially in this day of the AIDS, and looks like Sodom and Gomorrah would have been lesson enough. As though checking over what was just said for telltale sinning, she gazed out at the sunny fields of red bitterweeds like tilled clay.

Mama Sharon talked on, bearing heavy on the r's. "A lawyer hain't out for but one thing. Money. As good a raising as Archie Wall had, a body'd expect better. Big family of born-again Christians. Hardworking farm people. He'll do anything for a dime. Hain't never made a honest cent." She sat up, holding her bad leg, and watched as a gray car stopped before the white, warehousey recreation building. "What money he come by was from getting divorces for women so they could go out and sin." Rearing back, Mama Sharon gave half a dozen examples, leaving Chanell out. She seemed satisfied now that the rumor wasn't true, but since they were on the subject of Archie Wall . . .

Pete roused, resetting his work boots on the porch post, and tipped his cap bill, and in a sleepy, unctuous voice told how Archie Wall had once won a case for his client by simply wearing the court down with two weeks of nonsense. Ponderously dragging out pieced-together details from two ornery old Swanoochee Countians, Archie Wall had laid his case before the carefully sifted jury and an out-of-town judge. Every hour or so, he'd step back and let the two farmed-out oldtimers rage at one another, cuss words like backed-up sewage issuing around the clank of the gavel. A semblance of order restored, Archie Wall would begin again, eking out the story of how Zeke Parrish, his client, had borrowed fifty dollars from Dilmus Sharpe, putting up some undecided-upon tract of his two-hundred-acre sand-soaked farm as collateral. When the time came to pay up and Zeke didn't have the money, Dilmus set in to claim what was his. With the leathery toughness of two old gators, the men tangled over the land. Each gaining and losing just enough strength to hold the dispute over another day. Late one evening, Zeke finally agreed to grant the crusty, crippled-up man all the land he could walk over before nightfall. Old Dilmus, known for hoarding land against debts, set out shuffling along the fencejambs of blackberry thickets, his walking stick poking around the raw dirt of gopher holes and starveling cedars, intending to claim the whole farm. When he didn't show up by sundown, Zeke brushed the cornseed meal from his hands and, chuckling, went inside his house. Archie Wall, on the side of right, no matter how wrong, argued in court that by law for the sake of law and no law named, the debt was settled, that greed had doomed Dilmus Sharpe. Adding enough "furthermores" to frustrate the circuit judge and twelve tired jurors, Archie Wall won his case and put an end to Dilmus's land hoarding.

Later that afternoon, Bell went home to nap before church, and Chanell decided to walk back to her house. She didn't feel mad now, but passing the cedar-hedged, cinder-block Church of God, she entertained images of herself going inside and posting an announcement that T.P. was lying and she wasn't about to marry Archie Wall.

When she got to the end of Mama Sharon's road, taking the sidewalk in front of the gym, she saw T.P.'s elevated pickup parked under the huge oak among several other trucks. The hollow bounce of basketballs sounded from the floor inside. Chanell started to cross the highway and have it out with T.P. then and there, but he'd have some way around it. Besides, she didn't like to fight with him in front of his buddies, who always made it seem she was making up excuses to see T.P.

She went on, walking fast along the sidewalk, past the strip of neat white houses in front of the old school, past the Baptist parsonage and on toward Joy Beth's roomy frame house, next to the Baptist Church. She would take the first oak-lined road running around the loop to her house, she decided, and not have to walk in front of Archie's Wall's to get to the other turnoff. But when she got to Joy Beth's, and the first entrance to the loop, she spied her peacock strutting along the shoulder of 94 toward the blinking red light at the crossing. She didn't want to shout at him, right there in front of Joy Beth's house, so she ran on past, hissing, "Shoo! Shoo!"

George cocked his head, sun glancing off his array of tail feathers, like grease on collard greens, and pranced on toward the intersection where the red light paled in the lowering sun. When Chanell got in front of Archie Wall's, still on her side of the road, George stopped before the post office, jigging in one spot, as though trying to decide whether to turn back or go on. Both arms flapping, Chanell eased out onto the highway, circling, to haze him up the road to her house.

He fanned his crayon-colored tail feathers, let out a high-pitched holler, and flew halfway across 94, then tipped along the courtyard sidewalk toward the intersection.

"Shoo, shoo!" Chanell shouted. At least nobody was around—only a few cars parked in front of the Delta store, west of 129—at least she was well past Archie Wall's house.

"Let a big truck come by and squash you," she called out to George. "See if I care." She picked up an oak twig and hurled it over his craned head.

Sweeping the sidewalk with his drooped iridescent plumes, George streaked across 129 to the Delta, rounded the gas tanks, and cut behind the two-story brick Masonic building with blue window shades. Chanell stood in front of the court-yard with her foot on the metal rail, waiting for him to skirt the triangle of connected store lots or head for the rise of sun-beamed houses beyond the shortcut that merged with 94. In a few minutes, he showed around the rear of the Masonic building, then waddled up the dirt alley between the wall of red brick and the concrete-block store.

She kept still, watching as he straggled confusedly across 129 to the south end of the courthouse square, where the adjacent white-brick county health department sat just off the school-bus shortcut. Maybe if she left him alone he'd make the square by Archie Wall's hotel, bank, and house, then toddle home.

She slipped through the courthouse breezeway, coming out in front of Archie Wall's bank, all the while keeping George in sight, and hid behind one of the moss-swagged liveoaks. He strolled past the leaning two-story hotel, his shadow ostrichlike and lonesome on the gray dirt yard, and then straight in front of the bank. But when he got to Archie Wall's pickup, parked between the house and the bank, he stopped, cocking his head from left to right. Then he waddled up the narrow dirt drive toward Archie Wall's backyard and garden.

"Damn!" Chanell said. If she let him go, he'd get into Archie Wall's cucumbers. Then what? She hunkered close along the wall with puckered white paint, like fungus on an oak, to the corner overlooking the level green garden, the sunny high-way, Joy Beth's tall white house, and the front of the red-brick church. Across 94, cars were pulling up at the church for Bap-tist Training Union. Joy Beth came out of her house and slammed the screen door, crossing the full-length porch to the doorsteps, then headed east up the sidewalk toward the church.

George was now situated in the sprawl of vines, scratching them aside till the gray dirt shone with inlays of green cucumbers the color of his breast. Pecking, he'd lift his head, cone fringed like the bloom of a mimosa, blare his bead eyes, then peck again, tatting lacy holes in the scattered cucumbers.

Suddenly, Chanell heard Archie Wall's heels pounding on the floor inside, picking up in quick thumps as he neared the backdoor. She had to decide. She could either let the peacock go—let whatever would be just be between that fool bird and that fool Archie Wall—or she could run out there and try to chase him out of the cucumber patch and make a big to-do in front of Joy Beth.

"You a dead sonofabitch now!" Archie Wall hollered from the door. Chanell heard the breaching of a shotgun—*schl-lup*.

Joy Beth stopped in front of the church to watch, just as T.P.'s black pickup passed between and blocked her view. T.P., leering from the sun-spackled cab, slammed on his brakes and smacked the door with his fist and drove on. The frantic peacock hollered like a woman and fluttered to the corner fence post, then kited down to the sidewalk and scuttled across the highway in the wake of the truck's blasting glass packs.

"Archie Wall," Chanell yelled, coming quick around the corner of the house, where the red-faced lawyer now stood on the porch with the barrel of his rabbit-eared shotgun tilted at the peacock. "Archie Wall, don't! Don't shoot him!"

Joy Beth shook her head, wheeled, and pranced up the church walkway.

"Archie Wall," Chanell said, now facing him on the doorsteps, "if my peacock ruined your cucumbers, I'll trim your hair for free."

He lowered the shotgun, squinting out at the tattered garden. "I'd say two, three trims and we'll be even." He turned and ambled back inside, his white-socked feet whumping on the floor.

chapter five

Chanell could vouch for the stress on beauticians. Especially from women. Like a preacher, a beautician is supposed to be perfect—to look good and act good and make them look good too. She should make them the picture in their heads. How they hope they look, or hope sometime to look. Every woman has an image of a restaurant or a mall or a theater, maybe, where she'll be when she finally looks right, and it's up to the beautician to make that image real. One strand of bangs combed over the wrong eye and it's the beautician's fault.

Men, they look for peace. When they get enough money and power they'll be happy. When they get their women situated, walking in the line they've drawn, they'll be at peace. Unlike women, men think they look good anyway. It's up to the beautician to keep them looking that way. If she fails, she's shit.

Things rocked smoothly on through the first week of August. By Friday, Chanell figured that the rumor had worn itself out,

as Bell had predicted. T.P. hadn't been by since the Sunday
before, when Chanell's peacock had ravaged Archie Wall's
cucumber patch. They'd had a big blowup in front of Mr. Jim
and Miss Neida—right out in the front yard—and he'd left
mad because she wouldn't go inside so they could talk.

That morning, Chanell switched on the air-conditioner
early to get a jump on the heat. One day it would rain and
the next day the sun would bake down in a drawing smelter.
She had six standing appointments—Joy Beth and Linda Gay
included—a hair straightening, a curly perm, and a dye job.

Every day she turned on the soap operas to check the
styles, what her customers wanted to look like. And most of
the actresses were wearing their hair tame and straight. Natural with lots of body and sheen. Chanell knew, of course, that
the Hollywood styles wouldn't really catch on around Cornerville for two or three years. Most were still attached to the
curly dos that came out in the eighties, hairstyles she'd had
to talk them into then. She even had some calls for teasing
and wave sets, techniques picked up in beauty school a
decade ago.

While waiting for Miss Lou, who still wore the same
wash-water blue permed hairdo, Chanell decided to put on a
load of towels to wash. Hang them to dry in the sun. She bent
over to gather the dirty towels from the bin under the shampoo bowl, and standing again, saw Archie Wall wandering
around the south wing of Miss Pansy's house and disappearing
behind a hedge of reeds.

She stood there with the sun in her eyes, waiting for him
to show again. Was he checking out the house to buy? When
he didn't come, after a few minutes, she went on into the
kitchen and put the towels in the washer and got a glass of

iced tea. Starting back through the living room, she heard the door of the beauty shop squeak open and shut. Only eight o'clock; not yet time for Miss Lou. Maybe Archie Wall had come in for that free trim she'd promised in exchange for damage to his cucumbers. Good. She'd get him out of the way before the other customers got there.

But when she got to the shop, there sat Miss Lou, frail and slumped, clutching her bone-white triangular pocketbook.

Chanell always tried to tone down her loud, coarse voice for older, more delicate customers. But she never failed to feel awkward and hasty, like a phony apt to rupture their fragile beliefs. She flipped on the fluorescent light switch by the door.

"You're early, Miss Lou," she said.

"Yes 'um," said Miss Lou. "Got to run by the post office. Get a letter off to Mae."

"How's she doing?" Chanell walked over to the shampoo bowl. "Step over here, will you, Miss Lou?"

The old woman started over, straightening the cloth belt on her blue plaid frock.

"Here, I'll take your pocketbook and put it over there." Chanell reached for the strap, but Miss Lou hugged the body of the bag close.

"I'll just hang onto it," she said.

Chanell wrapped the green plastic cape around Miss Lou's shoulders and smoothed it while the bent old lady wrested the pocketbook from beneath the cape and clutched it to her withered bosom. As Chanell gently cranked the chair back, Miss Lou resisted by stiffening her neck, then let go, staring up with melty blue eyes.

Always before Chanell had taken the old lady's pocketbook. What was going on here? "Say Mae's doing good, huh?"

Miss Lou closed her eyes; the crepe-papery lids twitched. "Ain't had no hearing from her in a while."

"Did she get that child-support money for your grandbabies yet?" Chanell said.

With the water rushing around her ears, maybe she couldn't hear.

"I say, Miss Lou," Chanell spoke up, "did Mae get that mess with her husband straightened out?"

Miss Lou gripped her pocketbook tighter. "That water's a mite hot, honey."

"Yes 'um." Chanell adjusted the hot spigot till the water ran cool, testing with her wrist, then pressed the sprayer to Miss Lou's peeking pink scalp.

The old woman flinched and shivered.

Something was wrong. Miss Lou had always gone on and on about her daughter and the grandbabies; last visit to the shop she'd detailed every day since Mae's divorce from that rascal who she'd known was a rascal—he'd dropped Mae for a younger woman, a hussy—from the time they got married. So strange how Miss Lou would unself-consciously dump her woes in the beauty shop, yet self-consciously refrain from complaining about Chanell's occasional slip-ups. Once Chanell had left the perm solution on too long, literally searing the poor lady's scalp, and she'd not said a word. Lord help! Chanell thought. If Miss Lou, this sweet old saint, has turned against me, what about the others? She always gave Chanell Christmas gifts, brought her cake or eggs. No tipper, but thoughtful and loving. Good friends with Mama Sharon. What was going on here? Was the old rumor still alive, had a new one been born?

Feeling like a fool, not talking, Chanell finished shampooing the thready white hair while Miss Lou lay stiff and mute.

Above all, a beautician, in Chanell's book, should talk after she got done listening.

Chanell set Miss Lou's hair on bobby pins—perfect circles like pencil drawings—then placed her under the drier with a *Woman's Day* magazine on her lap. Without a lapse in motion, Chanell covered the exposed *Cosmopolitan* on the stack beside Miss Lou with *Southern Living*. Miss Lou was cradling her pocketbook like a baby. Chanell crossed to the counter and switched on the tiny TV. (Some of her customers even sang along with the McDonald's jingles.)

The magazine stayed closed on Miss Lou's skinny thighs—square-toed bone shoes primly set—while Chanell sorted clips from rollers in the portable bin. The old lady's eyes Ping-Ponged from Chanell to the pocketbook on her lap.

Chanell looked out the window for Archie Wall, but couldn't spot him in the nimbus of sun around Miss Pansy's white house.

"This here drier's burning my ears," Miss Lou said, scrunching her sloped shoulders.

Chanell went over and turned the drier knob to low. Miss Lou's hair was so thin it should dry within a matter of minutes, but those wet-wound bobby-pinned strands could fool you. "You want something to drink, Miss Lou?"

"I don't." She closed her eyes, sun striking her callused nose.

Next, Aunt Ruth—not Chanell's real aunt—came in, and they went through much the same thing. She held her pocketbook and practically barked at Chanell, a fussy old lady with a rimed, lilting voice, and made no pretenses about how last month's body wave hadn't held. Chanell offered the tall, straight woman a free one, but she said, "No thanks," then wilted back in the chair like a scalded gladiolus. That old budget perm had made her break out in hives and she'd had to go the doctor. Thirty-five dollars down the drain.

Chanell doused Aunt Ruth's short, silky hair in blue rinse, set it with wave clips, and stuck her under the drier next to Miss Lou. No *Southern Living*, no iced tea, nothing.

Both driers going at once, the shop was about the same temperature as inside the house. Chanell felt like cooking the two old grouches, but she carried the floor fan from the house to the shop and turned it straight on them, frocktails blowing over their clutched pocketbooks. Stepping out to the stoop again, Chanell leaned in the corner between doors and breathed, in through the nose and out through the mouth, five times. From her spot, she could see George the peacock following Archie Wall across Miss Pansy's red-brick porch. Archie Wall stood, sizing up the oak door, the frame of leaded glass window lights, then backing, almost tripped over the peacock. He wheeled and kicked at the bird. George shrieked and dropped his burden of feathers, circled the porch, then trailed Archie Wall to the south end.

"George!" Chanell called, stepping to the edge of her stoop. "George!" The peacock strutted on in Archie Wall's tracks. "Dumb peacock," Chanell said low, "just like a man— hears only what he wants to."

She started to chase after him, but hearing Miss Lou's timer bell chime on the drier, changed her mind.

"Shit!" she said, turning to the shop door and Miss Lou's stricken face.

The old lady stepped aside to let Chanell pass, then toddled behind her to the combout station. Oh, Lord! Chanell had cursed in front of her two main church ladies. She'd never be forgiven. No matter what she said now—and she'd just about made up her mind to tell everybody the straight of the story, or at least tell them off—they wouldn't believe a word. Chanell brushed out Miss Lou's hair, picking the feathery ringlets till the scalp ceased to show, sprayed it stiff, and lit into Aunt Ruth's crimped waves with a zeal born of being damned.

Archie Wall was stepping off ground between Miss Pansy's house and the Baptist Church as the two li'l ole ladies toddled past and angled right toward the post office. They turned and watched as he crossed the road, heading for the shop.

Leaving the ever-swinging door open, because she might as well, Chanell marched over to the shampoo bowl and began spraying gray hairs from the fake marble. Not even looking up as Archie Wall came through the door, as he closed it, as he stood there like a granite statue of himself— only lawyer in Swanoochee County.

"Archie Wall, I can't get to you just yet," she finally said. "I got a perm coming in any minute."

Flushed and round as a dog tick, he still stood there.

"You want to come back later?" she said.

"I'll wait." He took off his hat, sat down in the nearest drier chair, and stogged the felt fedora on one knee.

The time had come. Chanell had to say something. Or burst. "Archie Wall," she said, drying her hands, "I reckon you've heard all the talk."

He dug a handkerchief from his hip pocket and mopped his face, with his worn black lawyer shoes crossed and laid on their sides.

"Course you have," she said. "It's all over Cornerville."

He sat forward, shook his head.

"What I said that evening to T.P. . . ." she began.

"He come by my place yesterday." Archie Wall spoke as if speaking of something else entirely.

"What for?"

"To get me to check out Miss Pansy's place for you. Said you was hoping to buy it."

"Me?" Chanell stepped closer, stooping with her hands on her knees to stare him in the eyes.

"Yes 'um." Archie Wall looked down at his hat. "Said you was looking to buy it."

"I'm gone kill that sonofabitch, Archie Wall," she shouted. "I am. I'm sick and tired of him ruining my life." She pawed the floor, blew at her forehead, and spinning with her hands on her hips, spied Shirley Dees, her perm customer, peeping through a slit in the door. Her ashy black hair was fluffed on top and pinned on the sides, shocked eyes looming in her long white face. After what seemed like an hour of taking it all in, as if getting a bead on how to tell what she would tell to whoever she would tell it to, she eased the shop door shut and sallied off the stoop, heels of her sandals slapping along the hard road.

"Archie Wall," Chanell said, "get up here in this chair. I'm gone trim you now."

Chanell knew it was time for Joy Beth; she'd booked her with Shirley Dees in order to set her hair while waiting for Shirley's perm to take. And sure enough, Joy Beth strolled in just as Chanell was blowing the trimmings off Archie Wall's stuffed red neck.

Joy Beth acted as always, tender pink smile and all. No mention of the trick announcement in the church program, no reaction to Archie Wall—long gone now—no reference to the rumor. But Chanell knew Joy Beth was taking everything down in her head. She went on about what season she was— she and Chanell were both Winters, she'd learned from some fashion magazine, both brunettes, regardless of their opposite skin tones—her way, Chanell supposed, of finally putting the two of them on the same level—and could Chanell get her frizzy hair to lay close like Joan Collins's? Chanell couldn't. It was too fine for body, too brittle for sheen. Chanell straightened her hair anyway, then blew it dry. Hair the drab black of charcoal bloused around Joy Beth's tapered face, ends fried bad, bangs flattened to the penciled brows of her close-set blue eyes. Still, she smiled and acted as if she loved it. She'd done that before, then left to show everybody how Chanell had ruined her.

In junior high, when dressing up had taken the place of dressing paper dolls, Joy Beth had become jealous of Chanell. First warm spells in March, they would lie out in bikinis on an old chenille spread in one of their backyards, the spread's nubby weave transferring to Joy Beth's doughy flesh. Joy Beth would blister sore-red, while Chanell colored smoky brown. Joy Beth, checking the red line on her straight thigh, would say, "Honey, don't I wish I tanned like you!" Then after Chanell won the Future Homemakers of America beauty contest, a mandatory, fund-raising competition of all members, Joy Beth became spiteful and went around telling that Chanell had mixed baby oil with iodine to get that tanned look.

Joy Beth rose from the combout chair, handing Chanell a three-dollar tip, and brushed the hair from her royal blue rayon dress. Their color. Throughout the entire afternoon, Chanell spoke little to her customers, other than "Step over here," "Is that too hot?" and "Do you want it trimmed or just set?" No tea, no pocketbook taking, no magazines.

Three o'clock and five customers to go, and nobody's hair had come out like they wanted. One girl, who'd left school early to get her long, kinky hair trimmed, changed her mind after seeing a bobbed actress on *Search for Tomorrow* and had

Chanell whack off her blond locks and shave her nape and above her ears.

Miss Neida, back for what she called "a shaping," shook her head at the shorn girl in the mirror. "A woman's hair is her crown and glory," she said.

By knockoff time, Chanell's feet were burning from standing all day, her head ached, her jutted breasts were raw from sweating inside her double-D bra cups. She'd made $92 with tips, not a bad day. But, judging by her customers' reactions to the rumor—if that was what it was—she feared tomorrow she might earn half that. To keep her regulars, she generally charged less than the shops did in Valdosta, and, corny or not, she held prices down so that anybody could afford at least a trim.

The next day only a few of her regulars showed, including Bell—the others didn't even bother to call to break their appointments—with nothing eventful except the rain, a peaceful, traveling series of showers that cooled the bungalow and revived the wilted vines and grass. No thunder, even. Only the off-and-on patter on the roof, soothing Chanell. Nothing eventful, that is, except T.P. not showing on a Saturday night, setting Chanell on edge.

Something told Chanell to skip Sunday school the next morning; whether it was God or the devil, she should have listened.

But she went anyway, went on in and sat down in the same third pew from the front and sang with the saints, trying to key in on Bell's quavery soprano to keep from thinking about what everybody was thinking. But her mind kept wandering out the window and four side roads over to the Church of God, where, maybe right this very minute, they could be listening to T.P.'s special prayer request for his wayward ex-wife. "Our Father who art in heaven . . ." she intoned.

The choir trailed from the alcove behind the pulpit, Bell's jewelry jingling from ears to wrists; she flashed her green eyes, smiling slyly, and slid into the pew next to Chanell. The preacher got up and made the announcements—nothing in them about her upcoming marriage to Archie Wall—a special prayer request for Miss Pansy. There was a rumor going around that somebody would be buying her house. "But then," he added timidly, "there will be wars and rumors of wars."

Chanell sat back, took the skinny red pencil from the donation-card slot, and wrote a note to Bell on the program (no mention of Chanell there either, just a drawing by Linda Gay of the church twenty years ago, before the bricks, before the steeple with the hard-ringing bell). "T.P.'s got it out that I'm buying Miss Pansy's house," Chanell wrote. "Did you know that?"

Bell wrote back, "His ass!" underlining "ass." "Act like you don't care and everybody'll quit talking."

Chanell settled in for the sermon, growing drowsy and cool, the hum of the air-conditioner meshing with the rasp of Bell's nails scratching on her nylons. "The deacons have asked me on their behalf," the preacher said, "to bring before the church a little matter of violence in our good community." His reddish hair was pink in the holy aura of sunlit pine. "We need to be in special prayer, I say, that we won't fall into the world's ways. All the violence and hatred out there. We're living in the last days. Yes, we are, brethren. Mother against daughter, father against son . . . wives against their husbands. A shooting, Sunday was a week ago, I'm told, right here in front of this very church." He was looking everywhere but at Chanell.

Even before she could figure out what he meant, tingling had begun in her fingertips, traveling to her face. Like hearing the rumble of a coming train and being stuck on the tracks.

Bell placed a hand on Chanell's knee; Chanell's foot twitched and hit the seat ahead. "Some man, right here in our own community, it seems," the preacher went on in a tweety voice, "tried to defend his right to his wife against another, and that heathen shot at him."

Pictured in Chanell's mind was Archie Wall with the shotgun, Joy Beth on the sidewalk, T.P. driving past and ramming his fist on the truck door. She waited for the preacher to mention the peacock.

That evening, Chanell set out to look for T. P. Foster.

Beneath the leaning shed behind her house, she tamped down the battery cable connectors on her 1973 Datsun with the base of a Coca-Cola bottle. First time the rust-speckled car with the shedding vinyl roof had been started in more than a month. What she had in mind was to kill T.P., to lay him as low as her reputation. A beautician's business depended on her good name, and there was that matter of pride, and even, God help her, fear of feeling left out. That old fear rising up from the gut and bringing with it hot, liquid memories of when she was little—or big enough to care—and trying to fit in, in Cornerville.

Most camp families, outsiders in the county, had no known grandmothers and grandfathers, uncles and aunts, or cousins by the dozen, to ground them by name. No home base in the game of community tag. Usually the old-family kids stuck together, so did the camp kids, but Chanell became curious about the insiders—Joy Beth and Linda Gay—at Sunday school. Her mother understood that, and before Chanell began public school, she would take her to play in Cornerville, visiting with the mothers inside the white frame houses while the little girls tested each other in the playhouses.

Chanell never knew what kind of testing took place inside the real houses, which seemed no fancier, no finer, than her own—what went on between those women, who also seemed the same: stout, clean, and motherly. But after two or three visits, Chanell's mother would venture away to visit with other outsiders, newcomers from Alabama or Tennessee, maybe Florida. Not just in the camp, but outside the camp. Jo Ann Davis, for one.

A pulpwooder's wife in a cramped rented house east of town, Jo Ann was flashy and friendly, all teeth, with black wavy hair billowing on her shoulders. Her four boys, all younger than Chanell, seemed not to have come from Jo Ann; chunky and solemn in shrunk striped shirts, they spirited about the house, like moss fed by the air of their mother's loose laughter. Rumor was that Jo Ann had whored one Christmas to get money for her children's Santa Claus. Chanell never knew for sure, but she did remember as a child walking into Jo Ann's pine-paneled bedroom once and feeling her scalp prickle. Jo Ann was leaning into the mirror of a blocky dresser, slathering on makeup for a trip to Valdosta with Chanell and her mother. She was wearing spike heels and a tight black skirt with a lacy black bra contraption that pinched her waist. Chatting and laughing as she mascaraed her eyes, she called Chanell's mother "Alene"—"Alene, I'd give my eyeteeth for a trip to Vegas"—then slipped on a short black jacket and buttoned it to the marshmallowy mounds of her pushed-up breasts. There was something secretive and daring about Jo Ann calling Chanell's mother by name; about that black bra worn instead of a blouse, something never done;

about all that thick tan makeup, her red lips. And when they got to town, when she got out behind the courthouse, there was something else never done about her marching up that backstreet, waving bye-bye.

When Chanell had asked her mother about the rumor, she'd simply said, "How people talk! Jo Ann's just all fun."

But shortly afterward they'd gone back to Joy Beth's and Linda Gay's and their dull, stooped mothers, though Alene soon lapsed into visiting outsiders again. Like Patty Aimes, a single woman in her forties, fresh from New Orleans: a wizened, pot-bellied painter with bleached hair, who smoked perfumed cigarettes and drank imported beer from green bottles. It didn't take Chanell long to catch on that her mother was getting out too, not just getting Chanell out to play. She also caught on then that the other woman in her house was "Alene" first, "mama" second.

By the time her mother died, Chanell was sixteen and at that stage in which she had one foot in the camp and the other across Troublesome Creek in Cornerville. After winning the beauty contest, she became popular and had moments of finding it hard to believe that she wasn't universally known and loved. Other times she felt nobody cared. Not even her daddy, who always protested Chanell's attempts to fit in with those "close-minded fools." And hadn't Chanell witnessed this very morning exactly what her daddy had been talking about? She'd felt it from the first mention of the deacons' meeting, before finding out the matter pertained to her. She'd heard it all before, some outsider, like Jesus, being brought before the uppity-ups, then pressed till he left of his own seemingly free will. Something inside and tricky as the whitish camp sand turning black on a child's face.

Chanell had never been madder or hotter. The air-conditioner in the Datsun didn't work. She had kept her mouth shut long enough, taking Bell's advice. Now she would have it out with T.P., then go back to night church and make her own announcement. She figured they'd be having another deacons' meeting before next Sunday to discuss throwing her out of the church.

First, she drove by the gym. No sign of T.P.; the door was closed, the moss on the old oak, still, dry streamers holding heat. Rather than turn around in front and risk stalling the Datsun, she took the horseshoe road behind the schoolyard, where the row shanties of the Negro quarters faced the south end of the school grounds. Sometimes on Sundays, the overgrown county boys—little boys with beards—would buy beer from the juke, a windowless gray shack at the start of the row shanties. No sign of T.P.'s or his buddies' pickups. A bevy of barefoot black children, licking grape Popsicles, skirled across the hot gravel road to the run-together dirt yards, eyeing the car as it passed. Next, Chanell drove halfway up Mama Sharon's road, checking for T.P.'s truck, and turned in front of the recreation center when she saw only Bell's blue Buick parked before the house. When she got to the red light and didn't find him at the Delta store, she headed south on 129 toward the Georgia-Florida line. Driving too fast, all of sixty in a forty-mile-per-hour car. The engine kept pinging and cutting out, the rusty body juttering from that one tire with a knot she hadn't been able to locate.

Suddenly she remembered that the beer joint at the state line would be closed on Sunday. Still, T.P. might be there. Sometimes all the fellows would gang up on Sundays to drink and drag race, speculating on some mischief to shock their wives or mothers. On each side of 129 were spaced houses on plots cleared out of the woods, where the low sun rayed through tall pines and scrub oaks. Farming and timber country.

Coming up on the cinder-block beer joint, to her right, she spotted T.P.'s big-wheel pickup parked just off the highway that switched black to white in a blink, designating Georgia from Florida. Other pickups were parked at odd angles before the one-room building surrounded by pinewoods. From that direction, she couldn't locate a place to wedge the Datsun into the sprawl of trucks, and had to speed up to keep a semi from kissing her rear. As she gunned past, figuring to turn around at the next ramp, she saw T.P. and his buddies dossing at the tailgate of T.P.'s pickup. They jerked their heads high in surprise, then scrambled like dogs caught snitching meat at a hogkilling. Singed by the hot wind of the semi, as it passed, she started back, slipping the Datsun into the narrow space between T.P.'s black truck and a blue one with a Dixie flag decal. Her car was steadily pinging and sputtering now, sounded like a little boy with a hammer under the hood, and she regretted coming, dreaded facing T.P. and his buddies. They'd only make fun of her and make her feel worse. What had she hoped to accomplish? Already she could pick out six or eight guys who had tried to go with her on the sly (of course, she'd never told T.P.). She switched off the car—if it quit now, T.P. would restart it.

Foot propped on his tailgate, T.P. glared at her and went on talking to Alex Herndon. "Well, I gotta be getting on home to the old lady." Alex shoved off from the tailgate, slapping the side of his pickup parked parallel to the Datsun. "How you, Chanell?" he said, lifting one hand. He spat to the side; a circle on the rear pocket of his jeans showed a can of Skoal dip. He got into his truck and sped north up 129 in a gust of gravel.

One at a time, the others got ready to go, nodding at Chanell and hopping into their trucks, till only T.P. was left. At first, he simply stood there in his tight blue jeans and green

T-shirt and frown. Then, wagging his head, he lumbered toward the passenger side of the car, leaning in the open window. The mask of skin between his beard and hair was waxy-white, his brown eyes sunken like he was overing the flu.

"What you want, Chanell?" He stared out at the road, then off at the deep, soughing pinewoods.

"What do I want?" she said, ungluing her hair from her sweaty neck. "I want you to quit spreading rumors about me and Archie Wall."

"Gotcha!" He looked down at his boots drawing circles in the packed sand and gravel.

"I mean it, T.P.," she said. "I'm sick of you messing with me. We're divorced now."

"Mighty right." He stood tall, straightening his belt, head hid above the roof of the car.

Something was wrong. Was he drunk? He didn't smell like it, didn't act like it. In fact, to Chanell, he seemed too sober. "What the hell's going on, T.P.?"

"Nothing."

"Don't give me that!" she said.

"Don't you bow up at me, girl!" He stuck his head into the car again. "Trying to put the blame on me, after you the one messed up my life."

"Messed up your life?" Chanell repeated, keeping the emphasis off "your" to keep him from thinking her petty and redundant.

He still did. "Well, you won't be bothered up with me no more," he said, voice throwing like a ventriloquist's over the car.

"Good." My God, she thought, what is going on now? Through all manner of loving and fighting, spunkless tirades, he'd sneered and spat and sulked, but had never given in. And just how had she messed up his life?

"I'm gone hold you to it," she said and started the Datsun, gray smoke shooting from the tail pipe, a miracle.

He stalked off and got into his truck.

Chanell drove slowly north up 129, watching in the rearview mirror as T.P. drove slowly south into Florida.

All the way home, she felt feverish. Her face, hot and dry, appeared flushed under her dark skin when she looked up in the mirror. All at once, her world had gone quiet, a deadness that bloomed inside, the rattling of the old Datsun like the last sound she'd ever hear. T.P., always after her, now was dodging her. She thought about the few regulars who had shown up yesterday, no walk-ins or calls.

At the turnoff to her house, where the sun stenciled lonesome shadows of skinny trees on the road, cars were already pulling up at the church. She didn't even consider stopping, and hoped nobody noticed her car. She eased past, the hot car brattling gravel toward her house, and parked under the dim shed in the sideyard, got out, and crept to the back stoop. As she sat in the webbed lawn chair by the kitchen door, George strutted up and stood, dead-still and staring. He looked like a diagram of colors coded to body parts: emerald for the chest, sapphire for the back, and an almond patch where his heart would be. The sun was almost down, ruches of fire burning through the green gums and bays along Troublesome Creek. A light breeze rustling in the vines seemed to work up the whine of mosquitoes, the tired keening of crickets. From the church, frail strains of a hymn filtered through the waxy leaves of the sideyard magnolia.

All the petty stuff was over; she could feel it in her soul. Whatever was wrong now had little or nothing to do with Archie Wall. It was something else, something serious that she could feel inside, a dread set to ripen into the real thing.

part

two

chapter six

Days and weeks passed with no change. Then Monday through Wednesday of the last week in August only three customers wandered in—none of them Chanell's regulars. None of them talking about anything but hairdos—not food, not sex, not TV. Real specific, as specific as Chanell was in her headcount.

Even Bell hadn't called.

On Thursday Chanell considered calling her. No, not yet. If Chanell could depend on anybody, it was Bell. But what if she had sided with the others? Chanell didn't think so. Maybe she was just busy; maybe all of Chanell's customers were. The new school year had started that week and everybody was probably adjusting to different routines, kids back in school, that stuff. Or maybe Chanell was imagining things. She wanted to laugh and make light of the whole silly business, but inside something nagged like a nerve in a bad tooth.

Keeping busy, Chanell rearranged the beauty shop, cater-cornering the side-by-side drier chairs to give the room fresh angles, to offset the sameness. Then she pried open the paint-stuck double windows over the shampoo bowl and combout station, airing out scents of hair spray and ammonia. No screens on those windows, but it wouldn't hurt to leave them open since the bugs and mosquitoes were beginning to dwindle. She would open all the windows inside the house, too. Not yet autumn, but close: cool nights and hot days, days lessening by degrees of light that signaled the crop changeover from summer to fall flowers—goldenrod and purple tasseled rabbit tobacco—in the lot between Chanell's and the post office. Late evenings the cooling dirt radiated a rooty smell, and during the day, a sagey fragrance of cured weeds. Usually on first days between summer and fall, when Chanell could tell a change was in the air, she would feel peppy and new, nostalgia glazing good over bad until she was almost happy. She tried hard to recapture that, to set aside the sadness welling up. She cleaned out the refrigerator and swept down cobwebs, then dusted all the furniture and the living-room mantel, even the two little pickaninnies with dusty scrunched faces that Joy Beth had brought back from a trip to Plains, Georgia. The sheer white curtains filled with air, showing gaps of smeary glass. She could clean windows—she should. She wouldn't.

That afternoon, she mopped the speckled-white tile floors, washed bed sheets and hung them to dry on the sagging clothesline where the woods met the yard. Beyond the fountains of vines in the gums and bays, she could hear the school buses shift from stop to start at the red light, then pick up speed as they cranked north across Troublesome Creek. A familiar sound that should excite good feelings over bad and associate fall with school just starting. Basketball games coming up. The Halloween Carnival in October. Beauty contest in a couple of weeks. But all she felt was drain and dread. Having no children of her own to use as an excuse to trail along to school-related events, she often used her customers' children like tickets. Not that she'd ever wanted children of her own—she hadn't. Who knew better than Chanell what a trial children were, especially in the beauty shop? But she did their hair free, put up with their plundering and mess, even fussed over them.

To rid herself of feelings of doom, of persecution—what?—she polished her toenails on the back stoop, breathing in the ferny green air off the creek. She'd quit polishing her fingernails long ago; perm solutions and dyes ruined the polish and she never had time to keep them up. Now she did; now she polished her fingernails too. A muted pink shade that made the skin above her nails look stained.

She thought about Joy Beth's mother, Sandra Kaye, whose thick nails were ridged and parched yellow with tobacco stains, and one thought led to another, without order, nostalgia tricking Chanell into blending the last with the first and the good with the bad. And really there were so few good memories to retrieve from the bank of what was and what would be with either Joy Beth or her mother, an overbearing motherly type who somehow linked the ordinary with the extraordinary. Not all that important to Chanell, but in whatever form, there, begging to speak.

When Chanell started beauty school, with no car and no way to get to Valdosta except by catching rides with the local mail carrier, she had worked out an arrangement with Sandra Kaye to drop her off two streets over from the business school where both Joy Beth and Sandra Kaye were taking courses. So strange, it seemed to Chanell, that Sandra Kaye, whose other six children were grown and gone, had suddenly come out of the low frame house after years of holing up with only TV talk shows for company. The raddle-faced, dumpy woman, with twenty-five pounds of extra potato-chip weight on her thighs, began walking prissy and talking fast, carrying textbooks on accounting and business English in her solid arms. She began humming tunelessly with her hardened nether lip stuck out. Chanell would sit in the backseat of Sandra Kaye's chocolate Chevrolet and crank the windows down to keep from smelling the hot woolly seats. She'd felt sorry for Joy Beth, both sad and glad that her own mother wasn't living to follow her to beauty school on a quest of one last chance. Though Chanell knew that her own mother would never have gone, would never have needed to renew herself. Chanell paid two dollars for every round trip, keeping an eye on Joy Beth for some sign of daughterly disgust. Chanell felt guilty then for no longer missing her own mother, but never guilty for being critical of Sandra Kaye.

In first grade, Chanell's mother had dropped her off at Miss Booth's room, paying for her workbooks and the first week of lunches, then left to practice being "Alene" again, Chanell supposed. Alone and waiting for somebody she knew—anybody would do—Chanell had stood against the cool, gray concrete wall, between a poster about teeth and one with the ABCs in both caps and lowercase letters. Warm smells of milk, white bread, bologna, and fear made her tongue mist a vomit taste. When Joy Beth came through the gray door, ushered ahead by Sandra Kaye, whose belly pushed her waist to her bust, Chanell had sidled over and caught Joy Beth's clammy white hand and walked her to the first row of mutilated pine desks. They sat, Chanell in front and Joy Beth behind, the hooked-together seat and desk top wobbling from Chanell's runaway fright.

Sandra Kaye, waiting in the line of other mothers for her turn to pay fees, kept winking at Joy Beth, who was tapping on her desk with a giant red pencil. After Sandra Kaye had paid and given the teacher instructions on how to deal with her little girl's "sensitive disposition," she sashayed over and squatted beside Joy Beth, whispering excitedly. Chanell turned and caught Sandra Kaye's yellowish bug eyes, and the hard-lipped woman slapped Chanell on the thigh. "Face the front, you!" she said low. Chanell stared ahead, marking in her mind that moment and how mothers could turn nasty, showing their true feelings, out of earshot of other adults. A preshow of what was to come from the teacher, Miss Booth, who favored the camp children and the poor kids with her paddle over those belonging to the members of the board of education.

After Chanell's nails had dried, she went into the shop and shampooed her shoulder-length black hair, blowing it dry before the mirror to a smooth pageboy that emphasized sprinklings of gray. A classic style that framed her unlined face: right after buffing, her skin would look tight from swollen tissue, but later it seemed to crumble, showing up faint creases under her slanted brown eyes, on her high forehead, telling on her twenty-odd years of scrubbing. Well, she would still scrub, in spite of the skin doctors' dispute over whether to pamper or punish, and when her face wore out . . . She couldn't afford a face-lift, wouldn't have one anyway because she feared doctors, surgery, the aloneness and unknownness of death.

Trying to think healthy, she put on a pink polo shirt and a pair of white shorts. Her legs were shapely, dark and firm, but too heavy for shorts, which had never stopped her from wearing them, or sundresses that showed her muscled square shoulders, her thick arms.

Looking good and smelling the fresh house made her feel uplifted, but when she started dusting in the shop, when she got to the black telephone, she realized it hadn't rung all day and felt low again. Low and lonely. She'd call Bell tomorrow if Bell hadn't called by tonight.

Bell didn't call.

And in bed that night, while the green breeze from the creek drifted through the single window, Chanell fought back feelings of what it had been like as the only child of a sick mother. How she'd get off the school bus at the Sampson commissary—she was maybe ten then—and go inside the spacey, shelf-lined store for a Coke and a Zero candy bar, then walk alone to her look-alike house under cold shadow of cedars and oaks. Going inside to the warm closed house, which smelled like warm water tasted, she would first check on her mother.

Perpetually dozing, with her mouth open to breathe, she would lie bogged in a raft of pillows, skin so sore, she'd say, that even the sculpting of the mattress made her ache. Groans would wrest from her sucked-in throat, her dark hair permanently pushed up from a balding circle on the back of her head. The room, dimmed by rollup shades to a cave-brown tint, smelled of acid fever and stale sweat. She couldn't stand the light.

In the kitchen, Chanell would begin washing from the top the piled dishes in the sink, seldom getting to even the heart, much less the bottom, where knives and forks rattled in ropy suds. The ancient decay of dust on the dark wood tables and chests, handed down from Chanell's mother's mother, would remain another sick year.

Chanell would start supper when the sun lay in slants across the green-linoleumed kitchen counter. Her daddy would be in soon, around six. She'd watch for him through the window over the sink, not with eagerness, but with dread of him knowing she was alone and lonesome. Not that he would pity her or care—he didn't think like that. For supper, she would turn hamburger into casseroles or sweet-sauced spaghetti. French fries for herself. Canned English peas for mama. Whatever could be charged at the commissary, whatever she could figure to fix.

Outside, where the sun always sank early behind the woods, she would hear the other children tittering and laughing, and the house would seem quieter, a stillness that arched against the trill of play over the camp. Things seemed crazy then, off course, while Chanell waited for her mother to die—it would take another five years—and sometimes she felt crazy, too. Afraid her mother would die, afraid she would linger.

When her daddy came in, he'd take off his Sampson cap, hook it on the nail behind the kitchen door, tease her about being ugly, if he was in a good mood, then go to the bathroom to wash up. He'd always peep in at her mother, his face long and sun-drawn, then disappear into the musty blue bathroom that separated the two bedrooms.

Chanell would wake her mama and sit while she ate. The sick woman's face the shade of the overcooked peas. "You oughta be out playing with the other children," she'd say, leaning forward to cup Chanell's chin with her fevered hand.

"I'll play on Saturday," Chanell would promise.

"Go on, eat with your daddy." Her mother, propped on the pillows at her back, ate slowly, painfully. "Make some racket in this house," she'd say, then cackle dully and quit as if it hurt her throat. Her cancer was the slow kind, starting with the uterus and eating its way out.

Chanell couldn't remember when the cancer had started,

only when it had stopped. That Sunday evening, she'd talked her daddy into letting her drive the car to church. Linda Gay had walked over earlier and they'd been plotting in Chanell's bedroom all afternoon, back and forth with Joy Beth on the phone. What Chanell had privately dreaded was not that her daddy might refuse them, but that he might blow up in front of her friend and tell them both to go to hell. Possibly say something like, How could you think of leaving your mama right now? to the background hiss of the oxygen tank in the next room. But if she didn't ask, Linda Gay would think she wasn't cool. Not that Linda Gay was all that cool, but cool was the role Chanell had chosen for herself, like she'd chosen the new name, her sole intrigue and allure. But in the living room, where her daddy was watching TV, when Chanell asked he'd not said a word. Finally he stood and fished the keys from his pocket, telegraphing a warning to Chanell and Linda Gay with his eyes: Just to church and nowhere else. They stood there squirming while he twisted the car key from a ring of rattling keys, then dashed out of the house before he could change his mind. The sun was going down behind the camp, and its orange light rayed through the rear glass of the car while Chanell worked the key in the ignition, concentrating on the clutch—don't snatch the car into first, not right here in the yard—and Linda Gay worked the radio. They'd leaned together and giggled, then motored along the rows of houses and around the commissary and onto 129, like two li'l ole ladies bound for church.

Crossing Troublesome Creek, Linda Gay had turned the radio up, the deep, snappy voice of the disc jockey jolting in their brains. At the traffic light, Chanell took a left. "Cut the radio down a jiff," she said. She pulled in behind the church, in the grove of pecan trees, both girls scooting low in the seat to wait for Joy Beth. The sun was almost down and people were walking in sets and singly through the summer dusk toward the red-brick church, the whine of mosquitoes giving voice to the twinkling of lightning bugs. In a few minutes, they saw Joy Beth crouching along the rear wall of the church, dodging among the trees. She slipped into the backseat, shutting the door with a whispery snib, and Chanell backed up and pulled out onto the highway with only the tops of Joy Beth's and Linda Gay's heads showing through the windows of the big Ford. When they got to Valdosta, which took twenty minutes flying, they cruised Ashley Street another thirty, counting off the two-hour church time allotment on the courthouse clock, then spent another thirty at WVLD radio station, pestering the puny disc jockey who'd sounded tough on the radio. Linda Gay got tickled and wet her panties when a carload of Valdosta boys pulled alongside, daring Chanell to pull over. By the time the girls got back to the traffic light in Cornerville, pushing the Fair-lane at 75 mph, Chanell could see her daddy standing in the churchyard, alone in the crowd of churchgoers. "Oh, my God!" she'd said, braking the car as she neared. "We're not late," Joy Beth said from the rear seat. "What're they all doing outside?"

"Shit!" Linda Gay lay against the door. "I vote we don't go back."

Chanell drove on, eyes locking with her daddy's. The worst feeling in the world, worse than him knowing she'd lied, was his shrunken look of loss, rather than disgust.

By Friday morning, Chanell was beginning to panic. Not so lonely as desperate to know why everybody had turned against her.

Mr. Jim and Miss Neida were in the backyard trimming the fox-grape vines that snaked from the creek in summer, and when Chanell went out to feed George some stale bread, they rambled around the other side of the jailhouse. To keep from speaking?

Chanell shook the crumbs from the plastic bag into the high, rank grass and went inside again, brushed her hair and put on lipstick. Then she went out the front and walked the gravel road to the post office.

The gray sky was swollen and low, clouds swagged to the carved steeple of the church and the tops of the pecan trees. A pulpwood truck, stacked high with a uniform dome of poles, wobbled east along 94, snorting a mix of burned diesel and raw resin. Across the highway, the usual cars were parked on the oak island between Archie Wall's house and the courtyard, where the red brick looked darker in the dampness. Moss hung in still clots from the laden oaks. Chanell dreaded the rain and being closed up inside with nobody to talk to and nothing to do. The soggy air already was causing her hair to frizz. Stepping from the grass to the walk, she took a deep breath and pushed through the heavy glass post-office door. She could hear Miss Cleta sorting mail behind the wall of black mailboxes, the fluorescent lights humming overhead.

Chanell crossed the hollow dove-colored room to the window on the end and peeked around the partition of black cubes. Three green plastic pots of bristly African violets stood on the white counter. "Miss Cleta?" she called into the dim backroom, unable to locate the postmistress among the cramped boxes and shelves, where tones of light composed from brown parcel paper.

From the other end of the partition, the clicking and shuffling continued, then stopped. Ghostly white, the tall woman with a stony face glided to the window, her charcoal hair just so. She cleared her throat, "Can I help you?"

"Just come to pick up my mail." Oh, Lord, Chanell thought, Miss Cleta had always been solemn, but at least she'd smiled before, at least she'd talked about the weather before.

A test: "Looks like rain, don't it?" said Chanell.

Straight-faced, straight ahead, Miss Cleta spirited along the partition of mailboxes, white rayon blouse gathered at the waist of her narrow navy skirt—her trim body thinning and blending into the marrow of shadows. Had she left for good? Was she dismissing Chanell? Then within minutes, maybe seconds, she was back, ghosting into the framed window like a picture of a dead aunt retired to the attic, and passed Chanell's mail to her. Then disappeared again, as if finally the face had faded.

"Thank you," called Chanell. Itching all over, she started out, sorting through the stack of mail from beauty-supply houses, her monthly electricity bill, *car-rt sort* nothing mail.

Now she had to know what was going on. She had to. Fumes of fear rose in her head, her knees began quivering as if worms were burrowing under the caps. Taking the shortcut across the field of goldenrod and rabbit tobacco, on her way home, she suddenly stopped. She had it! Somebody must have started a rumor that she had AIDS. Yes, if she had AIDS, this is how she would be treated. She almost dropped to the dirt with relief: when she didn't get sick and didn't die, say, within six months or a year, everybody would know the rumor wasn't true, how they'd wronged her. She could almost taste their shame for having shunned her for no good reason. Still she had to know, had to be told if this was the latest gossip.

Bell. She'd go to Bell, make her tell the truth. But slamming into the house and slapping the mail down on the kitchen table, Chanell was no longer so eager to see Bell. She hadn't called in how many days—time, usually timelessness, was now slow-sliding vapors—which could mean she didn't want to see Chanell anymore.

Only one way to find out.

Under the car shed, Chanell again had to tamp the cable connectors with the Coke bottle to get the battery to fire, but once the Datsun got going, it ran almost smoothly, except for that same rapping racket under the hood, that little boy with a hammer. At least she was going somewhere, finally taking charge. Why not take advantage of this break from the beauty shop while she could? Soon the AIDS rumor would pass—rumors, always abundant in Cornerville, always passed. She should go shopping, get out among people, maybe at the mall in Valdosta. She should hold her head up high and go visiting like her mama and the other women in Cornerville used to. But she didn't want to shop, she didn't want to visit, she wanted her life back, the business she'd smithed from iron determination, her good name. She started to cry, then laughed. Oh, hell! She sat tall, taking a left at the Baptist Church. Ridiculous! Getting so worked up over nothing. She'd have an AIDS test—as soon as Bell verified the rumor—and when it came back negative, she'd show it around, set everything straight. But what if it was positive? Oh, shit! What if T.P., who was always hanging with whores, had for a fact given Chanell AIDS? Maybe that was why he was avoiding her—the blood in her head heated up—or maybe he'd heard the rumor and thought Chanell had passed AIDS on to him.

She had often pondered the general issue of AIDS—a frequent topic among her customers—and specifically how it might pertain to her, listing in her mind every girl she'd heard about or known of T.P. having sex with. Even going so far as to conjure up chainlike links of those partners' partners, how they could hook up to her through T.P. (she'd never had sex with anybody else, yet). Going way back to before they got married, to the Negro-quarter whores T.P. had bragged about, Chanell lost count.

Actually, this whole stinking rumor was funny. She could picture herself laughing with Bell as she passed the old school and turned down Mama Sharon's road, as she parked in front of Bell's mobile home, got out, and started across the mowed dandelions and grass of the fenced yard. And then she stiffened, taking the wobbly steps up to the peened aluminum door—this is it!—knocking and waiting with her misty eyes fixed on a blue wooden plaque—"Backdoor friends are best"—shaped in a heart.

"Come on in," Bell called.

Inside, the depreciating double-wide looked like a scaled-down cheap model of some overdecorated country home. Busy with blue and mauve carpets, chintz upholstery, and drapes that duplicated the silk flower arrangements on flimsy tables set about the longish room, which ran into kitchen and dining. Lots of gilt and glass and would-be wood. What Bell called "shit" when the country look went out as fast as it came in.

Along the rear wall of windows, in the living room, Bell sat behind a massive new Queen Anne desk, her latest attempt to crowd out the country junk. One gold hoop earring lay next to a mauve telephone.

"How you, priss?" Bell kept on printing figures in a green ledger with her head low.

Chanell no longer felt like laughing, no longer believed they'd laugh together, and Bell's big-sister tone made her feel like crying. She stopped before the desk. "I don't have AIDS, Bell," she said.

Bell's head shot up, green eyes wide and liquid in the lamplight.

Lord, let her say something, Chanell thought, let her laugh.

Bell stood, clipping on the earring as she came around the desk, and wrapped both strong hairy arms about Chanell's shoulders. "I know you don't have AIDS, sugar."

Chanell hugged her too, rocking. "Then what, Bell? What's come over everybody?"

"Crazy! Just crazy!"

"What are they saying, Bell?" Chanell pulled away and dropped in the ladder-back chair facing the desk, embarrassed. They'd never hugged before. "What's going on."

Bell strolled around the other side of the desk, brushing the glassy surface with her hand. "I don't know."

"You do, Bell." Chanell sat forward. "I can tell you do. Besides, around here, you hear everything."

"I don't." She sat, shuffling receipts into stacks.

"If it's not AIDS, what is it?"

Bell shrugged. "Don't worry, it'll all come out in the wash."

"I'll be on welfare by then."

"Crazy!" Bell grinned, then frowned, showing paper-cut wrinkles above her pink top lip. "Nobody's been coming to the shop?"

"None to speak of."

"Well, I am. Tomorrow." She laughed, but it wasn't the laugh Chanell had hoped for.

"Mama Sharon . . . ?"

Bell waved a ringed hand. "Give her time."

"T.P.? Why is T.P. shunning me?" Chanell waited for her to say, His ass! Bell shook her head and swallowed, the knot in her throat rising like a bubble in water.

chapter seven

In the summer of 1976 even Cornerville had been settling into the Big Change that had the rest of the world swinging free from the tightrope of do-right and bank what you make. Except for a few boys having gone to Vietnam and come back scarred where it didn't always show, Cornerville ignored the world outside; effects of the Big Change filtered through TV and movies like syphilis and nobody knew how it got started or even that it had. They voted and paid taxes, but the world for them stopped where the dome of blue sky met the green pines of Swanoochee County.

After five years married to Pete and two miscarriages, Bell had gotten pregnant again, and she put her foot down about the church giving her another baby shower until after her eighth month. Having little to do with superstition, unlike Mama Sharon, Bell simply believed that life being the bitch it was, she didn't want to tempt fate by looking forward to the event—let whoever was in charge of dashing good think she didn't give a damn one way or the other. Not God—she didn't dare blaspheme—maybe the devil. So for eight whole months she waddled around and griped about her liver-pied face and jutted belly. Her ankles puffed up like mashed pota- toes. She acted as if her doctor in Valdosta was God, and God rained down manna in the form of diuretics and diet pills. Weighing in every two weeks was the height of her summer. She would starve for two days before to keep Dr. Knowles from being disappointed, but still she gained too much weight. Following weigh-ins at the doctor's office, she would stop by the Dairy Queen for a Brazier Deluxe and a Peanut Buster Parfait, and when she got home, jaded and bored, she'd round up Pete and Chanell and T.P. and head back to Valdosta to eat at Western Sizzling: T-bones and baked pota- toes and all-you-can-eat salad bar. Then during the ride home, she'd groan about the weigh-in coming up. She'd pick fights with T.P., Mama Sharon, and Pete, and they'd just sit there, mum and fuming. Only Chanell was spared Bell's venomous jabs.

The diet pills kept Bell wide awake and talky, and she'd sit up with Chanell half the night in Mama Sharon's living room, smoking Kools, lamenting her swollen body, and cursing Pete for getting her pregnant. But Chanell knew that deep down Bell was scared of losing this baby too, and at the same time excited—maybe this time. It was like waiting for a bottle of frozen pop to blow.

In July, her eighth month, Bell let Chanell, Joy Beth, and Linda Gay give the baby shower. She was beginning to talk about the baby as a girl, one to dress up in frilly dresses and pink bows. Still swollen head to toe—her face filling out like the moon—she'd shop at the mall in Valdosta for baby clothes, fussing about the heat from the mall door to the new

Buick Pete had bought because the air-conditioner in the '73 model wasn't cool enough. He treated her like a tyrant queen and tried to stay out of her way, but what she wanted she got, and then some. She picked over the few maternity clothes in the Valdosta shops, then scouted for more in Tallahassee and Jacksonville, Florida. Tents and empire dresses in every fabric from brocade silk to madras-plaid cotton, even a swimsuit with a bubble top, which she never put on. Said it made her look like an elephant, but still strutted her belly, proud.

Late Friday evening, the last week in July, she showed up for the shower at the Baptist Church reception hall wearing the black brocade silk, feet stuffed into black patent spikes. The minute she flopped, surrounded by little and big presents tied with pink bows, she plucked off the high heels and placed one puffy bluish foot on top of the other.

All the women gabbing and laughing gathered round in the long white room, two or three fanning Bell with cardboard fans—the air-conditioner didn't cool to suit her—while another brought a glass of sweet strawberry punch with ice. As much as Bell moaned and groaned at home, in public she didn't make a peep, but all day she'd been holding her back and walking the floor, swearing to God that she was going into labor. She'd called the doctor's office twice and had Chanell call four times, and he'd told the receptionist to tell Miss Avery to lie down with her feet up. By the fourth call, Chanell had concluded that Bell's god-doctor didn't actually exist, though the receptionist's voice had that same quality of adoration and awe as Bell's. You had to have faith in the unseen god.

Bell kept blowing at her liver-pied forehead and dabbing sweat with a cherub-print napkin while she unwrapped lace-edged blankets and hand-smocked dresses. All pink. Each opened box was passed from woman to woman in the circle of chairs, then on to Linda Gay, who'd assigned herself the honor of displaying the gifts on a table set along one wall.

"Precious, just precious." Linda Gay placed a tissue-wrapped crocheted bib in its box, propped on the lid, and fussed with the straight rows of other boxes. She'd recently lost ten pounds, which didn't show, and was feeling prissy, and everybody should notice how her safe-blue skirt bagged on her flat behind.

Bell opened an electric bottle warmer, thanked Mae Spivey for the gift, then passed it to Chanell to pass to Mama Sharon. Mama Sharon stared inside the pink coil-lined cup, examined the folded bound cord, and passed it on to Miss Lou, who was nibbling on a cheese straw. And so on around the circle till the bottle warmer got to Linda Gay, hovering over the table like a crow in a pecan orchard.

"Precious," she gushed, "just precious." Linda Gay placed the bottle warmer beside the crocheted bib. "No card," she said. "Bell, where's the card?"

Bell spread her legs and peeped between her knees at the floor decorated in bows and God-bless-this-child gift wrap. "It's from Mae," Bell said, sat back, and swabbed her melting makeup again. She sucked in, her splayed feet thrashing in the paper.

Only Chanell seemed to catch on that Bell was about to blow.

"Here's another one," Joy Beth said, and they all turned to watch Aunt Ruth glide in with her nose up as if she smelled a mess.

Bell waited for the old lady to brush cheeks and smack, then stripped off the blue bow and shucked the paper. Two tiny blue bath cloths and a towel. "Thank you, Aunt Ruth," Bell said in a teeny voice and smiled and passed the box to Chanell.

Bell's dark downy mustache was dewy with sweat. She flapped her arms, showing wet rings on the bunched black brocade.

"Bell, see if you can't locate Mae's card somewhere." Linda Gay, pink-faced and excited, leaned over Mae's shoulder, pointing at the nest of paper and bows. She took the bath cloth and towel set and placed it on the table. "Precious. Just precious."

Bell inched to the edge of the chair, struggling to stand.

"Did you find that card yet, Bell?" Linda Gay asked sweetly.

Bell made a big show of patting her hips, her bosom. "What the hell difference does it make, Linda Gay?" She kicked the paper, a pink bow curling around her scorchy stockinged toes. "Make another card."

All the ladies scrambled up and made for the refreshment table: trays of Bisquick sausage-cheese balls; cheese ring spiked with nuts and onion and filled with strawberry jam—everybody just had to have the recipe—and a pinwheel of Ritz crackers; a huge bowl of strawberry Jell-O punch, thick enough to eat; dips and chips and pink cake squares with the same cherub as the napkins. Linda Gay tiptoed to the end of the lingering line, flushed and tittering like nothing had happened. She was finally thin. Thin!

"Chanell," Bell said, sucking air like a landed mullet, "get me to the hospital. I'm sick of this shit, had it up to here." She marked her froggy chin with her jeweled hand.

Chanell didn't know whether Bell had "had it" with the shower or the pregnancy—she looked like somebody who'd been partying eight months straight. "You want me to go get Pete?"

"Hell, no, he ain't having this baby, I am." She struggled to her feet again. "Well, y'all, I reckon I'll mosey on to the house," she announced to the flock around the punch bowl.

"Oh," Linda Gay cooed, "little mama not feeling good?"

"I'm fine," Bell said at the door, "just beat."

"What about all these gifts?" Linda Gay tripped toward Bell with her arms fanned. "You can't leave till . . ."

"I'm putting you in charge, Linda Gay."

"Oh!" Linda Gay crossed her raspberry-knuckled hands on her chest, honored, and then confusion bloomed in her flushed face as if on second thought maybe she'd been duped.

By the time they got to Valdosta, Bell was stretched out in the plush front seat, groaning and panting like a dog. During the twenty-minute drive in, which usually took thirty for Chanell, Bell's pains had alternated from five minutes apart to two minutes apart, and back to five.

After learning that Bell still had a month to go, the clerk behind the desk in the emergency room kept probing for insurance information while Bell in a wheelchair plundered through her giant black Aigner bag for an insurance card. Patience spent, she zipped the bag with shaking hands, "Forget that shit. Call the doctor."

"Mrs. Avery," the clerk with flossy black bangs said, "I've had the doctor paged. He's at a football game."

Bell, a nervous white, cocked her head as if she was hard of hearing. "A football game?"

To the left of the reception desk, a panel of glass doors slid wide with a hum, and a nurse with a broad, blanched face appeared. "I'll take you up to the labor room and have them check to see if you're dilated yet," she said.

She started to wheel Bell away, and Bell reached out and seized Chanell's hand, so that Chanell had to pace alongside the wheelchair, trying to keep her toes from beneath the wheels, trying to categorize this meeker, weaker version of Big Bad Bell in Cornerville.

"Don't leave me, Chanell," Bell said, rising in the chair with a grunt as though she'd sat on something sharp.

"I won't," Chanell promised.

When they got off the elevator on the second floor, the nurse told Chanell to wait in the lobby on their left, but Bell still clung to her hand.

"Mrs. Avery," the nurse said loudly, "she'll have to wait till they check and prep you, if need be. Then you can walk out here and sit with her awhile."

"I ain't in no shape to be walking, hear me?" barked Bell. "And if I'm paying this bill, I'm gone have who I please with me."

"Mrs. Avery, nobody's allowed in the labor room," said the nurse, ready to roll. "Policy, you know."

"I'll go call Pete," Chanell said, stepping aside.

"Hell, no!" Bell tightened her clasp on Chanell's hand, groaned, and towed her along as the disgruntled nurse wheeled the chair up the long pink hall toward the double doors at the end with a sign that read KEEP OUT.

"Dr. Knowles won't like this." The nurse clicked her tongue and pushed through the flapping doors to a glaring white section of hall.

In the labor room, Bell released Chanell's hand long enough to go to the bathroom and change into a knee-length turquoise gown with string ties in back. While she was changing, Chanell wandered out to the fluorescent-lit hall with like rooms along each side to the nurses' station on the south end, a glassed alcove where nurses revolved on crepe-soled shoes from station to rooms to hall and back again. Blanched faces were trained on carts and charts, and muted voices spirited through the antiseptic whiteness, like cold fumes of ether. Scanning the faces, Chanell picked out a spry one with a country-innocent face and asked her to call Pete. Though it was against "policy," the woman said she would. The nurse who'd brought Bell up now stood at the double doors with her hands on the wheelchair handles, talking to another nurse, who looked like Cinderella's stepmother: tall and bony with a crow chest and beak and jeweled glasses on a gold chain. Chanell figured they were talking about her and Bell, maybe how to get rid of the extra on the floor.

When Chanell got to the labor room again, another nurse with the same dour look cloned from Cinderella's stepmother was stationed by the smooth white bed, checking Bell for progress. One hand under the starched sheet, the other on Bell's propped knee. Bell was still panting and groaning with her eyes rolled up—not in pain so much as a concentrated disgrace.

Chanell stepped outside and started to go on to the waiting room. A pair of bristling uniformed nurses glided by in soft white shoes and eyed her.

"Chanell!" Bell called out.

Chanell started through the door and the nurse who'd been checking Bell pushed past. "When Dr. Knowles gets here, you'll have to go," she said.

"Okay," said Chanell. She hadn't been to a doctor since she was a child with an earache.

Bell, lying to one side of the bed, wiggled to the middle and reached for Chanell's hand. "I'm scared shitless, honey."

"Are you dilated much?"

"I don't know."

"I thought she was checking you."

"She wrote it down on my chart and said the doctor would be on after the football game."

"That must mean you're all right, huh?"

"Must." Bell arched forward, panting, her face red with trapped blood.

"You want some water, something?"

"Said I can't have nothing till after the baby comes. What time is it?"

Chanell gazed at her watch. "Five till ten."

Bell let go of Chanell's hand and seized the hard foreign mound of her belly, almost sitting up. "Ga—ga—god!" she stammered, staring off at the wall of first-aid posters as if for explanation.

"Breathe in and out, Bell," Chanell said, not knowing why all the women in the soaps did that.

Bell breathed in and out in jagged, aimless breaths, lay back, then jerked forward again, this time hollering and even whooping as if she was having fun.

"I'll go get the nurse," Chanell said, trotting to the door. "Nurse!" she called down the empty white hall.

Cinderella's stepmother peeped from the nurses' station alcove and cocked her head.

"How 'bout coming in here and checking . . . uh . . . Miss Avery?"

The nurse looked at her watch. "Miss Avery was examined only five minutes ago." Then vanished behind the glass partition.

Chanell stepped into Bell's room again just as she let out another whoop. Now sitting up, propped on her hands.

"Bell, they said it's not time yet to check you again," said Chanell.

"Shit they say!" Bell puffed quick, aiming for a rhythm, her green eyes lit, hairdo wilted, and who cared. "Tell 'um to call the doctor."

This time Chanell would walk all the way down to the nurses' station, but before she reached the recessed alcove on

the left side of the hall, she heard Cinderella's stepmother talking to another nurse—something about Mrs. Avery, about
hicks—in secretive, twisty tones that charged Chanell's hick
instincts like electricity. She stepped to the inset water fountain, one white plaster wall away from the nurses' station,
leaving her shaky shadow on the scrubbed tile floor, and listened to the gossip unraveling around the corner.

"All that weight!" the bow-chested nurse said. "These
hicks bring it on themselves, then bellyache to the doctor."
The other nurse said something about Dr. Knowles perscribing
diet pills for her—she'd actually lost weight while she was
pregnant.

Chanell held her breath, mad. Mad as hell, for Bell. Maybe
what they said was true, maybe Bell had made her labor more
difficult by gaining so much weight, but Chanell didn't have
to be a doctor to figure that Bell's up-and-down appetite had
been affected by the diet pills. And what about the baby,
tube-fed diet pills and diuretics?

Chanell toggled the switch on the water fountain and slurped.

In the lit nurses' alcove, everything got quiet; Cinderella's
stepmother stepped around the corner to the fountain, immac-
ulate white shoes planted on Chanell's shadow.

Chanell turned and glowered, wiping her mouth with the
back of her hand. "Mrs. Hick Avery said for you to call the
doctor." The nurse's sleek, wry face revealed nothing, not fear,
not remorse. Her pupils grafted onto black irises. "Miss, you'll
have to go out to the waiting room."

Bell's hollering whoops rent the buzzy white silence of the
hall.

Chanell ran back, followed by the bow-chested nurse, and
found Bell standing on the other side of the bed, with both
arms out, gazing down at her popped belly as if she won-

dered what was inside. "Get Dr. Knowles here right now," she screamed at the nurse.

"Miss Avery, you'll have to relax and behave yourself." The nurse waltzed around the bed toward Bell. "Maybe we'll check you again now." Chanell just stood there, watching Bell watch her belly.

"Wait outside," the nurse said through gritted teeth. She stepped around Chanell and went to the rubber-glove dispenser on the wall above the sink, snatched two gloves from the metal holder and tugged them on. Bell, no longer waiting for the next pain, whooped some more. Chanell eased out and left the heavy door half open.

When the nurse finished, she breezed past, letting Chanell in like a cat, and closed the door as though she didn't want to wake her patient, whose screaming now linked to screaming. Not at all like Bell's true whooping and hollering, more like some dainty girl's put-on shrieks.

Chanell leaned over Bell on the bed, shrieks piercing her eardrums till they roared. Bell's eyes were squinted as though she couldn't scream and look at the same time. Her eyelids twitched. "Bell," Chanell shouted, "you hurting that bad?"

She opened her eyes, yanked her head from the stiff white pillow and gazed about. "Hell, no," she whispered in a hoarse voice, "not all the time, but if I let up they won't never do nothing." She lay back down and picked up screaming where she had left off.

"You want anything?" Chanell said with her fingers plugging her ears.

"Drugs," Bell said, as if she was begging for water. "I want drugs. Run go tell 'um." She smiled and screamed in the fresh soprano of her singing voice.

In a few minutes, Bell began that honest whooping and

hollering again, thrashing about and clutching her stomach with her eyes closed and her mouth wide.

Chanell wet a rough brown paper towel and wiped Bell's face. Her green eyes flew open, pain etched in blood.

"Sugar," she said gravely, "they better call the doctor this time. I swear I'm having this baby."

"Bell, you probably just having labor pains; they'd know if it was time."

"I'm telling you, I feel it." She looked down at her tented belly. A newborn scream sundering the room in two. Her singing voice.

Now Chanell was really mad. Whether or not it was time for Bell's baby, she needed some relief, and if not relief at least respect. The hollering of a hurt dog would have drawn more attention. She marched out, listening to Bell whoop and holler and give voice to the newborn scream, and even though the bow-chested nurse picked up a chart from the counter at the nurses' station and appeared to be walking toward her, Chanell kept going, swinging her arms. "Hey, you!" She shook her finger, feeling her face grow light in the cold alcohol air. "Get your highfalutin behind over there and call the doctor and tell him to get his ass here this minute."

"Call security," Cinderella's stepmother said to the other nurse behind the desk.

"Yeah, do"—Chanell had reached the alcove and the terrified eyes of the other nurse, whose scrubbed hand rested on the black phone—"and while you're at it call the newspaper. I want to give them a story about how one hick woman is fixing to sue this hospital because two gossipy nurses neglected her friend who was having a baby."

"I doubt there's sufficient evidence to support such an allegation," Cinderella's stepmother said.

"Maybe not," Chanell said, "but Dr. Knowles might find it believable." Another bosh shot?

The nurse behind the desk withdrew her hand from the phone. By the time Chanell got back to the wailing labor room, she could hear the squeals of cart wheels bearing prep trays down the hall. Four nurses, who if not polite were less pointed, bustled about the room on the pivot of Chanell's gaze. And in less than thirty minutes, Bell was enemaed, shaved, and hooked up to an IV, which apparently dripped some kind of sedative-doped solution into the fat arm flattened on a board. Bell quit whooping and hollering between pains, and even dozed in two-minute intervals, while Chanell sat quietly beside the bed.

Between screams, Chanell heard out in the hall strange static and electric yells, and a man's excited garble getting closer and closer—talk of yards and sidelines and touchdowns. Names and numbers called. And in walked a slight man with dark wavy hair carrying a Walkman radio. He had on a brown tweed sports coat the color of his sleepy eyes. He sauntered over to Bell's bed, ironic and lazy, with a lopsided smile. The coat askew on one slouched shoulder made his arms look uneven.

Bell, with her eyes closed, whooped.

"Mrs. Avery," he said, setting the radio on the side table. Somebody made a touchdown and the yells of the crowd matched Bell's. The doctor stood listening, lazy brown eyes resting on the radio. "Ten to two, Valdosta's favor," he said.

Bell looked up and brought one hand over her eyes, then fluffed her bangs. "I'm bad off, doc," she said, "I swear."

"Sugar, what you doing messing up my football night?" He winked at her.

"I'm sorry." She turned her head and whooped the way

she'd look off to cough. Then turned again, smiling.

He patted her hard stomach. "Now, I've been told you're giving a little trouble . . ."

"I'm sorry."

"If you don't quieten down, we'll have to restrain you." He winked at Chanell this time and lifted the chart from a rack attached to the metal bed rail.

"Yessir." A pain hit Bell and she sat up, as if shocked.

"Your friend here'll have to step out in the waiting room," said the doctor, droopy and dazed as if doped. "I just spoke to Mr. Avery . . ." he stopped talking to listen to the speedy, bright voice of the game announcer. "Said to tell you he's waiting."

"For what?" Bell huffed.

"A baby, of course." The voice was cultured but wilted. He winked.

"I want Chanell to stay," Bell said.

"Dr. Knowles," he said to Chanell, sticking his hand out to shake. "Wait outside." Chanell went out and stood by the door, listening to Bell scream and the doctor talk slow and unconcerned around screams and over the racket of the radio. "Miss Avery, I'm going to break your water and speed things up." Somebody scored a touchdown and the radio roared in the room, at odds with the humming white hall where nurses glided past like women in a harem.

Pete was sitting on the brown vinyl couch in the waiting room at the end of the pink hall, one work boot crossed on his knee. Eyes on Chanell as she approached. When she got to him, he sat up and laced his fingers.

Mama Sharon, shimmed into a chair by the couch, stood, hugging her stuffed bone pocketbook. "How's she coming along, sweetie?"

"Okay," Chanell said, feeling she was lying. Bell was not at all okay and could be, for all Chanell knew, dying this very moment. Chanell would never have a baby, never; never again would she miss taking her birth-control pills—no more swallowing two to make up for missing the day before, to catch up dates on the plastic dial.

Mama Sharon hissed, "Jesus, Jesus," with her eyes closed behind the bubble glasses, while Pete alternated between sitting up and back on the squeaky vinyl couch. Chanell sat with her arms folded, feeling guilty for sinking into the bliss of silence. Peace. It was as if Bell had suddenly stopped screaming and gone to sleep, as if all sound had taken on a silent pitch, as if the Walkman radio had been switched off and the heel-dragging doctor-god had conjured peace from pandemonium.

"Pete," Chanell said, "you got any change on you for the Coke machine?"

"Yeah, sugar." He stretched one long leg, exposing a stark white sock that didn't go with his dirty work boot, and reached deep into his pocket. When he handed her the change, his hand was shaking.

Chanell took three quarters. "Y'all want anything?"

"No, sweetie," Mama Sharon said.

Chanell could feel them watching as she walked away, cutting left at the cross halls. She stood around the drink machine a minute, then headed back, to the left rather than right, and again felt their eyes as she kept walking up the long pink hall to the double doors that said KEEP OUT.

As the doors swung inward, she could hear Bell cursing and shouting, the god-doctor now a god-damned doctor. One of the nurses at the station looked up from a chart, then down again.

Bell screamed and the doctor mumbled something about her weight.

Chanell walked on up the KEEP OUT hall, watching the bow-chested nurse charging toward her. "*He* said I could come in," Chanell said before the protests could pass between the nurse's parted lips and marched on, stopping at the the labor-room door.

The radio was off now. "We're going to put you under good in just a minute," the doctor was saying to Bell. "First, we've got to let those contractions get a little stronger." From the closed door, it sounded as if they were tussling.

"You sonofabitch, put me under now!"

"Calm down."

"You're a shit, man. Shitman," Bell screamed. "You touch me again and you gone draw back a nub."

He laughed.

"Don't you laugh at me, you sissy little chipmunk!"

"Chipmunk, eh?"

Bell's screams were now slubbed with little hooks on the end.

"If you'd breathe in and out like I told you," said the doctor, "you wouldn't have such harsh contractions."

"Save it, buster." She screamed, the sound tapering to a yodeling croon.

Chanell heard him scuffing to the door and scooted away, walking fast back down the KEEP OUT hall.

Shortly after midnight, Chanell saw the doctor step through the double doors at the end of the hall, heading toward the lobby. She wasn't sure it was him at first. Shuffling toward them, even smaller than she'd thought, he was wearing a turquoise cap and a gown like Bell's.

Pete and Mama Sharon seemed not to recognize him either, or maybe they were too scared to move, because from the weary look on the doctor's face the news couldn't be good. He took off his cap and ruffed his brown hair, looking left to right where the halls crossed.

Pete stood, rimming the waist of his green twills with his thumbs, then Mama Sharon and Chanell stood.

"Mr. Avery," Dr. Knowles said in that level nothing voice, "your wife's fine, just fine. Resting now."

"Thank you, Jesus," Mama Sharon said and dropped to the chair, hugging her pocketbook.

"Asleep, huh?" Pete reset his black cap.

"Well, drifting out and in." Dr. Knowles rocked his out-stretched hand. "In recovery. She lost some blood . . ."

"Blood!" Mama Sharon sat up. "Don't give her no blood."

Chanell waited for someone to mention the baby; on TV the doctor always brought the baby out when he spoke to the father.

"Give her a couple of hours, Mr. Avery," the doctor said. "She's been through a lot . . ."

Chanell knew what was coming now, so she slipped off up the hall, hearing Mama Sharon sobbing, "Jesus, Jesus," by the time Chanell reached the double doors. She pushed through, hearing the rubber seals flap, and waved the bow-chested nurse away as she waltzed out of the alcove. "Just tell me where's recovery," Chanell said.

"You can't . . ."

"I'll find it." Chanell marched on.

"Next hall on your right," the nurse called. "Don't stay too long."

At the recovery-room door, Chanell caught her breath and peeped in at a quiet, flat Bell on the bed, her toes tented under the white sheet, tubes trailing from her arms to a metal tree hung with clear bags and bottles. She was trembling, with her eyes shut, but there was a resigned peace about her. Chanell eased to the head of the bed, touching Bell's puffy limp hand on the sheet. Chanell hoped the humming white lights overhead accounted for Bell's splotchy pallor. "Bell?" she said.

Bell rocked her head and opened her eyes. "How 'bout fixing my hair, girl. Make me look good for Pete." It was the one romantic reference to Pete that Chanell had ever heard from Bell. It made her want to cry.

Chanell brushed back Bell's damp Persian Gold hair, exposing more liver-pieds on her high forehead. Bell's shoulders shook.

"She weighed just under three pounds, never even cried," Bell choked out. "Can you believe all this weight was pure fat?"

Good at her word, Bell came on Saturday after Chanell had confronted her about the rumor; and good at her word, Bell still claimed not to know what was going on, trying too hard to make light of the whole rumor business.

Usually Bell smoked only at night, but that evening, while Chanell trimmed her hair, she smoked an entire pack of Kools. Balancing a tiny glass ashtray on one knee, she would light one cigarette from another, lipping the filter of the burned cigarette and sucking at the end as the next borrowed fire, then smash the first in the hub of butts, spilling ashes to her brown gabardine pants leg. A tidy messy ritual that required concentration, involvement.

Chanell decided not to press her about the rumor. They talked around it, steering past suggestive words, but somehow it would pop up and block the turns of their offtrack conversation. Bell brought up the subject of flowers for the church— she had to run into town and pick up an arrangement—and the matter of whether Chanell would or would not go back to church was there between them like cold water rushing around their feet. Would Chanell like to go with her to Valdosta? No, she wasn't in the mood. . . . The reason why was left begging to be stated in the form of the question: What in the hell is going on?

Chanell shampooed and blow-dried Bell's hair and manicured her polish-stained nails, and Bell paid her fifty dollars. Chanell tried to give back her change, but she refused. Chanell did need it to pay her electricity bill.

"See you at church," Bell said, going out to the somber supper smells of evening in Cornerville.

But Chanell didn't go to church on Sunday. She lay in her bed listening to the singing and regretted not getting up and getting dressed. Now she'd given in and made the final break final.

chapter eight

Chanell was waiting for the rumors to wear themselves out, not crazy yet but curious. Even a cow's tail has an end, she'd always heard.

On Friday morning, a woman from Southern Bell called to say Chanell's phone would be cut off is she didn't pay the bill. She had two more days and two hundred dollars in her savings account. Four hundred just withdrawn from checking to pay the beauty-supply houses. She might not keep the phone; she might not need to reorder supplies.

The shop was clean and stark in the sun through the east windows, where a small bowl of amber vinegar pooled light. She'd put it on the sill to absorb the stale smoke of customers' cigarettes, and now carried it out to the front stoop, pouring the vinegar into the bed of withering glads. Looking up, she saw Jimmie Mae Bruce, the Negro woman who used to keep house for Miss Pansy, walking up the sunny gravel road with her little girl. Both the color of creamed coffee, Jimmie Mae was tall and trim in a black skirt and white shirt, head held high like a snake in water. The little girl stopped to pick a sandspur from her white sock and Jimmie Mae waited, then bent down to buckle the child's black patent shoe.

Chanell started to go back inside. Probably Miss Pansy's brother had hired Jimmie Mae to check on the house. But when she saw them crossing the road, her side, she waited.

"Miss Chanell," Jimmie Mae said, her tilted eyes lighting like sudden birds on Chanell.

"How you, Jimmie Mae?" said Chanell.

"Doing awright." Jimmie Mae's haughty head lifted with her voice. Her neck was long and jointed, the collar of her starched white shirt folded back on her brown throat. Everybody accused her of being uppity because she took such pride in how she looked. Other way around, they wouldn't have hired her.

"This here my baby girl, Miss Chanell." Jimmie Mae glanced down at the little girl with a mix of pride and mere introduction. The little girl gyrated like a top, black patent shoes planted on the withering grass. Dozens of knurled braids seemed to rotate on her ball head.

"She's mighty pretty." Chanell wondered why Jimmie Mae had stopped to talk; before she'd only nod when Chanell spoke.

"She gone be in a beauty contest at the school tonight." Jimmie Mae turned her attention to retying the sash on the child's lace-trimmed red dress as if to put an end to such meaningless chitchat. The child stood lock-kneed, gazing off at the woods behind the house, at the blown-glass sky of September.

"I guess it is about time for the beauty contest." Chanell hadn't forgotten about the contest that night, had gotten up early hoping her customers would get frantic and call her to do their children's hair. So far, nothing.

"I come to get you to do Sabrina's hair." Jimmie Mae stared at Chanell, no shame in those stretched, liquid eyes.

Chanell leaned against a porch post. My God! She'd never done Negro hair before, had never been asked, and couldn't even imagine it. She'd always looked forward to seeing how much her hairdos had to do with the outcome of the contest, and now this. Would this be her only beauty-contest customer, her sole involvement? A step down.

"I reckon I could, Jimmie Mae," she said. Did Jimmie Mae know Chanell didn't have any customers? What did she know? Caring about that was like caring what some outsider knew. But Chanell trusted that Jimmie Mae would pay her, and she needed the money. "Bring her on in here."

Inside the shop the little girl twisted and stood back with eyes bright and quick as a cornered rabbit's.

Chanell turned on the sprayer, feeling the water till it warmed.

She'd have to loosen all the braids first. She placed the pine plank seat kept for children across the chair arms.

"Get on up there," Jimmie Mae said to the girl, stooping and speaking in a private tone, rough but not harsh.

The child backed to the door, gnawing a finger, and still gazed at Chanell.

Jimmie Mae scooped her up in long spindly arms, the child's legs stiff in lace-trimmed socks, and set her on the pine plank. "Behave yo'self now."

The child sat like a plastic doll while Chanell unwound the rubber bands from each brittle braid, fixing her face not to show that she'd never done this before, that she'd never touched kinky hair before. She wasn't scared of messing up—

not at all—simply felt she'd sunk to a new low. Her chest felt tight, a cage for her fluttering heart. Her only customer on beauty-contest day!

"You got any notion how you want it done?" Chanell figured straight; she figured all Negroes wanted hair like whites.

"What suit you suit me." Jimmie Mae leaned in the doorway.

Each unfastened braid stood up, threatening to rebraid. Maybe, when Chanell wet it . . . "I'm gone lay you back now, honey," she said.

The little girl stiffened like somebody levitated in a magic act. Chanell sprayed the braids and they wilted only slightly, water beading on the coarse strands. Shampoo, maybe shampoo would relax the crimps. She doused the shrunken-looking head with shampoo and felt to the scalp with a chill running from tailbone to neck.

The child's eyes were wide and scared, pupils overflowing to honey irises.

"Close your eyes, sugar," Chanell said. "Don't want to get soap in them."

The little girl squinched them shut. Her elfin face looked cut from a mold of Jimmie Mae's larger face; her brown skin was as smooth as cocoa icing. The braid marks seemed to drain from her hair with the water, and after a good dousing of creme rinse, felt almost as fine as Chanell's white customers' hair. Ringlets circled Chanell's fingers like curled satin ribbons. So black, just the shade of black Chanell hoped to develop to cover her own gray. She cut the water off and took a white towel and tented it over the little girl's head.

"You can set up now," Chanell said. She held the little girl's back and raised her, still stiff as a doll with legs that twist to sitting position.

Chanell's eyes kept wandering to the squat blue jar of pomade that she used on her own hair in damp weather. She didn't know what it would do on the child's hair, and she didn't know if Jimmie Mae would consider pomade an insult. She reached for the jar, opened it, and dug into the lardy white gunk, then rubbed it between her palms till it turned clear, talking as she smeared it into the nylony locks.

"I bet you miss Miss Pansy," she said to Jimmie Mae.

"Yes 'um," Jimmie Mae said, "in a way I do."

It wouldn't hurt to do a little picking, Chanell figured, while she had the chance; talking to Jimmie Mae was like talking to one of the drier chairs. Jimmie Mae didn't matter, what she thought didn't matter. "I hear tell her house is up for sale."

"That what they say." Jimmie Mae eyed the child, whose hair now glittered and curled around her babyish face.

Should Chanell roll her hair on curlers or blow dry it straight? "What you reckon they're asking?" she asked.

"I don't know now." Jimmie Mae folded her arms and leaned around the door frame, staring out.

Chanell was beginning to have a feel for how the hair would look. Curly, yes, curly. Loose curls with a big bow on one side. Get rid of some of those flowery hair bows Alma Jean Wright had palmed off on Chanell to sell on consignment.

"What color's her dress?" Chanell asked.

"Who that?"

"Your girl here. Sabrina."

"Red, it be red. Got it off Miss Linda Gay. One of her little girl's."

"I see." Oh, so now Chanell could get down to some real gossip. "You working for her now?"

"Yes 'um. Tuesday and Thursday, now she be back in school."

How could Chanell ask without giving away that she had no customers? Jimmie Mae didn't matter. "I reckon she's all up in the air over this beauty contest, her little girl maybe winning and all."

"Say she ain't." Jimmie Mae laughed low, a thick after-laugh sounding from her smooth throat.

"I bet." Chanell hoped the "I bet" hadn't sounded mad. "She staying busy with school?"

"Say she be. Say she working on that his'try book the younguns put out ever' year."

"Well, it's a job I wouldn't have," Chanell said. "Hold still, honey, I'm nearly 'bout done."

"Behave yo'self!" Jimmie Mae's tone switched from polite to pithy.

Thinking of Linda Gay, Chanell had yanked the child's hair, and felt terrible for letting her take the blame. "That too tight?" She patted the last large pink roller.

The little girl sat like hardened wax, gazing down at her black patent shoes. Chanell wondered if Linda Gay had given those shoes to Jimmie Mae too. Probably, knowing stingy Linda Gay, she'd paid Jimmie Mae in kids' clothes.

"This your only youngun, Jimmie Mae?" Chanell was rolling the crown now, almost through, and the child was beginning to look more innocent and white with her hair in rollers.

"Got four more at home," Jimmie Mae said.

"My goodness!" All on welfare, Chanell thought, and thought about her property taxes coming due on her house and lot, and wondered if property taxes were applied to welfare and if so was she giving Jimmie Mae the money to pay for the hairdo.

"Okay." Chanell removed the damp towel from the child's lace-trimmed yoke and lifted her down, rubbery stiff. "Let's put you under the drier." She placed the pine board across the arms of the drier chair, turned the drier on, and picked the child up, her black patent shoes sticking out in the window-stencil of sunlight.

"It'll take about thirty minutes for her to dry, Jimmie Mae." Chanell had no idea how long it would take; generally fifteen, twenty minutes would do on a white child's hair. "You want to have a seat, look at a magazine?"

"Nome, I's fine." Jimmie Mae still stood by the door, proud and straight as a spear.

Chanell went to the shampoo bowl and rinsed the woolly black hair from the mock gray marble. After Jimmie Mae and the girl left, she would Clorox the bowl, sweep around the chair, deodorize the room. But really they didn't smell, not at all.

"I'll be back in a minute." Chanell edged out the shop door around Jimmie Mae and went into the house, closing the wood door for the first time that morning. Her hands were shaking. She sat in the crackling green vinyl recliner—T.P.'s old throne—by the mantel, staring out the south window at the road. What if somebody came by?

As much as she'd hoped they would, she now hoped they wouldn't. Her business would be ruined. And what did this mean? Would the Ku Klux Klan burn a cross in her yard?

Chanell would give that hair fifteen minutes to dry, five for combout, and get Jimmie Mae out of there. How dare she do this to me? she thought. Drumming her fingers on the vinyl chair arms, she checked her watch, 11:15. At 11:30, she'd go in there, maybe ask Jimmie Mae not to tell she'd done the child's hair. She watched the sulfur butterflies tangle like tiny kites around the crepe myrtle trees at the church. She wondered if they still expected her to place flowers on the altar table next month in memory of her mother. Everybody took months, and Chanell's was October, one of those months you had to buy flowers because none were in bloom. Maybe by then . . .

Eleven-thirty. Chanell got up and went into the beauty shop. Jimmie Mae still stood by the door. Chanell felt almost mad at her.

"I expect she's dry." Chanell switched off the drier, flipped the hood back, and unwound a roller, testing the curl. Glossy black and dry. "Okay, let's go over to the combout station."

The little girl twitched her toes, peering down under lash-heavy eyelids.

"Get up like the lady say," Jimmie Mae barked.

The child climbed down from the drier chair and followed Chanell with the pine perch to the combout station.

Chanell began unwinding the rollers, then brushed the smooth hair straight back over her hand, but when she let go, it sprang again to the molds of rollers. Channel tousled it with her fingers to diffuse the broad curls, arranged tiny tendrils around her face, then unclipped a fluffy red hair bow from the standing cardboard display on the counter. "You want to buy one of these, Jimmie Mae?" she said. "Three-fifty." The bow had a dozen loops of red satin ribbon.

"What that come to with the hair?" Jimmie Mae asked.

"That'll be eight-fifty."

"Yes 'um, I reckon so," Jimmie Mae said.

Chanell clipped the bow on the left side of the little girl's black patent curls, freeing a few more wisps for bangs. "She looks precious." She really did, like a colored Christmas doll.

Jimmie Mae pulled a small fold of bills from her black skirt pocket and shelled nine ones into Chanell's outstretched hand while the child scampered down. Slinking toward her mother and hugging her legs, the child's pouty lips parted in a shy smile.

Chanell started to say thank you, she started to ask Jimmie Mae not to tell, but she only handed her fifty cents in change and watched as they marched out the door and up the road, Jimmie Mae no more or less beholding than when she came.

That evening Chanell was in a dither over whether to go to the contest or not. She couldn't stand staying home; she couldn't stand being so set apart. But what if she got to the school auditorium and no one spoke. But going might just be the thing to break the grip of those rumors. If she made a real effort to get back in with everybody, if she did as Bell said and ignored the whole silly business, everything might get back to normal.

She dressed in a long white piqué romper, which she hated but her customers loved, one she'd bought because it was in style. A bloomer jumpsuit that would look fine on a little girl but on a grown woman, especially one as hippy as Chanell, looked silly.

She brushed her hair in a high bushy ponytail and clipped on blocky gold earrings. She did her makeup just right, more foundation and blush than she liked, less than her customers liked. She felt like a fool. It had been years since she'd tried so physically to fit in. She'd never dressed quite as up-to-date as Bell, but she'd managed to keep up with most trends.

Her knees shook as she took off walking up the gravel road to the sidewalk that led to the school. The weather was fair, dry, and cool, squirrels spiraling up the pecan trees in the Baptist churchyard. She kept telling herself how crazy it was to feel so nerved-up and naked—same sidewalk and houses, same people—but before she got to Joy Beth's house with the empty, sloping front porch, she crossed the highway to the corner fence post of Archie Wall's cucumber patch. She wondered what he'd heard. She figured that if he'd heard anything about himself he probably didn't care.

He never seemed to care that people still talked about him defending Cliffie Flowers in that murder trial thirty years ago, and you had to give him credit for standing by her when she'd got pregnant by her own half-brother—that's what some people said, some said not. Some said the daddy of her baby was her own preacher, who left town when the church came down on him for messing with a seventeen-year-old girl. Others said he took the blame to keep Cliffie's shameful secret. They said her half-brother, not Cliffie, had set fire to the flatwoods shanty with his three deformed stepbrothers inside, and Aunt Teat, his mother, the old beggarwoman, had burned up trying to rescue them. Cliffie claimed it was an accident. Yes, you had to give Archie Wall credit for that case. He got Cliffie off and not for the money. Pappy Ocain, her daddy and daddy to half the flatwoods, had nothing but pride. But, Chanell figured, if anybody in Swanoochee County did have money, Archie Wall would probably take their cases ahead of people with none.

At the break in the sidewalk where the gravel horseshoe road hooked around the schoolyard and Negro quarters, cars and trucks were parked in front of the high school auditorium, an appendage on the hip-roofed, winged schoolhouse. All school doings, except basketball games, were held in the port-wine brick auditorium, built before Chanell was born.

She scooted across the road, ahead of a white car, and joined the crowd thronging toward the arched auditorium entrance. Her face felt hot, her body seemed to draw back. She shuffled elbow to elbow with the others, smiling with her head high.

Almost every girl in the combined-grade school took part in the beauty contest, and so it took two nights running to get through all three categories: Little Miss, Junior Miss, and Miss Swanoochee County High. Chanell would know by the way things went at the Little Miss contest tonight whether she'd go back Saturday night. Maybe her going tonight would get all the big girls in her shop tomorrow. It wasn't just the money—she didn't care so much about that—but the rejection. What was going on? What? What was everybody thinking? She kept smiling as she shouldered through the arched entrance with the crowd. The same auditorium where she'd won the same beauty contest twenty-three years ago. Same Vaselined smile. Chanell—beauty queen, beauty consultant, beautician, sometime wedding director (for friends, for free). She loved all her titles, had earned them, her place in Cornerville as the beauty connection. God, how she loved these beauty contests! Pointless as they seemed on the surface, as damning as they were to the poor losers' pride, Chanell could vouch for their value on one score: pageants got the pageantry out of a girl's system prior to her wedding-day investment of gowns and flowers and crowns disguised as wedding veil attachments. Chanell had directed enough weddings for friends to spot the difference in contesters and noncontesters; she wondered if she'd ever be asked to do another wedding.

A woman with a ruddy face—nobody Chanell knew—brushed arms with Chanell as they shuffled inside. Chanell spoke, the woman didn't. Chanell cringed, mincing on the concrete floor, not looking at the others who faced her as they crisscrossed toward the two side aisles. Chanell tried to place the woman who hadn't spoken, now filing with the crowd along the left aisle. Maybe the woman was irritated by the crush at the entrance. When Chanell reached the ticket table, set up along the back center row, she handed one of the Future Farmers of America in a blue corduroy jacket her two dollars. A couple of seats among the rear center rows was empty, but she forced herself to walk on up the aisle of the buzzing auditorium, fans overhead billowing the drawn green velvet curtains on the stage at the other end.

Don't stop, she told herself, spotting an aisle seat in the center row. She could feel eyes. Just my imagination, she thought, walking fast on the downslope of concrete to avoid recognizing anybody, to keep from singling anybody out, though she knew most of their faces, the shape and shades of their heads, like her own. She wished she hadn't worn the silly white romper. Did she imagine too that she heard her name whispered by somebody on the right? She found a seat next to the aisle halfway up and sat, looking because she had to at who she'd sat down beside.

Ima Jean Coats, a girlish woman with a flat nose, who had gone to school with Chanell. Chanell started with how good it was to see Ima Jean, touching her arm on the armrest every other word, and Ima Jean smiled and nodded, answering yes and no, but adding nothing. Ima Jean had always been so timid and neutral that Chanell couldn't tell if she was being friendly or unfriendly or merely tolerant. But at least Chanell, by acting bubbly, did become more comfortable and knew she looked comfortable—she was that sure everybody was looking. In school, she'd always considered homely Ima Jean beneath her. Same as with Jimmie Mae. At least Chanell recognized that in herself right away—she could say that much for herself.

She scanned the crowd for Bell, for Joy Beth, for Linda

Gay, and spied Mama Sharon's round brown bun like a hair wreath set among the rows of heads in the middle near the front. She was fanning with a hand fan, facing the curtained stage. People still milled along the two aisles; a few mothers of the contestants trekked in and out of the exit doors that led backstage and along the darkened halls of the old school.

At last, the show started. The principal stepped from behind the Kelly green velvet curtains and welcomed everybody, then in a muffled voice, dulled by the whispering crowd, began bragging about the school, about the Future Farmers and Future Homemakers of America, who sponsored the contest every year. He went on about Cornerville's being so proud of its beauties, its clean name. Same old stuff said at graduation about Cornerville's brains.

After he finished, the pleated curtains parted, and all forty little girls were paraded across the stage, each dipping into a quick curtsy and tripping on the hem of her frothy pastel tulle dress. The piano played a repetitious melody on the ground level below stage, tinny as rain in the din of chatter and clapping. The glisten of laughter. It was plain to see that Linda Gay's frail blond child was a favorite with the crowd. When she stepped up onstage and turned, whistles and oohs cut through the chatter of the stuffy auditorium. She wore a stiff pink hooped gown with bows on the shoulders; her weak blue eyes were stark with fear and makeup. Her long spunglass hair cascaded down her back in soft curls.

Chanell wondered who did her hair.

Sure enough, Linda Gay's little girl was called back out with the semifinalists, twenty tiny would-be women, among them Jimmie Mae's dark Sabrina, whose red fluffy bow was now set too close to the crown. Her red gown hung limp, unseasonable, and stale in the line of crisp, flouncy pastels.

Chanell noticed that the out-of-town judges, who were now huddled in the front center row, always threw in a Negro contestant for semifinalist. Keep everybody happy.

After one hour and a fifteen-minute intermission, which Chanell spent squirming in her seat, the finalists of the Little Miss contest were called onstage again, and still Linda Gay's and Jimmie Mae's were in the top ten. The little girls in the off-hue rainbow line stepped forward as the circled numbers pinned to their skirts were called. Jimmie Mae's drooped and dwarfed Sabrina took second place, and Linda Gay's stiffly smiling number 21 took first. The audience clapped as last year's redheaded Little Miss crowned the blond child, both mechanical as dolls in shop-window displays. Then everybody rose and filed up the aisles toward the sidestage entrances; Chanell, in the line on the right, carried along to keep from pushing toward the front and facing friends who might snub her. Also, she kept step with the crowd in hopes of mingling and putting an end to whatever rumor was going round. Shuffling forward, with the focus off her and on the beauty-contest winner, she hadn't felt so at ease in ages, so at ease that she almost forgot she'd been shunned.

At the east exit, where the short flight of stairs up led on the left backstage and ahead to the dim classroom halls, everybody grouped to wait their turns to speak to the winner. Over the crowd in the wings, Chanell could see Linda Gay and Joy Beth onstage, where flashbulbs flickered like faulty fluorescent lighting. Head to head against the back curtains, they were grinning and talking, Linda Gay with her stout arms crossed and Joy Beth gesturing with her hands. Others hovered about the winners, now seated in white wrought-iron lawn chairs, center stage. On the far end of the stage, separated by a white wicker standing planter of pink glads and ferns, Bell stood talking with Lonnie Hughes, the FFA sponsor.

Chanell eased out of the group at the sidestage entrance, sidling between the back curtains and the wainscoted wall, to speak to Bell. After every contest, Chanell had always gone backstage with the winners, whose winning she credited to her creative hairdos. She felt sure now that if she could get out there, right in the heat of the winning fever, everything would be all right, everything would be like it was.

Halfway along the dim alley of green curtains and brown wall, she could hear Joy Beth and Linda Gay talking on the other side; and without meaning to eavesdrop, at first, she stopped to listen. It was as if a hand had shot up before her face in the cave-brownness of the tunnel and blocked her from reaching the light at the other end. A blessed privilege to hear, granted, without being seen.

"I know you can't hardly stand it," Joy Beth said to Linda Gay, her voice like the hum of a harmonica.

"I'm so proud I could bust," Linda Gay tittered, "you know."

"Honey, I just knew that little colored girl had it," said Joy Beth.

"Well," Linda Gay said in her reedy voice, "I've got to admit, I was a little worried myself."

"I can imagine!" Linda Gay said.

A high school boy reporting for the yearbook interrupted to ask Linda Gay what her little girl wanted to be when she grew up. She said a teacher of course and laughed, and the boy laughed, Joy Beth laughed.

Chanell listened as the reporter wrapped up his interview with Linda Gay, then started on toward the end, careful not to bump the green velvet curtains with their sloughed nap.

"Guess you know who did the little colored girl's hair?" said

Linda Gay in the same secret tone as before the interruption.

Chanell stopped.

"Well"—Joy Beth clicked her tongue—"what can you expect and her part nigger herself?"

Chanell leaned into the wall, feeling blood beat in her ears. She closed her eyes, waiting, waiting for more, for the words just said to unsay, for the words now teletyping in her mind to reverse or delete, for her jellied bones to form again. On the other side of the curtain, somebody else came up and began weaving a trail of different voices into Linda Gay's and Joy Beth's public trillings. No more mention of Sabrina; no more mention of her beautician. Chanell decided she had heard wrong, she had missed something. Her face was on fire, her ears needed to pop. Maybe they'd been talking about the child being part Negro. That was it. Had to be. How white Sabrina looked. But something rang true for the first time in weeks. Some explanation for what Chanell had been going through.

"These fools have it out that I'm part colored," she whispered, then began laughing out loud. She could fix this. No AIDS. No engagement to Archie Wall. It was all so funny.

Beyond the green velvet curtains, they must have heard her laughing, because they scattered, hissing frantically. Either Joy Beth or Linda Gay saying, "God, Chanell! Chanell heard—shit!"

Chanell bumped her head against the wall, laughter crossed with crying, and closed her eyes to the starts of brightness at each end of the tunnel.

"Chanell!" somebody called. "Chanell."

She opened her eyes to see Bell teetering toward her from the north wing.

Bell grabbed her by the shoulders and shook her as if she was mad, then hugged her. "Chanell, no, no."

"Bell," she said. "Listen, I'm all right, really I am." She wagged her head, feeling her heavy ponytail sag. "It's okay. Now that I know, I can handle it."

"They're a pile of shit." Bell said it loud, for them, not for Chanell. She kicked the curtains and they billowed center to ends, like wind you could see. All quiet on the other side.

"It's a lie!" Chanell hollered. "It's a fucking lie!" She'd never used that word before, had never needed to call it from the stash of never-used words in her brain.

Bell drove Chanell home, the two of them awkward together for the first time, in the car, in the house. Not saying a word. Chanell could tell Bell believed the rumor too. She didn't say that.

"How in the world did something like that get started?" Chanell laughed, her throat so parched from fighting back retching it felt like she'd drunk something hot.

"Linda Gay." Bell, in a deep green jersey dress, sat on the couch, smoking, while Chanell paced back and forth, back and forth, from kitchen to living-room doors. She had the urge to walk through the front and out into the dark, to head for the river bridge, out of town, out of Georgia, out of the South. To Detroit maybe. Was that where they said all Negroes wanted to go?

Bell lit cigarette from cigarette. "Linda Gay took her class to Folks-Huxford Library in Homerville to check out backgrounds on people to go in her stinking old history book."

"Yeah, but . . ." Chanell stomped to the front door, back to the kitchen.

"She looked up your mama's family and found out they was part French and something."

"French, yeah," Chanell said, stopping. "I'm French; that's not colored."

Bell got up and crossed the room.

Chanell dodged and circled, hugging herself, thinking, thinking, thinking. She'd always been proud of being part French. It was exotic. The reason she'd changed her name from Betty Jean to Chanell. Now the name seemed as foolish as the white romper. And she felt poor and pitiable, inferior to Bell in the green fall dress.

"I'd rather be French than, than . . ." Chanell wanted to say white, white trash, felt all mixed up.

"I don't think it was the French business, honey," Bell said, smart camel pumps planted in the center of the floor. "What bothered them was the other. I can't remember what, I was too mad."

So Bell had stood up for her, but Chanell found little comfort in that fact. "What was it, Bell? Try to think. What?" Chanell stopped and stared at Bell.

She jangled her bracelets, drawing smoke from her cigarette like oxygen through a tube. "I don't know," sorted through the smoke. "Just let . . ."

"Let it go!" Chanell screamed. "Let it go! How can I stay here and let it go?" She took off to the bedroom, switching on the light by the door, and dragged her scratched brown Samsonite from under the bed, brushing dust as she cried from that sore place in her throat.

Bell knelt beside her, holding both her hands, and shoved the suitcase back under the bed. Then she stood up, tugging Chanell to her feet. They sat on the bed and she hugged Chanell while she cried. The bedsprings squeaked with the honking of bullfrogs on Troublesome Creek. It might rain.

"Call up your daddy, sugar," Bell said. "Get the straight of it from him, then go from there."

"I can't, Bell. I can't bother him," Chanell bawled. "He's just married and . . ."

"Listen here, sugar." Bell pressed Chanell's cheeks between warm palms, staring into her eyes. "Listen. You gone make yourself sick. I don't no more believe you're part-colored than nothing."

"If you did," Chanell said, "would you be here now?"

chapter nine

Chanell was no longer proud.

Bell offered to pay her telephone bill and Chanell let her. She had to call her daddy, and without a phone at home she would have to use the pay phone in front of the courthouse. Still, she kicked around the house for two weeks, crying and cursing, before she got right down to calling. It was like second-guessing a winning lottery ticket, or calling the president, the way she kept going to the phone in the shop, setting it just so, picking up the receiver, and putting it down.

Meanwhile, Bell was coming by regularly, bringing Chanell plates from the café or from home as though she was in jail— Chanell no more shut-in than before the beauty contest, but her mind was.

One day, she'd get out her suitcase to pack; the next day she'd get dressed to go to the post office, to church. But she would always end up staying home in the same old rip-kneed blue jeans and gray sweatshirt, walking the floor and thinking.

Not thinking to solve the problem, just thinking over all that had been said and done, same as she had done after her mother had died. What had Chanell been doing at that exact moment? What had she been doing when Linda Gay had looked up or stumbled onto the information, or when she told the others? Who was told first, who last, how had it spread? Over the telephone lines, or from door to door? Who knew, who didn't? If Archie Wall knew, what did he think? Poor Archie Wall, nobody had ever cared before what he thought.

Gazing out the window and up the road, she would think about going to his house and getting him to sue them. But she'd have to sue all of Swanoochee County, she supposed, and who would sit on the jury if the case went to trial? Then she'd laugh and head for the telephone to get her daddy to set the story straight. And it was on one of those trips, on the upswing of one of those moods, that she finally got up the nerve to call. The nerve to take it, truth or lie.

It was Wednesday, the first cold day of fall—not freezing but bright and by comparison cold—around six in the evening. That time when the loneliness generally peaked for the day and the week. A middle of the week loneliness she remembered when her daddy used to come home from work and eat with her in front of the TV to satisfy her mama that he was keeping Chanell company.

Hand on the phone and clocking his daily routine—he should be coming in from work about now—she stalled to give him time to get through the door of his new house, which she pictured in the same floor plan as their old house across Troublesome Creek, give him time to hang his black Sampson cap on the nail behind his new door, and wash up for supper with his new wife. She waited, watching the clock above the combout station. She thought about the time of

year and how her daddy, to keep from turning on the heat at
the first hint of winter, would sit buttoned up in his black
jacket before the TV morning news, drinking black coffee. She
could smell the coffee, hear the rattle of the cup on the
saucer, feel his silence swell around TV voices as familiar as
family.

Keeping an image of him calm like that, she dialed his
number in Blountstown, Florida. His wife, Rose, answered.

"Hey, Rose," Chanell said, "it's me," and felt stupid sounding
so intimate and chirpy. Chanell didn't like Rose; she didn't dis-
like Rose. She didn't know her. Rose was daddy's wife, not
Chanell's stepmother. She'd met her—a lean, washed-out, attrac-
tive school secretary trying out a fourth husband—just once.

"Rose, is Daddy home?" Chanell asked evenly.

He was, wait a minute.

Chanell could hear high heels tapping away from the phone,
heavy work boots pounding back. Haunted by the slice of sun
on the shop floor, Chanell could hear their TV and imagined
she could smell wieners and beans and light bread, what Rose
was maybe keeping warm for him now. What Chanell and he
had eaten together while watching *All in the Family* on other
Wednesdays.

"Hello?" he said, his voice shrill for a man's.

"Daddy?" Chanell almost started to cry. "It's me, Betty
Jean."

"What's the matter?"

"Nothing, Daddy. Nothing." Chanell thought she sounded
like one of those college girls on TV calling home for money.
She'd never asked for a dime.

"Uh," he said, "you sick or something?" His face would
be bright, wrinkled, and inert from hard listening, that rind
mouth hinged above the receiver.

"No sir, I'm not sick," she said. She sat down on a bar stool by the shop door, then let it all go, whether it would sound stupid or like begging. She'd always prided herself on being independent, above hurt.

"Shit!" he said before she got done. "That bunch is always looking for a nigger in the woodpile." His favorite saying; he didn't even catch the pun. "I can't believe you let 'em get to you."

"I'm not, Daddy." She sat up. "I just . . ."

"Let me give you the straight of it, gal." He sounded mad with Chanell. "And I better not never hear no more of this putting your mama's bunch down. Good people, worked hard for a living. Like me. If other people had to work like I do, they wouldn't have time to run their mouths and mess in other people's business."

She hung her head, listening to how he spoke more than what he said, and watched the dust sift down in the narrowing band of light on the white tiles. "Yes sir, I'm sorry." He didn't even hear her. "Your mama's grandmama was French Creole. From up around Louisiana way. They's done been some talk about this before . . .

"Hell! Folks don't never get done stirring up stuff. You tell 'um I said to go to grass." He said something to Rose, just as sharp, then to Chanell, "I gotta go."

"Daddy, wait." Chanell stood up.

"What?"

"I might need to come see you for a little while. Okay?"

"How come? You gone let that bunch of shitheads break up your home?"

"Daddy, listen. Me and T.P. broke up. . . ."

"Over this shit?"

"No sir, we . . ."

"Ain't you got enough grit to stand up for yourself?"

Chanell placed the receiver on the hook, valuing the silence, and watched the sun straw on the floor dwindle to nothing.

She didn't know how long she'd sat there, but when she got up the house inside was as dusky as outside. The hum of the refrigerator the only sound except for the locusts' drone closing outside in.

She slipped on a sweater and went out the front, listening for traffic, for voices. George, the peacock, roosting on the wood settee of the stoop, looked drooped and dull as papier mâché with his tail feathers shed. A dog was barking at its echo across the creek where the afterlight of the fallen sun played still in the tops of the sweetgums. Dark was grafting onto the dusk from the house to the highway, and layering fog and leaf smoke hefting in stolen places of the pecan orchard behind the church.

Hiding behind one of the trees, she waited for two pickups to pass on 94, then dashed across to Archie Wall's dirt yard and onto the front porch.

She couldn't keep wavering over what to do or she'd do nothing. She'd almost given up the idea of leaving Cornerville, now that she had nowhere to go. She'd have to fight, but she didn't have a single weapon in mind.

Through the two front windows over the porch, she could see a light at the rear of the house. She knocked on the four-panel wood door and stood back, listening for Archie Wall's steps. But all she heard was the rattle and clank of a pump in the backyard and two girls giggling in the house behind Archie Wall's. She started to knock again, but the door opened, and there stood Archie Wall, wearing a hat but no shoes.

"You going somewhere, Archie Wall?" she asked.

He opened the door wider and stepped aside. "Done been."

"Oh, you're just getting home." Chanell eased inside. The tall dim room was walled in books and stacks of newspapers, parchment shades rolled halfway down on the tall windows. No furniture, except for an old heavy desk with a sprung swivel chair behind and a straight chair before it. On the north wall, the fireplace was boarded up, and a gas space heater stood on the scabby concrete hearth. A maroon wool rug, with faded roses and bruised blue leaves, covered the center of the wood floor, which peeked from an edging of junk. An odd effluvium of book mold and cooked eggs.

"Have you got a minute, Archie Wall?"

He shut the door, head down and mincing on white socked feet.

Suddenly it occurred to Chanell that he might have heard she was part-Negro and might not want her in his house. "I don't want to take up your time," she said.

"I was just about to eat a mouthful." He nodded toward the hazy narrow hall where the light welled with the eggy smell from the kitchen. "Come on in."

She followed him to the high-ceilinged kitchen and pulled out a chair at a square table cobbled from odd-sized boards. A loaf of white bread and a set of café-style salt and pepper shakers were scrunched to the end, where the table sat flush with the mildewed yellow wall.

He crossed to the greasy white range covered in dirty pots and pans, and spooned some dry scrambled eggs, like popcorn, from a cast-iron skillet to his plate. Then he took a fork from a drawer under the scratched green-linoleumed counter and sat down at the table. Mind on his business, he sprinkled his yellow eggs white and black with salt and pepper, then took a slice of white bread from the loaf and started eating as if Chanell wasn't there.

She tried not to watch, but somehow it didn't matter. What he thought or did, what she thought or did, didn't matter. "Archie Wall, I reckon you heard what's going on."

His unblinking eyes shifted from his plate to her. "What's that, Betty Jean?"

"The rumor," she said, thinking that she'd start from the beginning, where the dreamlike funny stuff had turned into a nightmare.

He snorted and coughed into his fist, either choking or laughing, then gulped some water from a jelly glass and set it down. "Which rumor?"

"Sir?"

"Which rumor?" He folded his bread and bit off the end.

Chanell swallowed for him. "The one about me being part-colored."

"Oh." He ate more eggs, bit more bread, and washed it all down with water.

"I guess you're wondering how come me to be here."

He looked up but went on eating. Then, like a man switching hats, he sat back and crossed his stubby arms over his tight, round paunch. "What can I do for you, Betty Jean?"

"Well, I don't know . . . I mean I don't know where to start. I don't know what to do." She waited for him to read her mind. Did she want to sue? Did she want to tell him, the true stranger in Cornerville, her troubles?

"I guess," she finally said, "for starters, I'd like you to tell me what 'Creole' means."

He got up and left the room, padding down the hall to the front. She could hear papers rustling, books sliding to the floor. Had he left for good? Did he want her to leave? She'd known he was peculiar but not abrupt. But then she thought about his quick-change approach to 1-75 exits on the way to the farmers' market and let her mind dawdle off into one of Pete's Archie Wall tales.

Several years ago, Archie Wall had defended Miss Mattie Kirkland, a stingy, cantankerous old widow, in a landline dispute with her only living brother. Known for overseeing her timber business from her front-porch rocker, Miss Mattie had got her hired man to keep slipping the landline further onto her brother's inherited plot, which she claimed was rightfully hers, and when her brother tried to take her to court she refused to go and commanded Archie Wall to fight the case by proxy. No such precedent, the judge cried, and sent the sheriff out to her falling-down house on the Florida line to cite her for contempt. From the front-porch rocker, she spied the sheriff's car coming round the dirt-road curve and jerked up her shotgun kept by the door, firing as the sheriff braked and backed up, coming and going dust colliding. A few hours later, the sheriff returned, sneaking through the woods to the back of the house with two deputies. They nabbed Miss Mattie from behind and hustled her off to jail in Cornerville. That evening, Archie Wall took her rocking chair to the tiny cell overlooking the school-bus route. Fighting mad, she cussed him black and blue. Regardless, Archie Wall had begged the court for mercy on her behalf—after all, she was a widow alone, couldn't have more than four or five years left in which to be cantankerous, and following her death the land would pass on to her brother, as next of kin, anyway. Furthermore, Archie Wall brought to the attention of the court, what if the old widow should die in jail? How would that look with the Baptist Church within seeing distance? Winter was coming and her heart was bad. Freedom granted, Miss

Mattie, obsessed now and unrepentant, still owning up to no wrong, refused to leave the drafty cell, refused to eat, and rocked bundled in a shawl in the open door for another two months, until her brother begged her forgiveness rather than watch her wither before his very eyes as he drove the school bus past the jail every day.

Archie Wall was still rustling papers like a rat building a nest in the living room, and Chanell was about to get up and go out the backdoor when she heard him coming up the hall. She perched on the edge of the chair. He walked around the table, licking a pointer finger and turning pages in a thick blue book.

She couldn't see the cover for the shelf of his belly. Was he looking up something in a law book? "I don't know exactly that I want to sue," she said.

"Says right here in the *American Heritage*," he mumbled to himself, thumping a page, "Creole means . . . a person of European descent born in the West Indies or Spanish America. A person descended from or culturally related to the original French settlers of the southern United States, especially Louisiana. The French dialect spoken by these people. A person descended from or culturally related to the Spanish and Portuguese settlers of the Gulf States. A person of mixed European and Negro ancestry who speaks a Creole dialect. A black slave born in the Americas as opposed to one brought from Africa." Keeping his finger on the dictionary entry, he looked up.

Chanell's scalp stung as if her ponytail had been yanked. She'd been proud of being French, and would have been proud of being Creole if she hadn't known what it meant. "Read the last part again, Archie Wall," she said.

He reread the whole thing and even read on about Creole cooking, lost in a courtly chant. "A creolized language. Haitian

Creole. Of, relating to, or characteristic of the Creoles. Creole. Cooked with a spicy sauce containing tomatoes, onions, and peppers . . ."

Chanell held up one hand. "I don't care about the cooking part, Archie Wall. And I ain't gone sue cause I'm guilty." She got up.

"You are, huh?" He sat down and reared back with his arms crossed, book open on top of his plate of eggs.

"I'll go now."

"You're not leaving Cornerville, are you?"

"No sir, not yet. I can't. No money; nowhere to go."

He nodded but still sat there, studying the empty chair with a stymied gaze as if confronted with yet another case by proxy.

First thing the next morning, Archie Wall was rapping on Chanell's front door.

Tripping through the living room, half asleep, she wrapped her blue terry robe over her T-shirt and panties, then stood back, talking to him through the door.

"I come to get that trim you owing me," he said.

"Archie Wall . . ." She'd already trimmed his hair in exchange for the ruined cucumbers. "I just got up . . . I . . . Go on in the shop and set down."

She got dressed in the same body-molded blue jeans and gray sweatshirt as the day before, brushed her teeth and hair, and hurried to the shop, flipping on the light switch by the door. It was dark and rainy outside, a gray dreariness seeping through the front wall of windows.

"Come on over here, Archie Wall." She stood next to the combout chair and yawned. "Gone rain, ain't it?"

"Looks like it." He dawdled over and sat down, holding his hat.

She began trimming the band of silvery hair below the crown, taking her time. It was short and thorny from the last cutting, and all she could do was make it shorter. "I'm sorry about last night," she said.

"Ain't no problem." He talked to her reflection in the standup mirror on the counter.

"I'm just gone take it like it comes, Archie Wall, long as I can." She held the flickering silver scissors still, talking to the mirrored image of his round red face.

"Yes 'um." He looked down, his waxy baldness gleaming beneath her chest and head in the mirror, as in a picture of a woman with a crystal ball.

She'd hoped he would come up with some legal way to banish all the mess. What way she didn't know.

When she got done trimming, he got up and brushed the yoke of his blue shirt, then shook the collar to sift down the silvery stubbles of hair on his neck.

"Want me to put some talcum on your neck, Archie Wall?"

"That's all right," he said, heading out the door.

"Be coming back," she said. Surely now they were even on the swap of hair trimming for cucumbers.

As she started out of the shop behind him, she saw a ten-dollar bill on the shelf above the shampoo bowl.

Mama Sharon had always said when it rains it pours, meaning trouble; so when Chanell woke up Saturday to a steady slow drizzle and a day getting darker instead of lighter, she expected the rain to pour down, her troubles to double.

She'd quit dressing up in the morning once she accepted as fact that her customers weren't coming. That nobody was. She hadn't shaved her legs in a couple of weeks, only under her arms. Her hair was clean but not fixed, pulled tight in a

ponytail to keep it from frizzing around her face and remind-
ing her that she had whatever degree of Negro blood. Creole
and French. She kept trying to figure in her head how much
Negro blood the mix would amount to as removed as the
connection was. But she'd never been good with fractions, or
estimations, could rely on just a guess that the Negro blood
reduced to very little. What difference did it make? She'd been
labeled part-nigger.

She wished she sewed or crocheted, wrote or painted,
instead of doing hair, so she could do it by herself and have
some way to dissolve the gelling time in her head. She
couldn't leave now, had nowhere to go, no money, so her
house was permanent. Yet in her mind she was still going,
and she didn't even care to paint her bedroom now that she
had time. The quart of purple paint, accidentally bought for
pink, sat in one corner of the living room.

Walking the floor while it rained, peeping through windows out of habit, she got on to herself for not being grateful
that she at least owned her house. She'd paid for it—took ten
years of doing hair—and when she and T.P. split up, he'd
tried to claim his half. But Archie Wall had fixed that: he told
T.P. that if he got the house, Chanell would get the pickup.
Community property, Archie Wall called it. So T.P. had let it
go. Besides, T.P. never expected to be gone long. He'd fully
believed that Chanell would get lonely and beg him back. He
knew she didn't like being by herself, but she'd been fine as
long as she had friends.

She turned on the overhead light in the living room, sat on
the couch, and started looking through a hairstyle magazine.
Too exotic for Cornerville, though many of the hairdos were
too simple for any of her customers, more suited to women
with confidence. A soft layered do on Joy Beth—providing

her hair would lie that way—would make her look merely undone and frumpy.

Chanell's back was to the window over the stoop as she heard car tires singing on the wet gravel from the church to her house, then fizzle out. A car door clapped. Her chest heated up, then her face. She turned on the couch and peered through the curtains.

Bell was dashing through the rain to the stoop, clutching something under her old green parka with its alligator emblem. Sometimes she wore her oldest, rattiest clothes, as if daring the changing styles.

Chanell opened the door. "How you, Bell?"

"Nothing extra." She pulled out a stack of mail and handed it to Chanell, then took off her parka, tossing it to the settee on the porch. "God, it's raining cats and dogs!" She came on in and shut the door while Chanell thumbed through the mail, looking for her gas bill.

"Miss Cleta said your mail was stacking up," said Bell. "Told me to bring it to you."

"Guess it's got around that we're still buddies, huh?" Chanell didn't know why that snagged in her mind, but looking down at Bell's muddy, worn Reeboks, it suddenly came to Chanell that Bell was taking a risk. Also, crazy as it was, Bell's association with Chanell now somehow diminished Bell, what she'd been. "I reckon I'll have to call about my gas bill."

"I paid it already," Bell said, plopping in the chair by the window, staring out with her sculpted, unfixed face in shadow. Her skin was liver-pied, with blue crescents under her ringed green eyes.

"You shouldn't of done that," Chanell said.

"Gone turn cold after this rain." Bell stood up and hugged herself with a put-on shiver.

"You should of asked." Chanell didn't really care; after all, she'd let Bell pay the telephone bill. But she still owed Bell and Mama Sharon for beauty school. Also, Chanell was picking for a fight.

Bell seemed to know. "We'll settle up later." She waved one hand, backing to the closed fireplace with the other fisted behind.

"You had no business going through my mail." Chanell slapped the sheaf of mail on the mantel next to the pair of pickaninny figurines with baked dusky faces, then crossed to the couch and perched on the arm by the door.

"What's got into you?" Bell sat in the recliner again, hands clasped between the knees of her too-blue Chic jeans. Her eyes were as out of focus as T.P.'s when he got mad.

"I don't want you feeling sorry for me," Chanell said. "Don't hang around just cause I'm your ex-sister-in-law."

"I'm not." Bell stood again and slid her fingers into her pockets.

"I can take care of myself."

"You're just feeling sorry for yourself, Chanell." Words puffed from Bell's mouth like smoke. "You're not the first person ever talked about around here. Why don't you get out and get a job, do something?"

"Got any ideas?"

"Go to Valdosta, check out the beauty shops, see if they're hiring."

"Sure!" Chanell walked over and got the mail from the mantel, then went back and sat on the couch with her legs hooked across the arm in the doorway. "I just want to be by myself, Bell."

"You want me to go?" Bell stepped a little forward, stopping in the middle of the room, fat humps on her thighs exploding.

"Yeah. Yeah, I do." Chanell opened a circular advertising aluminum house siding and acted as if she was reading.

"Well, move your feet then," Bell said.

Chanell swung them around, and Bell walked out, got in her car, and drove away.

"My gift to you, Bell," Chanell said. "You can go without feeling guilty and not be doomed with me."

Chanell sailed the circular across the room, picked up another, and sailed it, too. She started to sail the next envelope but noticed that it contained a letter. She ripped it open.

> Dear Mrs. Foster,
>
> As you know, Pansy Maine's property across from your own is up for sale, with a couple of prospective buyers who have expressed a desire to purchase the adjacent vacant lot and all surrounding and adjoining properties. Therefore, on behalf of my client, Ms. Maine's brother Alfred Maine, I would like to negotiate with you on an acceptable price—one I'm sure you will find most generous and fair. Please get in touch with me at your earliest convenience, so that we may further discuss the terms.
>
> Very truly yours,
> Archie Wall, Attorney at Law

Chanell dropped the letter to her lap. So Archie Wall was in on it too. And now they were going to clean up the old neighborhood. Nobody wanted to live next door to a part-nigger. Maybe they never believed that Chanell would buy Miss Pansy's house in the first place, that she could, or that Archie Wall would. They were just trying to get rid of the bad blood. Maybe all the other rumors were staged to pick at

Chanell. Not the last one, but the ones before. No. What started out was more mischief than maliciousness but had mushroomed into something serious. And now, now they wanted to get rid of the trash. The trash!

Chanell jumped up and stomped through the living room, through the kitchen, through the door to the back stoop, where rain gushed from the corner gutters and pooled on the white sand and grass, level with the concrete floor. She lifted her twenty-five-gallon green plastic garbage can and lugged it off the stoop, rain beating on her head, lashing her face and arms. She ripped off the lid, sailing it like a Frisbee across the yard to the border of fox-grape vines, where the rain sifted through the leaves in rapid ticks. As though sowing lawn fertilizer, she reached inside the can and grabbed a newspaper coated with coffee grounds and slung it toward the understood property line between her place and Miss Neida's. The flattened paper picked up the tune ticking from the vines and sogged into the grass.

Carrying the can toward the run-together grass seaming her yard to the vacant lot, another understood property line, she set it down and reached again inside, bringing up a double handful of jagged eggshells and a can with the Jolly Green Giant strutting on the label. She reared back and dashed the egg hulls and the tin can toward the car shed, then hobbled the garbage can around front, picking up speed with a rhythm, tossing a ketchup bottle to the side of the house, hearing it clink and smash and clink again in bits and pieces of glass as she tossed a couple of Campbell soup cans just short of the gravel road. Like a child picking out a model plane from a toy box, she pulled out a milk carton and sailed it to a puddle in her yard.

The rain smelled silvery tart, the coffee grounds and slop-soggy paper smelled sour. She kept walking, slinging trash around the house, keeping just this side of her landline, paper towels hanging from the leafless wisteria between her yard and Miss Neida's—Chanell's half of the woody trailing vine. She could see Miss Neida's gray head posed in one of the barred windows of the old jail like a ghost of one of the jail-birds wanting out.

Chanell hobbled on toward her backyard, scattering nap-kins and Coke cans over the wet grass and weeds. She hadn't mowed the grass since the rumors started, had let it grow wild with them. She picked up the garbage can and dumped the tea grounds on the bottom.

"Now, let 'um try to buy my house," she yelled. "Let my new neighbors see what real trash is."

She felt tired, her wet shoulders ripping at the sockets, and knew she'd be picking up the trash later, much like when she used to pack to leave T.P. following a fight, and then had to unpack and put it all back. But it felt good to be mad, and at least now she knew she'd be staying in Cornerville.

Idleness seeks action just as silence seeks sound.

chapter ten

Now Chanell had more to do than she could handle; her mind was working overtime. She couldn't wait for the rain to stop—literally couldn't wait. Saturday morning, while the wind picked up out of the west, blowing the trash east, she took the gallon of purple paint, which she'd accidentally bought for pink, out to the front stoop and, starting from the left corner, began brushing stripes of purple onto Eggshell White.

After several swipes with the paintbrush, she almost stopped. The purple looked so permanent, so forbidden, was surely an act she'd regret, one she couldn't take back. But she kept on painting, hearing the wind whisk drying napkins and newspapers across the gravel road to Miss Pansy's yard. Her legs were chilled below her cutoff overalls, so cold that the hair prickled and stung. Heart beating hot in her chest, she kept her eyes on the changing wall to keep from seeing if any of her neighbors were watching, but still she imagined eyes like camera lenses in every window along the crescent.

After the first round of zigzag brush strokes, sidling right along the square stoop, she began humming for courage and effect, painting as high as she could reach among swagged cobwebs and dirt daubers' adobe burrows.

Humming the first tune to pop into her head, which happened to be a song she and Joy Beth and Linda Gay used to sing in first grade. Then singing, singing loud because she might as well, singing loud for courage and effect, singing broken because, in truth, she was a coward.

> *Way down yonder in the pawpaw patch,*
> *The pawpaw patch, the pawpaw patch,*
> *Way down yonder in the pawpaw patch*
> *There sat little Chanell.*
> *Come on boys and let's go find her,*
> *Come on boys and let's go find her,*
> *Come on boys and let's go find her,*
> *Way down yonder in the pawpaw patch.*

She climbed up on the wood bench, bail in one hand and brush in the other, and painted above the living-room window, a delicious dribble of purple running all the way down the dusty window screen to the concrete floor. Slathering the ceiling beams, she felt paint trickle from her right wrist to her armpit and spatter her black hair. And the third verse of the song:

> *Picking up pawpaws, put 'em in your pockets,*
> *Picking up pawpaws, put 'em in your pockets,*
> *Picking up pawpaws, put 'em in your pockets,*
> *Way down yonder in the pawpaw patch.*

She had now painted the entire stucco wall of the front stoop with streaks of white peeping through purple, purple cobwebs draping like shredded party streamers from corner to corner. She started on the wall around the door to the beauty shop, working toward the outside corner, and then the jutted front of the shop with the double windows, where the paint was newer, whiter, more difficult to damage—she'd loved those windows that let the sun in, that let her look out when she tired of the tiny shop.

The wind had swept all the paper she'd scattered into Miss Pansy's yard, except for one sheet of newspaper now snagged on the camellia bush that Chanell thought of as a landmarker designating the bungalow yard from the old jail yard. Painting only as high as she could reach at the far corner, Chanell was socked by the force of the cold north wind. Her teeth chattered, maybe from the cold, maybe from fear. She had to keep singing—she had to. She could still feel her neighbors' eyes, a crescent of gazes along the curve to the highway. What if they called the sheriff? Would he arrest her? On what charge? She laughed, hysteria gathering in her throat with the words to the song.

> Way down yonder in the pawpaw patch,
> The pawpaw patch, the pawpaw patch,
> Way down yonder in the pawpaw patch
> There sat little Chanell.

And again she tasted her own name bubbling timidly between her lips. Such a crazy song, such a crazy situation. If she stopped now, she'd slink away like a dog caught stealing chickens and never step outside the house again.

Finally, out of paint, she stepped back and surveyed the

front of the house. Looked like the beginnings of a bad mural on a backwoods service station. Two soup cans rolled in the wind and clinked along the gravel road. The napkins in Miss Pansy's yard sailed toward the pecan orchard behind the church. George waddled along the sideyard, dull as a feather duster, glass eyes flicking from Chanell to the hedge of stemmy azaleas. The wind at his back ruffed his sparse bluish feathers as he pecked at tea grounds and wind-tumbled eggshells, some soggy saltine crackers melted into the grass.

Chanell stood a while longer, waiting to regret the trash and purple paint. She didn't.

Later that evening she watched while cars and trucks drove past to see the crazy part-black's part-purple house.

At first she had thought the passers-by were people looking to buy Miss Pansy's house, but when they kept coming, when she began recognizing certain cars, she caught on. But still she didn't regret the paint or the trash. It had been something to do, something to while away another miserable day, and she'd made her point. Now she would wait to see what they would do.

But she wasn't through.

Her mind was buzzing with notions, which really weren't plans but a jumble of nonsense, which like the words to the pawpaw song begged action more than thought, something to do until she could once again be. A steely after-ring of revenge in her ears. And in her mouth a vinegary taste of satisfaction.

Still cold, still in cutoff overalls, as the sun backlit the bullous vines and trees, she walked toward the creek along the narrow dirt path cobbled with russet grape and sweetgum leaves, stopping in a clearing of dog fennels before she got to the embedded black stream. The spindly stems of the weeds were turning wine and had ferny white blooms that shed when she broke the woody stalks. Gathering dog fennels, she listened to the traffic still passing by her house, to the traffic on 129, west of the clearing, where the creek gurgled through a culvert on its route to the river.

When she had a round lush bouquet of dog fennels, she followed the path up the slope to her yard, went through the kitchen door, and took a tall, green vase from the seldom-used cabinet over the refrigerator, filled the vase with water, and stuck the fistful of dog fennels inside. Sun reflecting on the chrome and glass of passing cars cast mobiles of light on the furniture and walls, little angels that made her feel like the devil.

Holding the bouquet in both hands, out from her body the way her mama had taught her, she sucked in and stepped out the kitchen door, angling across the south side of her yard and the gravel road. Two cars passed before she got to the pecan orchard of the church, but she didn't look up, didn't want to see the spectators come to view her act.

Inside the church, sun stenciled twelve-paned window patterns on the pine pews and aisles, squares of light in the holy round hush, with ruches of maroon from hymnals and the altar table runner at the pulpit. A fine sifting of dust and mold spores, like gnat swarms. Even the traffic outside the west windows was muted. She tiptoed to the altar table and centered the arrangement on the velvet runner, white petals snowing down like dandruff.

"Forgive me, Lord," she whispered, "but it is my month to place flowers in the church. I know you'll understand these weeds. Remember the money changers in the temple, Lord?"

Then she tipped up the aisle again, pawpaw song ringing in her head as if she'd yanked the bell pull in the holy twilight of the vestibule.

*   *   *

This time Archie Wall was seated like a big hairless rubber doll at the clunky scratched desk in his living room, writing on a yellow legal pad.

"Working on a case," he said.

"Is it mine, Archie Wall?" she asked softly, towering above the desk.

He kept on writing. "You ain't hired me yet."

"I mean Mr. Alfred's case, him trying to get my place."

"Don't take it personal." He looked up, then down, writing.

"It *is* personal."

"I gotta make a little cash somewheres."

"And he'll pay you, right?"

"I hope so." He put the pen down. "Understand?"

She did understand. She'd done hair for money and she'd done hair for free; she'd done hair for people she loved and she'd done hair for people she hated. "Yes sir, I understand, I'm just . . ."

"Hurt? Disappointed?"

"Mad." She started to leave.

"Sit down, Betty Jean."

"I ain't got time." She was at the door when she heard his chair roll back. She turned. He sat again, swiveling and rocking. He was all she had, maybe her only friend. Friend?

"I'm going over a landline dispute, right now. Nothing to do with you." He looked touched, but neither meekness nor sorrow lined that smooth bland face.

"Most of them don't pay you, do they, Archie Wall?"

He rocked, laughed.

She pulled the straight chair up to the desk and sat across from him, shaking cold. The gas space heater before the closed-off fireplace hissed waves of panicky heat in the drafty room. "Me and you's got a lot in common, Archie Wall."

He stared at her.

"I didn't mean . . ." she started. "Maybe you don't want to associate with me."

He waved his hand, still rearing. The chair squawked.

"What I mean is, a beautician and a lawyer's got a lot in common," she said. "Around here, they pay you when they can or give you junk."

Blue eyes shining, he slid open a drawer of the old desk and began rummaging through yellowed receipts, coils of string and gummy rubber bands, and brought forth a small jar of homemade pickles like tarnished coins he'd been hoarding.

She laughed. He set the jar on the desk. "Where'd this Creole business come in?" he said.

"You mean when did the rumor start?"

"No. Who in your family?"

"My great-grandmother, I think."

He locked his hands behind his head, tender white flesh of his underarms showing from the sleeves of his blue shirt. "So, that'd put you with about, say, somewheres in the neighborhood of having one-sixteenth Negro blood. If that."

"Ain't much for all this fuss."

"Just enough to start a stink over."

"I been thinking, Archie Wall." She tipped forward, elbows on his desk. "What if I don't leave? What if I stay put and fight? What you reckon would be my chances of them taking me back?"

He shook his head. "The way you were, the way they used to think of you?"

"Yeah."

"None."

"I know that."

"But painting your house purple and stringing trash at least let 'um know you won't be run off."

"You know?" She laughed. Of course he could see her purple-striped house from either of the north windows just by swiveling his chair around.

"Be careful." He drummed the jar of pickles on the ringed varnished surface of the desk.

"You mean, stay on the side of the law, right?"

"Huh uh." He looked at her hard. "Around here, they don't go by the law; the law goes by them."

"Yes sir." She got up to go.

"And look out behind your back."

"You think they gone try to get shed of me, don't you?"

"They gone do their darndest." He stood up too, easy in the soft hiss of the heater.

Walking up the dusky road home, she could see her trash blooming like strange winter flowers in the cold-cured weeds of the vacant lot, on the brown bed of pecan leaves in the churchyard, on her neighbors' frost-parched grass and pruned shrubs, point to point along the crescent. Even the newspaper from her landmark camellia had dislodged and now lay heaped on the gravel road between her place and Miss Pansy's. Almost night now, and Chanell couldn't wait to get home and lock her doors. She'd never locked her doors before, had never been afraid. But she didn't really believe anybody would harm her, not really, not in Cornerville.

The same lavender-bordered sky formed a dome over the little town, where the same clean-living people made ready for supper, a faint clatter of pots and pans and muted steps going off like distant thunder in the kept-up frame houses where dim lights glowed, slow traffic now passing at the red light only—all seemed to have passed Chanell's purple house and grown weary of the spectacle. The smell of frying ham steeping in the chilly twilight.

As she got nearer, she saw that the newspaper she thought had blown free was still trapped in the branches of the jointly owned camellia bush. Her eyes kept switching from the bush to the heap on the road. A sudden lift of air ruffled feathers on the speckled mound, and her breath caught. She inched closer, hoping, hoping that the heap on the road would prove to be flat, that the trick of dusk was responsible for the heaped image that could turn out to be only an oil spot on the gravel. Closer, close now, she could make out the broken body of her peacock. Hot bile pooling in her throat, she knelt and placed her hand under one crooked wing, feathers cold but warmth seeping from the queerly still body to her tingling fingers. No blood beating in his ribby breast, no pulse in the lumpy back-flung neck. His bead eyes were milky and lolled in his hard-ball head. His fringed cone felt wet, showed red on her hand when she held it up to Miss Pansy's security light. She scooped George up and cradled his body—lighter than he'd ever looked—to the front stoop and his favorite roost, the wood settee he'd claimed and she was always threatening to reclaim.

She'd always believed that the odds against anything bad happening after a warning, or right after thinking about something bad, were slim. But even odds didn't figure in this nightmare game. In her nightmare with the purple house and trashed yard, dog fennels in the church, her whole world caught up in back-flung action, the routine of regular living rocked. But, strangely, she wasn't spent, just dizzy from the crazy spinning motion. Sad, but all right, making the most of a bad situation, minute by minute. She'd been given no choices, so she took some.

Sunday morning, while they were singing at church, she got her shovel from the car shed and began digging in the front yard, vacant-lot side, facing the open stretch of wintering grass between Miss Pansy's house and the pecan orchard behind the church. A mild wind pushed east, flapped her blue chambray shirt, and scuttled a tin can along the gravel curve while church hymns kited eerily in the stark blue sky. Sunday didn't feel like Sunday, but she couldn't think what day it did feel like, no day she'd ever lived before. She tried to call up her sense of nostalgia, but even that didn't work to place her in some better time, on a better day to log in her memories for tomorrow. Her gums itched, her hands were blistering. Her eyes smarted from the shock of sun on clay, which smelled like copper tasted, or maybe hate.

When the hole was what she termed deep enough, wide enough, she stood the shovel up in the skived clods of clay and went to the stoop, where George lay wrapped in a pink chenille rug. She carried him to the hole and laid him gently inside, then stood and spaded the raw dirt over his body. She mounded dirt on top of the grave and marked it with the pink plastic flamingo Linda Gay had brought her from Florida last summer. White trash, Chanell had been told, displayed pink plastic flamingos in their yards, and wished she was even that well thought of.

No, a pet's not human, and no, a pet's life can't be measured by human worth, but George had been her last link with a breathing being around her.

While the preacher preached, a listless chant that barely carried on the wind, she wandered the yard and collected George's blue-green iridescent feathers. No problem to find because the sun picked them up all over the yard, like shimmering oil spills.

The eye dots winked from the hedge of azaleas, from the edges of the concrete stoops. After gathering all she could find in the yard, she walked the banks of the creek and the borders of Miss Neida's yard, finding feathers beneath the stemmy bullous vines, as surprisingly bright as Easter eggs or diamondback rattlers. At last, she had a tall, fanned bouquet of peacock feathers with stark living eyes. She took them inside and stuck them in a crock vase and set them by the living-room door. After church let out, between services, she would take them over and pick up the dog fennels. For more than just revenge this time.

But later, when she went back to the church, the door was locked. So she ended up at Archie Wall's house with the bouquet.

"Guess you know about my peacock?" she said.

"I heard."

"Who told you?"

He didn't answer, just stared at the crock vase of feathers on his desk.

"Who killed him then?"

"Could of been me, couldn't it?"

"I know it wadn't you, Archie Wall; happened while we was setting talking, right here."

He was at his desk again, this time reading from a thick law book stood on his lap. "If you hadn't been with me, would you have suspected me?"

"I don't know," she said, pausing. "No, not you."

"I had plenty of reason," he said.

"So did Mr. Jim, so did half of Cornerville—all that hollering in the middle of the night."

"Take your pick."

"I don't want to guess, I just want to live." She swallowed tears.

"What about the fact that the church doors have been locked, maybe because of you and your dog fennels?"

"Even that," she said. "I can't go back."

"Do you want to now?"

"Maybe. Maybe I miss being in on things—I don't know."

"Then go next time the doors are open, go and go till they ask you not to come back."

"I can't."

"Then stay home and wait for them to come to you."

"They won't—you know they won't."

"I don't; they always surprise me in spite of the fact that I've lived here all my life, that I know most secrets in this sorry town."

"Why don't you leave here, Archie Wall?"

"Same reason you don't, maybe, because *we are they*."

She snorted, laughed. "Not me."

He scraped his small feet, shifted the book supported by the desk edge. "Least I know what to expect here; besides, I'm a coward."

"Huh uh, Archie Wall. Staying's harder than going I'm beginning to believe."

"How're you faring financially?"

"Able to eat, that's about it."

"Come on by the bank sometime this week; let's write you up a loan."

"Ain't come to that yet, but if it does, I'll let you know. And I 'preciate it."

"That's what bankers are for."

She picked up the bouquet of feathers. "You're a good friend, Archie Wall."

He squirmed as though uncomfortable with the term. "That's a new one on me."

*   *   *

Once she got started hassling the town, she couldn't seem to stop. Maybe she would when it all quit hurting.

A couple of weeks later, she saw Sheriff Crosby's brown car turn in at the farthest start of the crescent and tool along the bend of white frame houses, as if making a routine check on each one. He'd never done that before; Chanell figured he was coming after her. By then, she'd done so much to aggravate people she couldn't guess what he'd get her for—disturbing the peace, loitering, or littering. Since burying George, she'd kept her radio tuned in to a rap station, full blast, and had been roaming up and down the sidewalk across from the courthouse, foraging for trouble, then slinking home to wait for her hunger to fester again.

As the sheriff pulled around the curve, getting closer, he gazed out at Miss Pansy's sun-spanked white house, one arm cocked in the window. Chanell knelt on the couch, peering between the drawn drapes. Sun sliced the darkened hideout of her living room.

He stopped his car in front of her house, still on the gravel road, and switched off the engine. He got out, strutted around, and propped himself on the brown fender with his arms crossed. A little man who behaved as if he dressed each morning before a full-length magnifying mirror. "Betty Jean!" he called.

Blood rushed to her face. She eased off the couch and crept to the door, opened it, and stepped to the stoop.

He reset his dull black Sunday shoes, gazing left to right. Not at her; he never looked at anybody. "How you this morning, Betty Jean?"

"Awright." She held to the open screen door. "Can I help you, sheriff?"

She used to cut his hair until he pinched her on the behind while she was stooping to get eggs from the cooler at Walters's store. After that, when he called for an appointment, she was booked solid.

Now he stood there stiff and foreign with the morning sun glinting off his badge. "Betty Jean, they's been a sight of complaints filed against you."

"You don't say." She stepped out to the edge of the stoop and leaned against the shop wall. She could smell the purple paint mixing with the chilled air.

"Yes ma'am." He stepped away from the car and knocked his fists together, whistling low and tuneless. "That your trash?" He motioned with an owl rotation of his knob head.

"Might be, might not be."

"I hear you!" His close-set eyes roved from the old jail to the purple bungalow. "They's a rumor going around that you're hassling folks."

Chanell decided to put an end to the hemhawing. "To my beknowest, sheriff, they ain't no law against throwing trash on your own property. It scattered by itself."

"Did, huh?"

"That's right."

"Ain't the way I heared it."

"Hearsay ain't evidence."

He cackled, ducked, stood back up. "Betty Jean, what we got here is a bunch of clean-living Christians don't cotton to being bothered. They like to get up in the morning and know which-a-way the wind's gone blow."

"Well, maybe by now they know that the wind's liable to change." She turned to go inside again.

"Betty Jean?"

"Am I under arrest, sheriff?"

"No 'um, can't say you are, but if I was you . . ."
"You ain't." She stepped through the door and slammed it.

That was Monday. On Tuesday morning, first frost, she got up
with all intentions of simply hanging around outside the post
office. Block the sidewalk awhile, speak to see who would
speak back. Maybe pick up her mail. She'd found that she was
more creative in the morning, before loneliness set in for the
evening. She knew what the town expected of a Negro, what
she used to expect herself, and decided to live up to the
name. She also felt braver on the morning side of noon.

She put on a long red paisley skirt—the only thing by
Ralph Lauren she'd ever bought, back when the styles were
baggy. She'd paid $75 for what now looked ready for the
quilting-scrap pile. With it she wore a white Kmart blouse and
a pair of rubber shower shoes. Her toes were freezing as she
headed out, shortcutting through the patch of cold-charred
goatspurs. Fog dulled the bluing sky overhead, where a flock of
blackbirds turned and cast themselves like a net over the pecan
trees behind the church. Under one arm, she carried a stuffed
black purse with one shoulder strap ripped loose to tail her.

In front of the post office, she stood around on the sloping
sidewalk, facing the courthouse square, sometimes swaying,
sometimes circling, and waited for the town to wake up. A
few cars and trucks stopped at the red light; some turned
west, some east, passing right by her, while others pulled up
at the Delta across from the intersection. But nobody seemed
to notice Chanell, and nobody was out walking the sidewalks
yet. She thought about how little the sidewalks were used
now, how everybody had cars and would usually drive if
going only next door. Then the pencil-yellow school buses
merged at the shortcut route on the south end of the court-

house square, site of the new library, site of the new jail, and she thought about herself as a schoolgirl, and felt as if she'd never been, had never been Chanell the beauty queen, had never been Chanell the lead character in the senior play. Somebody's best friend.

The sun was up good now, firing the tops of pines in the east, burning off the frost and beaming fanned rays through the fog over the highways.

Robins chirped in the gums on the creek. Two mocking-birds blessed the post office, then its sister, the contemporary red-brick courthouse, then dipped into the evergreen leaves of the ancient liveoak on the south end of the courtyard, where the black hip roof of the traditional-style library reared its head. The only new public building in Cornerville in possibly twenty years, the only change in the place that never changed, a state change for the sake of change, and the town would have been better served, Chanell decided, by a movie theater or a McDonald's. Nobody read books, not really; maybe gro-cery-store romances or horror. Chanell thought about the tex-tured bindings and heft of the books she used to read in the one-room library at the courthouse: books with gold-embossed titles she couldn't recall, just their ripe paper and ink smells, words that had suckered her into believing she could be, do, become. . . .

Soon everything was moving except Chanell, who stood solid in her rubber shower shoes. She thought she recognized T.P.'s pickup shooting through the diagonal strip behind the store fronts that linked 129 to 94. She heard Joy Beth's screen door screak open and slap shut on the other side of the church and watched as she pranced in a royal blue matching skirt and sweater across her porch and out to the sidewalk, bound for Chanell. But when Joy Beth got to the church, she dropped her head and crossed the street to Archie Wall's road and passed through the rear door of the courthouse. After two months of being ignored—it seemed like two years—Chanell was getting used to it. She knew Joy Beth had seen her, she knew Joy Beth well, how she'd hang her head to avoid somebody or when she was ashamed.

chapter eleven

School had been out for a couple of weeks, and Chanell (Betty Jean then and not even thinking like a Chanell), Joy Beth, and Linda Gay had a month free before Bible school to play under the water hose and read at the library, to roam the cemetery by the river and eat Popsicles. Nothing bad happened to children in the sixties—at least nothing that was told—and the mothers, calm and certain, would shell peas and pare peaches on their front porches, half watching along the sidewalks for each other's chaste little girls and understandably less-chaste little boys.

It was election year, 1962, the contests for county representative, sheriff, board of education, and superintendent coming up in the fall. Few of those running for local office did so out of love of justice or education, but for social come-uppance, big ducks in a little pond. Holding their hats, they would wander past scooters and doll carriages left on the sidewalks to park themselves on porches and lie to the women, half of whom had never registered to vote. But their husbands voted, and the politicians, idle, sharp, and country savvy, knew the power of those mothers in corn-smudged frocks.

That Monday morning, Chanell and her mother had driven to Joy Beth's house—the same lofty frame house with more ceiling space than rooms bequeathed to Joy Beth when her folks retired to their farmplace across the river. Usually Chanell played in Cornerville only in the afternoons, but her mother had gone early that day to help Joy Beth's mother put up cucumber pickles.

At dinnertime, the kids were fed from a giant aluminum stock pot of mixed spaghetti and sweet tomato sauce, then shooed out of the cloyingly warm kitchen spiced with sugary vinegar, cloves, and cumin. The women would be all day putting up twelve quarts of pickles, which they would divide up in the evening like the boys did marbles.

After dinner, Joy Beth, Linda Gay, and Chanell had gone straight to Walters's store and charged three Popsicles to Joy Beth's daddy, who like so many fathers back then was always gone, making an honest living for a big family by dabbling in timber, turpentine, and farming on land inherited like the neighbors. Grape Popsicles for Joy Beth and Chanell, banana for Linda Gay, a chubby, fair eleven-year-old with a thick tan braid down her back who was just beginning to smart off, what would later be termed an "attitude." Often they would quarrel and pair off: usually Joy Beth and Linda Gay, or Joy Beth and Chanell. But this time, Linda Gay poked fun at Joy Beth's mother's mixed spaghetti and sauce, and Joy Beth stalked off sullenly toward the old jail, vacant then and play-house to half the neighborhood. Her frizzy brown hair stuck out in two plaits above cup-handle ears, her faded print sun-suit wadded between fat-wedged legs.

Standing on the apron of blazing asphalt before the store, Linda Gay and Chanell watched Joy Beth vanish down the dirt road behind Mr. Hosier's piece-goods shop.

"She's so shitty, you know?" Linda Gay, pinking in the high hot sun, licked her Popsicle, her mean tongue banana-white.

"I guess you're gone say that word in front of Miss Lewis at Bible school, huh?" Chanell wandered off down the weed alley between Walters's store and the Masonic building, keeping to the shoulder of 94 on her way to the cemetery. A shock of white headstones and sand through a screen of heat waves in the west; and beyond, a ridge of hollies and bays on the river banks in cool green relief. Linda Gay trailing, slurping her banana Popsicle.

"I might not even go this year," she said, slurping. "Bible school's for babies. You going?"

"Have to," Chanell lied—she didn't have to do anything. Her mother was then at that stage of sickness that could be disguised as "a little under the weather," pale and drawn, having to lie down a lot, and Chanell was as revered as an angel and missed being just a child. Like Joy Beth, whose mother with her demon crew of six doorstep children, didn't have a qualm about knocking their heads together. Made them wear shoes year round. But even then Chanell suspected that if her own mother did lay down rules, she'd probably wish she didn't. Six of one, half dozen of the other, that's what the women said if something could go either way, a code of riddles they talked in when the kids got smart enough to put together spelled-out words. Chanell was glad that hot summer day that her mother was palling around with Joy Beth's mother—help toughen her up—and hoped she'd pick up whatever Joy Beth's mother did to make Joy Beth so popular at school. No doubt she'd be the class president when they started sixth grade in September, and it was definitely mothers who determined popularity. Chanell knew deep down that logic was flawed too, but it kept her mellow and unblamable in her heart.

After a stop-off at the cemetery, where Linda Gay and Chanell played step-over-the-graves and made fun of simple names carved in the simple granite headstones, they sneaked down the steep willowy banks of the river and hung back to watch the big boys swing from a tupelo branch and break the glass surface of umber current, then float downriver across the trick shadow of the bridge to the tea-tinted shallows.

The girls often watched from the bank and they never did it without Linda Gay elbowing everybody in the ribs and daring them to sidestep along the spring-riveted slope to talk to the boys. But she never suggested that they swing from the rope rigged to the bent tupelo, and never dared them to go swimming. She wasn't that brave. If girls went swimming in the river, it was with both parents present. Most mothers didn't swim; most mothers had been so brainwashed about the hazards of the black sucking whorls that they sat on the banks with tea-weed switches meant to tame the child who dared wander from the map of clear water radiating into opaque drop-offs.

Today, Linda Gay stood clutching the trunk of a willow and checking the weeping branches above for braiding moccasins, duck-chested in her pink cotton sunsuit.

"Go on and talk to the boys if you want to, Linda Gay," Chanell said. "I don't." That feeling of wanting to be alone—which would last all of six months—swept over her again like one of Linda Gay's mom's hot flashes, she imagined.

Chanell turned to trudge up the bank, listening to Linda Gay behind her. "You don't think I'll do it, do you?" she said.

"I doubt it." Chanell didn't look back but knew that Linda Gay would do it. Already, she was thrashing through reeds and brambles, downriver; she would do anything on a dare, then simper and play sweet in front of grownups. They always bought it, especially teachers.

Suddenly, Chanell felt close to Joy Beth. Like a sister, that's how she felt. Yeah, and look how Linda Gay had talked about her sister's mother's spaghetti, which Chanell had really liked. Red speckles as proof covered her shirtfront like raised dots on dotted swiss. She'd just learned what dotted swiss was, and the words kept hissing in her head—maybe the key to being popular—with the picture of the pink dress Joy Beth's mother had whipped up on her black treadle Singer.

Chanell walked back to town, along the prickly-pear-flanked path of row houses fronting 94, then tipped quickly across 129 at the intersection, with her feet on fire, and side-soled along the hot sidewalk that would take her to the looping dirt road and the old jail. Past the vacant lot of brown-eyed Susans, touched by crayon-marked butterflies, behind Mr. Hosier's piece-goods store, which with the aid of the federal government would end up the new post office, and on toward the empty stucco bungalow next door to the old jail, the little house that her mother's friend from New Orleans had just moved out of. Chanell's house later, her own jail later.

"Joy Beth," she called, keeping her eyes on the south door of the leached-brick, columnar building. Barred windows, some askew in their frames, were set in twos along both stories of the old jail, which had been throughly explored; and sometimes the off-again, on-again girlfriends played house in the dim, dusty cells, leaving dolls and tea sets in the gutted shadows for weeks at a time, or until they got scared their babies might be snatched up by the ghosts of the convicts.

There were always accommodating tales to validate their fears, the tales a litany on the little-town air, which could hardly be traced back to the bearer after a number of tellings. Glorified legends of innocent-enough men, after thirty or forty safe years went by. One rascally fellow—cousin so-and-so, celebrated for his leisurely brawling—had shot a drinking buddy ostensibly over five dollars and had managed to evade the law all summer by hiding on the family farm near the Florida line. And when he had to get out—for whatever reason rascals such as himself had to get out—his big brother would haul him around in a horse-drawn turpentine wagon, right past the courthouse in Cornerville.

The fugitive, something of a hero by then for outsmarting the dumb sheriff (all sheriffs were dumb, even the smart ones, just as all drunk drivers drove with their headlights on in daylight), would scrunch down in an empty turpentine barrel, surrounded by like barrels of shifting resin, all the way to the flatwoods near Fargo, where he'd visit with his wily grandmother, the purported perpetrator of the plot. When he finally got caught—not a salient point of the tale—the story went that he wheedled one of the awe-inspired guards at the old jail into carving out a hickory key to his cell, unlocked the door that still summer night, and hightailed it to the palmetto fringes of the Okefenokee Swamp. The end.

Under the beaming white sun in the clearing of the road, Chanell could feel her scalp blistering through the side part of her broomed black hair. She hobbled to the patchy parched grass before the empty bungalow, feeling a breathy void through the sprung-open screen door. Cooling in the flocked shade of a tall magnolia, she picked a sandspur thorn from her heel while listening for sounds from within the old jail, but heard only the locusts in the vines and reeds closing in on the run-together yards, and squirrels in the branches above, scamping and barking. Seedpod pickings sifted through the waxy magnolia leaves to the shoulders of Chanell's white shirt. She brushed them off, walking on toward the side door of the jail.

"Joy Beth!" Chanell stopped at the heavy domed door, halfway open, and whiffed the musty air inside, a smell that filtered through the sweet-soap scent of bay blooms from the creek.

"Joy Beth?" Chanell's voice sounded off in the hollow room where the children imagined a jailer had sat, where he beat all the gaunt shuffling convicts from the upstairs cells daily. Cobwebs swagged from corner to corner of the dun concrete walls, cobwebs important as the only evidence to link spook-infested places to those seen in tent-show movies the children went to some nights. What the playmate gang found to excite their imaginations were broken cola and whiskey bottles, rusty nails, and other old trash. No giant keys to fit the crumbling square locks of the cell doors, no whips, knives, and shackles or convict pants with stripes up the legs like those pictured on wanted posters at the blue gingerbread-trimmed post office with its steep shake roof.

Chanell didn't really like to play in the old jail—it was too nerve-racking. Once you got upstairs and playing good, Jack Maine and his gang of less-than-chaste little boys would sneak up and chunk rocks or whoop to see the girls jump. The only way down was past the sweat-reeking, jeering boys on the dark, twining metal stairs.

When Joy Beth didn't answer on the second call, and no other sounds came except the wind shifting through the barred windows, Chanell was glad. But just in case Joy Beth was hiding inside, Chanell would make it sound as if she hadn't gone in for more reasonable reasons. "Okay," Chanell said, "guess you went on home." She started off the slick concrete slab that caused the same grating effect in her head as the scratching of Jack Maine's fingernails on tin, and thought she heard her name called. Perking, with her soles on concrete making her cringe, she waited, hearing only the wind wailing down the stairwell in the middle room.

"Betty Jean." Joy Beth's voice—very dim and very low and sad—more eerily enchanting than the melody of the wind.

Chanell turned back without thinking into the snuffy room, pushing the heavy door inward till it stuck on the gritty floor. Peeping around, eyes twinkly in the shock of dense curried light, like firecracker sparklers, she spied Joy Beth sitting on a wood bench along the west wall. Eyes wide and ankles crossed with the strap of one white sandal broken and dangling. Plaits gone now, and in their place a bush of brown hair, face the color of canned Christmas snow.

"Joy Beth?" Chanell crept closer. "Why're you just setting there? Say something."

Joy Beth blinked and hung her head.

Chanell sat down beside her. "Linda Gay didn't mean what she said; she ate a bait of your mama's spaghetti." Even saying that, Chanell sensed that hurt feelings weren't the real problem. She just hoped they were; and whatever was the problem, it would be so serious that Joy Beth might die; Chanell herself might die. Hot spurs flashed along her spine.

Joy Beth wiped her nose on the back of her hand and held to the edge of the rough-hewn jailer's bench.

Chanell could smell something wild—maybe fear, maybe change—but not Joy Beth's usual bland soap smell. A Breck girl, she called herself, hair peaked with shampoo and frothy

as meringue, when she and Chanell bathed together in Joy
Beth's clawfoot tub. Chanell knew this smell was either vomit,
rust, or blood. She glanced down at the speckles of spaghetti
sauce on her own shirt.

"You want me to go away?" she said, praying Joy Beth
would say yes. "You want me to go get your mama?" Praying
again she'd say yes. Only a mama could fix this.

"No," Joy Beth said. She wiped her nose on the back of
her hand. Dry. Eyes fixed on the open door that led to the
darker middle room with the stairwell.

Chanell started to cry. She always cried, even before the
bad news was out, because she could sense things bad. "You
been hurt, Joy Beth?"

"No," Joy Beth said. "Well, my hair hurts." She touched
the tufts of hair around her wan face. "He pulled my hair."

"Who? Jack Maine?"

"Huh uh." Joy Beth crossed her plump straight legs prop-
erly. "My daddy's buddy, Frank Lewis."

"You mean that big ole man politicking at your house
before we left?"

She nodded.

Chanell pictured the giant man's head on runty Jack Maine;
Frank Lewis's sparse red hair and ample ruddy features, those
flared lips, in place of Jack Maine's scrunched tan face. "Why
did he pull your hair?"

"To make me suck him." Joy Beth stared up, gray-blue
irises a watery swarm.

"Suck him?"

"His thingamajigger."

Chanell's ears clanged, as if all twenty cell doors above and
below had slammed shut. "Why?" She honestly didn't know,
but something new and ugly stirred in her brain, and she

wanted to hear more, but at the same time didn't want to hear another word.

"See over here." Joy Beth hopped off the bench and duck-walked to the outside door, pushing it to, then pointed behind it with her broken sandal to a puddle of mingled red and white spaghetti, buzzing with blowflies. Strap and buckle dangling in the mess. "I vomited," she said.

"Come on," Chanell said, "let's go tell your mama right now." She believed suddenly with all her heart in fairness and justice, had faith that any daddy's buddy could be brought to a swift reckoning of what's right.

As she got to the door, swinging it wide, Joy Beth grabbed her from behind and buried her face in Chanell's back like a tick, crying, "No, no. Don't tell, don't tell. You can't never tell."

Chanell tried to unlatch Joy Beth's fingers, but she held tight, skidding and grinding sand on sickening concrete, while crying and begging, echoes begging back from bottom to top stories of the old jail.

"He bloodied my pants," she said. "Nobody can't see me."

"He bloodied your pants?" Free now, Chanell turned around and Joy Beth was standing straddle-legged, the crotch of her sunsuit bunched and blood-stained. "He told me he wouldn't own up to it," she babbled, again glancing at the middle-room door. "Said he'd tell my daddy it was Jack Maine done it, and he seen us playing nasty over here and come to tell Daddy, and soon as Jack left, he come in and . . ."

"Shit!" Chanell said and thought about Mrs. Lewis, Frank's wife, teaching them at Bible school and knew she'd never go now. "You're hurt," she said. Her eyes stayed on the wicking bloodstain of Joy Beth's crotch.

"No . . . he used his finger."

Chanell thought then and later that the saddest part was

Joy Beth's physical pain, kept private out of embarrassment, like the cheap broken sandal never mentioned, and how because they hadn't told, the shame was Joy Beth's alone, to live with always.

"I'll sneak through the back of your house and get you some more clothes," Chanell said, walking Joy Beth to the bench and brushing her springy hair from her forehead. "And a Kotex," she added. "If your mama notices, say your period started. We'll bury that." Chanell pointed to Joy Beth's ripped sunsuit, the last vestige of her little-girlness.

"Never tell," Joy Beth said, hanging her head. "Cross your heart and hope to die."

"Cross my heart and hope to die," Chanell said, crossing her heart with her arms. "Hide under the stairs if Linda Gay shows up—that chicken won't come in here by herself." Going to the door, Chanell felt heavy with the feeling that, since she was the one told, she too had been raped, or that it was she and not Frank Lewis who was party to Joy Beth's rape.

"Betty Jean, wait," Joy Beth called.

Chanell ducked around the door. "I said I won't tell and I won't."

Joy Beth hopped from the bench. "You want to see something?" She nodded toward the next room, where the door stood wide.

"What?" Chanell stepped inside again and waited for Joy Beth to hop from the bench again, then followed her through the middle-room door.

As Chanell passed into the darker room, facing the spiral stairs, Joy Beth stepped to one side, pointing to the landing, a round iron plate with a nap of scratched dust.

"What?" Chanell said, not meaning to be mean, but dern!

If it was a snake or spider, Joy Beth should say so. And then Chanell made out the head of a man next to the bottom stair, hair like fireworm fuzz, huge body gracefully curved around the back side of the stairs, white shirt coming clear as Chanell's eyes sorted images she expected from images actually there. Even his polished black shoe, which turned down and in at an angle that would be unbearable if he wasn't either unconscious or dead.

"Frank Lewis?" Chanell asked.

"Yeah," said Joy Beth, almost back to her old self, always loving to surprise. "He thought he heard somebody coming and got tangled up in his britches. Tripped down the stairs from up there." She peered up at the barred light shed from the top landing, a dun haze hovering in the ceiling of the room below.

"Is he dead?" Chanell whispered.

Joy Beth shrugged. "Broke his neck, I guess. Look ahere." She walked over to the landing, and with a practiced air, squatted and hefted the giant coppery head with blank rolled eyes and twisted it left to right and almost around.

"Shit, Joy Beth!" Chanell screamed, slinging her hands, and dashed through the door to the jailer's room.

Joy Beth dropped the head with a thunk, scooting behind Chanell with hands tucked under her chin like a begging puppy. "What?" she whispered, panting.

"You touched a dead man. God!" Chanell circled the room, and each time around peeped past Joy Beth in the doorway at the corpse sunken into the furry light.

"Yeah, I guess he likely is dead," said Joy Beth.

"Well, if he wadn't before, he sure is now. Don't you know not to never move nobody with a broke neck."

Joy Beth shrugged, almost calm now, as if she'd given over her burden to Chanell. "I didn't know that."

"Anyway," Chanell said, stopping in the doorway, "he had it coming to him. But *dead* . . . a *dead* man in the jail!" She circled some more. "Now what?"

"What's changed?" Joy Beth leaned in the middle-room doorway.

"Nothing new for you, I guess. But here I got to walk out there and look like nothing never happened." Chanell shivered. "God, Joy Beth! You go all to pieces over bloody pants, then act like a dead man ain't nothing. A dead man!"

"Does that mean you'll tell now?"

"No."

"Cross your heart and hope to die."

"Cross my heart," Chanell said.

The following Monday, both girls sat in the Baptist Church at the flower-banked funeral of Frank Lewis, now lauded as a great statesman. Funeralmongers from four counties crowded into the stifling little church, some even traveling down from Atlanta, and mention was made of all the incumbent representative had ever done, except being found in the old jail with his pants down. (An accident, everybody said. Good ole Frank Lewis, quintessential ombudsman, slipped and fell while checking out the old facility for possible renovation to save taxpayers' dollars.) And throughout the summer, both girls, maybe somewhat vindicated, faced posters on every telephone pole that read, LEWIS FOR REPRESENTATIVE, SEND A MAN TO DO A MAN'S JOB, his jowly face cropping up on every corner tree. The girls drifted apart—no more baths together—and maybe to keep Frank Lewis from surfacing, kept all conversations surface. Playing in the cemetery, they stepped around the glorified statesman's grave, and neither girl ever mentioned the incident again. Their secret.

*   *   *

Chanell stood in front of the post office with her mouth open a few more minutes, then flip-flopped inside and got her mail out of the box. She could see Miss Cleta through the chute in the black partition of boxes. She was sorting mail with her keen white face low over the stacks on the counter, acting as if she didn't know Chanell was on the place.

Chanell's box was full—bills, sale papers, three letters with no return addresses.

"Trash," she said loudly and crossed to the wastebasket under the wanted posters with faces of criminals clearly marked with scars, mussed hair, and hard eyes. She dropped the letters in the basket and slumped out.

Then she crossed the road to the rear of the courthouse and pushed through the double doors, thinking about Aunt Teat, the old beggarwoman, who used to make her rounds in Cornerville once a week. How the stooped old lady must have felt when the kids would yell, "Hey, you old heifer." Chanell remembered playing on the school grounds with her friends when Aunt Teat would come begging at the lunchroom, and how they'd laugh and tease each other with the tag of "Aunt Teat," filing it away for later to tease each other with as the need arose. As teenagers, to offset embarrassment, Chanell and friends sometimes even referred to themselves as Aunt Teat—"I look just like old Aunt Teat"—when their hair didn't look just right, when they got caught looking less than their best.

Scuffing along the dim green hall that gave off whiffs of heated dust and justice, Chanell didn't know what she'd do, which of the facing doors she'd stop at, until she reached the open door of Family and Children Services and saw Joy Beth's boxy back in royal blue, where she sat across from Missy Simpson at her desk.

Chanell stepped inside with the tail of her purse strap dragging. "Good moaning," she said.

They stopped talking; Joy Beth turned and gaped. Two streaks of orangish rouge stood out on her boneless cheeks.

Missy Simpson shot Chanell a disgusted look, lifted a bell-shaped paperweight and rapped it on her desk.

Joy Beth sat back, eyes on the wall of jalousied windows ahead, and placed both hands on the arms of the chair as if bracing for an earthquake.

"I come by to sign up for some food stamps," Chanell said, nearing the desk.

Joy Beth and Missy sat still, barely breathing, so that the scattering voices throughout the other offices filled the room. Chanell leaned into the desk, bumping it with her pelvis. Joy Beth was swinging her foot, right at Chanell's leg. Then, as though feeling the heat of Chanell's intent, she tucked it under her chair.

Missy Simpson, bug-eyed and buck-toothed, with fine black hair picked like a dandelion, pulled out a white sheet from her desk drawer, slammed it, and handed the form to Chanell. "Fill out the information and sign it."

Chanell took the form and wandered over to the windows covered in orange waffle-woven sheers. She studied the printed questions a minute, sucking air through her teeth, then turned, catching Joy Beth and Missy eyeing each other. "You got ery pencil on you?" Chanell said.

Missy Simpson passed her a ballpoint pen from a white glass mug with a picture of a disgruntled Garfield holding a banner that read, "Keep your paws off my pencils." Chanell tapped the form, scanning, then, clutching her tucked purse, placed the sheet against the sulfur-yellow concrete-block wall to the left of the desk and signed it with an X and delivered it back to Missy. "You gone have to fill out the rest; I can't read."

Missy took it, wheeling her blunt knees in mauve gabardine pants under the desk, and started writing with her head low. A sigh escaped from her poked-out lips.

Joy Beth stared down at her hands on her lap, face as white as it had been that day in the old jail.

"You out of work?" Missy Simpson went on writing with her head down.

"Been out of work," Chanell said and smacked her lips. She plopped her stuffed purse on the desk, overturning Garfield's mug of yellow pencils and ballpoint pens.

Joy Beth flinched, looked up at Missy, then down at her hands again.

Missy shook her head, writing with her gnawed pointer finger pressed hard on the pen. "Have you been looking for a job?" she asked.

"Ain't none round here," Chanell said. "But yeah I have. Been looking ever day."

"What skills . . . ?"

"I's a beautician."

"Got any other qualifications, Miss Foster, which might make you eligible for food stamps?"

"Yeah, I'm colored. Part-black."

Joy Beth shifted in the chair, her see-through hair drab in the light from the windows, and Chanell thought about her hair jerked from the plaits the day she was raped and almost felt sorry for her.

"I have to warn you," Missy said, "that falsification of

information can lead to imprisonment, fine, or both. You may be called on to produce facts to substantiate . . ."

"Rumor won't do?"

"No." Missy twiddled the pen, top then point drubbing on the desk.

"Miss Joy Beth here be my witness." Chanell stepped closer and gazed at Joy Beth's stricken face.

Joy Beth got up and sidled around the chair, wall side, then out of the office, with her hands in the pockets of her royal blue skirt. Their color.

Breathing hard, with her knees buckling, Chanell pushed through the rear double doors of the courthouse and made a beeline for Archie Wall's one-room bank: because his door was open, because she needed to sit down before she dropped, because her rubber shower shoes resisted making turns and the bank happened to be in the direction her feet were going when she stepped through the courthouse doors. Because she wanted to share her triumph, if it was triumph, or her defeat, if defeat was what it was.

He was sitting at his pine desk piled high with paper-stuffed manila folders, left side of the single-teller station in the cramped room, this time wearing his court-worn white shirt, same hat, same dour, doomed expression he sometimes wore to make you wonder whether he'd just as soon you take your business elsewhere or was grateful you had come to his bank, only banker in Swanoochee County, or to his office at the house, only lawyer in Swanoochee County.

"How you this morning, Archie Wall?" Chanell stepped inside.

"Awright," he said, rearing in his chair with his feet clear of the floor. "See you taking a interest in dressing up again."

Was he joking? Was he picking? Had he seen her out
traipsing the sidewalks? Of course he had. "This is old, Archie
Wall, I'm just wearing it to . . . to be wearing it."

"You here to take out that loan we talked about, or you
here just to jaw?"

He sounded mad at somebody, maybe Chanell. "You in a
bad mood, Archie Wall?" She looked around for another
chair, found none. No room for another chair, even if it could
be hung on the stale air between the desk and the low plyboard ceiling.

"Let's just put it this way." He sat forward, plopping his
feet to the floor, his stubby arms to the desktop. "I'd be a
fool to be in a good mood; ain't been two people passed
through that door there"—and at that point he pointed to the
door with the cardboard sign stating days and hours of business—"the whole day, and them two was here to withdraw
their money."

"Oh." Chanell figured why and was truly sorry. "I gotta
get home," she said, and turned to leave while reeling in her
purse strap.

"Betty Jean?" he called, standing and unbogging his bur-
dened belt from his paunch. "Don't go getting puffed up and
sorry for yourself over what I just told you; this ain't about
you, it's about business."

"I'm not sorry for myself, I . . ."

He broke in, "Feel sorry for me, I'm the one about to go
broke."

"I do, Archie Wall, I . . ."

"One day they come in droves, can't hardly beat 'um out
with a stick, then the next day . . ." He kicked the plyboard
wall of the teller station. It rocked.

"I gotta go, Archie Wall." Chanell stepped out the door to

the porch, then to the cooped noon shadow of the great oak.
"Hope your customers come back."

"Don't care if they do or don't," he said, going inside
again, mumbling.

She walked off, then circled back to the shelter of the
porch supported by four skinny metal poles, smiling as she
leaned through the door. "You're a good friend, Archie
Wall," she said. "Don't know what I'd do without you."

He was glazy-eyed but calm now, standing as if he'd been
about to go after her. "I like good company."

"I'm too stuck on myself to be good company, Archie
Wall, just like you said. I don't even know how anymore."

"You will," he said. "Give it time."

"Time's all I got."

"I'm glad to see you're getting out, even if only to pro-
voke them."

"Feels more like they're provoking me."

"They are," he said, "but you're holding your own."

Still smiling, she headed home. Archie Wall was a real
friend—one who would tell her like it was, one who would
share down days as well as up days, triumph and defeat.

chapter twelve

That night Chanell got dressed for the first high school basketball game of the season, by then so crazy she didn't give a flip
what anybody thought. She knew in her heart that all the crazy
stuff was what kept her going, without the luxury of feeling
she'd regret it. Should she stop now, she'd have to be sent off.

Tonight, her target would be T.P., who never missed a
game until November, when he would head for his camp in
the deer woods to winter till February.

First, she opened a tin of sardines, poured the oil into her
cupped right hand, and rubbed it over her face and neck, her
arms and legs, then put the sardines in the refrigerator for
lunch tomorrow. No longer did she eat for the thrill of taste;
she ate to keep up her strength and for the energy required of
revenge, and not even revenge entirely, mostly motion. Soon
she'd run out of food—she was down to using change from
the tip jar in the shop, leaving the fifty dollars in her checking
account at Archie Wall's bank for emergencies. She couldn't

imagine what emergency might compel her to withdraw it; she tried not to imagine any surprises of sickness or legal fines that could crop up. How far could she go? How much would the town take? When would they trap her in one of her get-back games? And who would play Judas? T.P.? While she smeared herself with the fishy oil, she fought against back-tracking over her life with T.P., how he used to play basket-ball in high school while she cheered—not for the team—for him. She shook her head, working the oil between her fingers like good lotion, while the memories fumed up, a sweet smell gone sardine sharp.

Even after they were married—after two days of honey-mooning south along the Florida east coast to T.P.'s Aunt Tillie's in Cocoa Beach—after he'd handed Chanell over to Mama Sharon like a new puppy, they would slip off some evenings to the county trash dump in the flatwoods and make eager, noisy love in his pickup. Afterward, he'd lounge, satis-fied, on the truck seat with his long white feet out the win-dow while Chanell stroked his thin hairy chest. But he'd never been really satisfied, not since they'd married. After making love at their old parking spot, he would drive her back to Mama Sharon's, get in his truck again, and be gone for the night. Got to where Chanell knew he was going before he went by the way he'd snap at her when she was late coming home from beauty school, making the fight her fault, by the way he'd amble out on the porch and gaze up the road, by the smell of his aftershave, or the way he would tuck his shirttail in instead of leaving it loose. He despised Sandra Kaye and Joy Beth, who made Chanell late getting home each Fri-day by stopping with her at the supermarket, not because he blamed them for making his wife late, but because he was sure they talked about him behind his back. He would have hated Bell too, who talked about him to his face, but she was his sassy blood kin and, woman or not, sassy kin got high marks from T.P. At family reunions he'd grin and hook an arm around Bell's waist, saying, "She stays on my case, gives me hell evertime I turn around."

When he would come back from wherever he went on those games of payback—Chanell didn't figure out where for a while—if she acted mad, if Mama Sharon shamed him, he'd stick around the house for a day or two, letting his blue-black beard grow, then take a bath and get dressed in his going jeans, and ease out. Said when he wanted a little piece he expected a little privacy. Chanell would feel bad—blame herself for not keeping up her man as *Redbook* preached—and maybe a little put out with Mama Sharon, who, each night after supper, made it a practice to sit in the squeaking porch swing while T.P. and Chanell made love in the room partitioned from the swing end of the porch by two gracious windows with clothespinned curtains. Slick with sweat and panting, they would wallow from the rattly bed to the floor, eyes on Mama Sharon through the sun-rotted curtains, her big bun like a warden's cap. She could have stepped right through one of the open windows. Did she suppose that each night after supper T.P. and Chanell went to their room to play checkers?

So Chanell had decided to buy a house and privacy, but it never made a dab of difference. Actually T.P. had thrilled more to the suspense of love on the sly. When Chanell would bitch about him sleeping around, it would excite a twitch over his right eyebrow. Sleeping with his own wife was like tasting paste.

Heady from the rich fish stench of sardines, Chanell set out in the cold late sun toward the ruins of shed pecan trees behind the church. Nut hulls, like dried tulips, were stuck to the bony branches, and above, an abyss of blue sky with white clouds scrolling up in pretty scenes. Crisp brown leaves crunched under her shoes with the walked-down backs, her heels slapping free, as she headed toward the trash barrel set in the midst of the orchard. Nobody around, not a sound, except for a flock of crows cawing over the creek, where the sun played tag with the shadows.

She stopped at the trash barrel, a concrete pipe screwed into the ashy dirt, reached inside, and began rubbing both hands along the velvety soot of the walls. Spurs of burned foil and carbon ash had settled on the bottom with a Sunday-school book parched in the shape of a fan. Drawing her shiny black hands from the drum, she smeared soot over her face and neck, the mix of sardine oil making her eyes smart, her skin draw. Again, she rubbed her hands along the inside of the barrel, then stroked an even coat of black acid soot on her arms, hands, feet, calves, and knees, on all contrasting white skin below the hem of her tattered black taffeta skirt, all skin peeping from the sleeves and neck of her silky purple blouse, which she'd worn to go with the purple house now beckoning from the curve on the crescent. A hoarse laugh caught in her throat, but she didn't feel like laughing. She just felt crazy, dizzy, and wild. She had no plans for tomorrow, so what she did today didn't matter.

In the lofty gym lobby, where everybody stood around waiting for the game to start, Chanell handed the high school boy at the ticket stand a dollar. He stared at her, shock showing on his tender round face, seeming to set off a collective stare from those milling about the lobby and lined up at the concession booth on the north wall. Not a sound except the hard bounce of balls from the main part of the gym as Chanell wandered through the crowd to the right door, home side, watching the Cornerville team girls warming up for the game. Balls dribbled on the yellow shellacked floor, bounced off the backboards, a gong sounded end to end of the barny lit gym, signaling that the game was about to start. The home girls in green and white shorts and T-shirts, with balls tucked under their arms, loped over to their coach on the center bottom bleacher and huddled, while the girls in red and black from the out-of-town team gathered on the other side of the court.

A few spectators wandered through the door from the lobby, shoving past Chanell, and climbed up toward the middle section of bleachers on her right. All tiers spottily filled with groups of only the most loyal fans, mostly family members of the basketball girls. In Cornerville, the girls' game was considered little more than a sideshow; the main attraction was the boys' game. The gong sounded again, and the girls from both sides squared off in playing positions on the court, guards flapping their arms like scrawny birds. The racket from both sides of the bleachers swelled and roared in Chanell's ears. Only a couple of Negroes played on the home-girls team, but the bleachers next to the home-side door were packed from ground to top levels with black faces. Chanell stepped inside and leaned against the wall, next to three stout Negro girls babbling on the bottom bleacher. Between bodies parading up and down bleachers, she scanned for T.P. among the white faces tiered on the other end.

As soon as she spotted him, sitting with his buddies about halfway up, she sashayed along the side court, the squeak of tennis shoes and the hard, lively bounce of the basketball keeping time with the *blap blap* of her heels on her walked-down shoe backs. Even moving now, even glad she was moving now—on her way to do unto others as they were doing unto her, what she had to do or die—she hated herself for doing unto the blacks as the whites were doing unto her. She parted two people on the bottom row, stepping around another on the second, in her zigzag climb up the bleachers. "Excuse me," Chanell said. A woman ducked, gazing up with questioning eyes, and punched the man beside her. Chanell tripped on up the bleachers, feeling their eyes following. A whistle blew and the screeching shoes and basketball *pop pop* stopped, and the girls huddled again with their team coaches.

Warm-up time was over.

"Excuse me," Chanell said to two madeup teenage girls, parting them like water from a dive, and tramped on up, not two bleachers down from T.P.

He was looking the other way, laughing with his buddies, his green plaid shirt like a signal for go. She quit saying "Excuse me" and stepped up the last bleacher, squeezing between a twelve-year-old boy—little man in training—and T.P.

"God amighty!" said the kid with a hard hat of sandy hair, and he jumped up, tweaking his nose so that his giant teeth showed. He sidled along the bleacher, away from Chanell, and wedged between two other boys, shoving the next one to Chanell. That boy took one look and whiff and did the same, leaving the next boy in the same predicament.

T.P. was still looking the other way, leaning across one of his buddies to talk to another one. The gong sounded and the home girls ganged on the north end of the court. T.P. sat up, watching the court, spellbound. Suddenly, he sniffed, stiffened, pupil-less eyes floating in dingy eye whites till they settled on Chanell, the whole process of looking without seeming to look taking all of two minutes, lips parting in his scraggly black beard like a fish sucking air, soon to die.

"What the shit!" he finally said.

Chanell smiled, shining her teeth.

"Get out from here, Chanell," he breathed. "What you think you're doing?"

She smiled.

"I mean it, Chanell, you better get yourself up from here."

"We're integrated now," she said.

He sat there, hanging his head. Sweat popped on his long tanned neck.

"What you want?" he mumbled, looking up at the shrill of a whistle for a foul against the home girls.

"Nothing," Chanell said.

"Go on home and I'll come by later. We'll talk."

"Nope." Eyes on the court, Chanell leaped to her feet, yelling at the referees, "That ain't fair!" What T.P. always said Negroes say.

The home girl shot the free foul basket and a girl from the other team, an outsider, dribbled up court, basketball shoes slapping on the brilliant floor.

Elbows propped on his knees now, T.P. followed the ball with his eyes, up and down the court. His cheeks, showing around his beard, red as Santa Claus's. "For the love of God, Chanell!" He shook his head, eyes rising and dipping with the ball. "Get to the house!"

One of the Negro home girls snatched the ball and shot it cleanly through the net. "Way to go!" Chanell hollered, jumping up and down and shaking the bleacher. Dizzy with triumph and terror—triumph, over how things were going, terror, over how things might go—she realized she was cheering both teams, but didn't care. Her head felt like a balloon and all that kept it from floating to the lengths of heater pipes in the ceiling was the frayed strings of her nerves. She could smell the soot and sardine oil, sharp and cold, could feel her face drawing.

T.P. sprang up in the standing throng of spectators and bulldozed a path to the bottom bleacher, swaggering down-court toward the door. Shoving a hand inside his tight jeans pocket, he used the other to punch up his truck keys.

Chanell sat casting her eyes about the gym. Nobody seemed to be noticing her except the three little boys swap-ping places and snickering on her left. Finally she spotted Linda Gay on the south end of the gym, yelling on her feet with the team of bouncy cheerleaders. So now she was cheer-leader sponsor. Chanell got up and edged down through the crowd till she was standing behind Linda Gay, who was rah-rahing every breath, same old safe-blue straight skirt hiked on her loaded hips. Socking the air and yelling, with white wat-tles of flesh swinging from her underarms, she stepped back to the bleacher as the players and the ball turned down court. So close now that Chanell could hear her winded sighs of sat-isfaction, and knowing she would sit now, Chanell sat, mak-ing room for the square buttocks lowering to the bleacher.

Linda Gay's turtle-lidded eyes traveled up court and down, then landed on Chanell.

"My God!" she said through clenched teeth, eyes roving over Chanell with her upper body stretched away. "Chanell Foster, what are you up to now?" She raised one hand as if to fend off a lick. Then, "I knew you were tacky when you changed your name to Chanell, but this beats all." She slapped her knees, depriving Chanell of her explosive regard by watching the court. "Why, you're nothing but"—she seemed to be searching for the right words—"but white trash!"

The most consoling thing said to Chanell in a while. The crowd roared.

*   *   *

During that phase of her craziness, Chanell was back and forth at Archie Wall's. Either telling him off—so he could tell them—or crying on his shoulder. To talk, to hear herself talk. She was that lonesome.

She kept lumping all the stuff she'd done since the rumor had started in July, all that had been done to her, letting it simmer in her head, on hold. For what, she didn't know. For some solution, maybe. For somebody to give in. But she knew better.

Like somebody mad at the IRS and refusing to pay, knowing, though it feels good at the moment, they'll come after you, she kept thinking of the letters she had thrown in the trash on Tuesday. Legally, nobody could take her house away—she knew that—but she fully expected the town to burn it down or have her arrested for something.

"Archie Wall"—she was sitting in his living-room office again—"did you write me another letter for Mr. Alfred?"

He backed up to warm at the space heater. "Yes 'um, I did."

"Well, I ain't got no hard feelings toward you, just now. But I do want to get the point across that I ain't going nowhere."

Round and bland, he turned and held his hands over the boxy gray heater.

"Can they make me?" she asked.

"Can't nobody make you do nothing, long as you stay on the right side of their law."

"That's all you care about, ain't it, Archie Wall?"

"What?"

"The law."

"I'm on the side of who's paying my 'lectricity bill."

"Ain't always the way it works."

"No 'um. You right about that."

"Tell me one thing, Archie Wall. Who's so deadset on getting Miss Pansy's house?"

"That's confidential."

"I've been took into the confidence. Wouldn't you say?"

"Yes 'um, I would." He faced her, locking his hands behind. "Linda Gay Sauls is the main one."

Chanell laughed, got up, and paced the path between stacks of old newspapers: The Atlanta Journal and Constitution, The Tampa Tribune, The Florida Times-Union. "She can't afford that big place."

"Credit's cheap right now." He watched her like a movie.

She took the walkway of papers to the first of the two front windows, peeping around the fly-specked shade. "Oh, Archie Wall, I feel something crazy coming on."

What she did next was the meanest, what she was later most ashamed of. Then, she was crazy, her only excuse. Or like some animal hurt.

Archie Wall once took a case for a man suing the Cato Timber & Turpentine Company in Withers, ten miles northeast of Cornerville, for injuries received on the job. But as with most suits it was more complex than it appeared in legal transcript. The slight redhaired fellow, on the dumb side, had worked twenty years for the company, which had developed a bad reputation for laying off employees prior to time of retirement. Nobody died there or even faded away, they got fired—uneducated flunkies who slaved one day in the turpentine woods, chipping boxes and dipping gum, and the next mechanicking on the company's Caterpillar tractors and trucks. Rain or shine. Sick or well. When a wildfire broke out in Cato forests, the men plowed firelines ahead of sweeping blazes, flames fueled by resin and shifting winds. Laid-off Cato men were a common sight around Cornerville: some poor old sucker loafing Monday mornings, maybe checking out a video at the Delta, lost outside his routine. Technically unskilled and too stove up to work anymore, too old to get another job—providing there were jobs in Swanoochee County, save starting their own logging crews, cutting fence posts, or hauling pulpwood. Providing they could come up with the cash.

So Archie Wall had either got a bait of the company policy of fire before they retire, or maybe hoped to get a little cash contingent on the outcome of the lawsuit for the hurt man, not even close to that age of early retirement, but fired because he literally broke his back on the job. Now bowbacked, whipped, and broke, the fellow had halfheartedly agreed to let Archie Wall test the local court for fairness, though half the jurors would work for Cato, the other half, landowners themselves. The way it went, according to Archie Wall, was that the redhaired fellow was mechanicking under a jacked-up Caterpillar tractor when the jack slipped and all twenty-five tons of steel had dropped on his back. When the other mechanics got the tractor jacked up again and the hurt man out, he'd dragged himself under the tractor, howling like a dog hit by a car. After several surgeries and a six-month rotation of different hospitals, the man went back to work, only to be laid off by the company with a pension, which amounted to just enough to keep him off welfare. Archie Wall claimed they laid the fellow off to keep from paying his ongoing medical and therapy bills, and because he posed a threat to the company. Every day he stayed with the company was another day the company faced the risk of a suit. Every day he stayed was another dollar spent that the company could invest in more foreclosed-on tracts of timber. Every day he stayed was another day the company had to put up with him dragging around—and they said Archie Wall demonstrated for the court the apelike slump and warped gait of the fellow, while preaching like a Baptist, using the pronoun "you" in place of "he" to hit home with the Cato employees, and as usual lots of "furthermores" to tire down the court.

The hurt man had won his case; Chanell never had the feeling she would.

Sunday morning was like most other Sundays, a certain brightness and lazy elasticity even when it's raining. Warm for October and sunny today. She got up to birds singing and got dressed for church in an old linenlike suit that she hoped didn't look too much like linen. Her knees were shaking so that she had to change from taupe pumps to flats. Besides, she'd have a good long walk to church this morning.

Setting out, she turned right at the post office, walking the sidewalk to 129, then right again along the shoulder and across Troublesome Creek. The highway dipped between boundaries of white metal stakes, some bent from brushes with automobile bumpers. Brimming from fall rains, the blackwater creek curled between banks of frost-curled water grass, where red cola cans and green bottles peeped, a shock of color against the woody vine cloaks of stripped gums and bays. White paper, dissolved to the texture of foamy dried scum, flagged the branches of the creek's ancient parting and pull toward the Alapaha River. Dewy dead weeds and grass along the shoulder made Chanell's shoes squeak, made her stockings mat to her miserable toes.

By the time she got to the lop-roofed, red-brick Negro school, closed since the token inaugural integration in the sixties, she could see dressed-up Negroes straggling with tail-wagging fice dogs from the dingy houses of the Sampson camp to the tin-roofed white church east of 129.

Against the backdrop of muted blue sky, scraggly, dusty

palms and white sand glared from the camp with expansive precision, like a desert or the site of a home sucked up by a recent tornado. Bare feet along the gravel-laced shoulders had tramped down tufts of brown grass, a shade that picked up in tawny tints along broomsage fencerows with the dull rust of walked-down wire, which stopped and started without purpose behind jammed-together junk cars and mobile homes and set-back board houses. Clothes hanging from pole-propped lines shouted color around bleak piles of old tires and bicycles and mangled burned trash. Power poles were strung with drooping black wires, where birds perched like big-chested women stopping for breath. There was an off-key ring of shoddy brilliance and sparseness about the birds' songs, about the racket from the camp, and from the facing houses and mobile homes leading to the steep-gabled, slender church with its boxy steeple. An everlasting odor of motor oil and asphalt and the hot, hissing wind of occasional semis.

Chanell followed the sandy path from the highway to the church, watching men, women, children, and dogs group and mill around the front of the stoop, flanked by two conical green cedars. An old mama dog with scabby, drooped tits lurched and barked, then slunk to meet Chanell as she approached. Chanell could have turned around then or cut across the vine-tented woods, between the off-set rows of house trailers, and been safe again in her own backyard. Just a hop and a skip across the creek. But she walked on with her head high, arms loose at her sides and begging to fold.

On the left side of the path, three men with sculpted-tar faces turned to watch. They were dressed in white tuxedo shirts and black patent shoes. Chanell took a deep breath and walked up the green-carpeted steps to the open double doors of the church. She wasn't afraid; she'd never been afraid of

Negroes. And she didn't feel uppity. Just ashamed. Not ashamed to be seen in a Negro church, but ashamed of using them.

At the door a stout woman, about Chanell's own age, handed her a pink program with a drawing of the church on the front. The woman was chewing gum; her hair, slicked back, stuck straight out. She glared at Chanell through rose-tinted lenses set in elaborate square frames. "Welcome to His Holiness Church of God," the woman said and assumed a haughty pose, looking beyond Chanell as if she were invisible. The woman's rich musk perfume hovered in the doorway.

Trying to look the way she would at the door of her own church, Chanell stepped to the side and stood a minute. An older woman in a straw hat with flowers and thick rolled stockings went around and up the center aisle, then sat down with a settling motion on a slatted pew and began talking with the woman on her right. A tiny boy with nappy square hair was passed from pew to pew, from lap to lap. The church was almost full; several heads turned, eyes grazing Chanell, then turned back, whispering.

Chanell had already decided to sit anywhere near the rear. But when she spotted Jimmie Mae and her little girl in the middle on the left, she eased up the green-carpeted aisle and sidled toward them, brushing knees with the three women on the end.

"How you, Jimmie Mae?" Chanell said and sat beside her, fanning with her program.

"Chanell." Jimmie Mae didn't say Miss Chanell this time, and nothing about her seemed friendly or even off-center reciprocal as before.

The little girl by the window poked her face around Jimmie Mae's slim body and grinned, then sat back where

Chanell could see only the toes of her black patent shoes.

Jimmie Mae was staring straight ahead, her handsome face tilted so that the light from the window showed up two black hairs on her brown matte chin. Those hairs were the only indication that Jimmie Mae could be older instead of younger than Chanell. Maybe Jimmie Mae ate better, couldn't afford expensive junk. Maybe what Chanell had read about the human body aging quicker from ingesting lots of foods and drink and drugs was true. Was Chanell's Frito and bologna diet wearing her immune system down, making her age? Jimmie Mae's eyes crossed with Chanell's. Well, Chanell thought, looking away, at least now I'm thinking of you as if you matter. Chanell fanned, hot in the body-warmed church, and thought about how much had happened since the day she'd fixed Jimmie Mae's little girl's hair. She set her eyes on the window, on a white fluffy cloud that seemed to whirl east to west with the whole blue sky. The motion made her dizzy and doubtful about coming, so she crossed her legs and stared straight ahead.

Double rows of slatted pine pews were set close to the altar, a raw plywood platform that stretched across the front like a stage. On the platform, below a gilt-framed picture of a white Jesus with a reddish beard, metal folding choir chairs stood in three rows on a background of fake-oak paneling. A podium, front and center of the choir chairs, was draped with a tasseled red velvet runner, and facing the podium, on the left end of the platform, were double rows of deacons' benches, shorter versions of the other slatted pine pews, which appeared to block a flimsy wood door.

A stout older woman with heavy rollicking hips waddled up the aisle and right at the front toward an upright piano in the corner. The rasping of her stockings and her nylon print dress seemed to preempt and consolidate the whispers and shuffling, to set off all previous sounds as static. She sat at the piano and sank her fingers into the keys, and peppy chords swelled in the stuffy church. The backdoor swung wide behind the deacons' benches, and a trail of haughty-faced women and men in white robes threaded into the metal choir chairs.

The three men in tuxedo shirts, who'd turned to watch Chanell out front, marched up the aisle, followed by several other men, some in pink and blue dress shirts, some in work plaid and khakis, all shuffling toward the front, sitting left and right with women and children who matched their postures and dress.

"Miss," a man behind Chanell hissed. "You, miss."

Chanell turned and stared into the oily black face of a slight man with close-knotted hair and a gold top tooth. He motioned for her to follow and side-stepped from the pew behind to the side aisle and stood waiting by the window. Chanell stood—oh God, were they asking her to leave?

A woman stood in the choir and in a loud, husky voice started singing, and the whole church came alive with clapping and tapping on the rickety wood floor. A net of humming dropped from the rough rafters.

"Come with me," the man waiting by the window whispered, and Chanell had to dodge around Jimmie Mae's little girl's shoes to get out. He shoved Chanell lightly along the wall toward the altar.

"I'll just go out the front," Chanell said, trying to turn but finding the narrow aisle blocked by his wiry body in a white tux shirt and black cumberband and trousers.

He grinned, mincing ahead with the music, the glint of his gold tooth oozing around a wide, happy grin.

At the front, Chanell's toes flush with the low platform, he leaned against the wall and pointed for her to sit on the front row of empty deacons' benches. She shook her head and tried to turn back again, but he took her arm and guided her onto the platform. She remembered suddenly having heard about Negroes placing whites up front at funerals, and questioned whether the practice was to honor wanted guests or to display the unwanted. A matter of spite?

She sat on the end of the front pew and stared ahead at the soloist with fat hair, at the choir chairs filled with charmed Negro men and women, some humming, some singing in a harmonic lilt. The congregation swayed and clapped, gazing up as if they could see the beat, and kept time with a constant thumping on the floor.

At the close of one song, they'd start in on another, all shouting amen, belching hallelujahs, clapping till the house shook, till the heat built up like fire caught from kindling. They appeared not to notice Chanell—she tried to take comfort in that—but she knew better. They still seemed to be listening on a higher plane, to be seeing with their ears, hearing with their eyes, some voice that fixed them in that powerful, reckless rhythm. She couldn't even flatter herself with being unwanted. She didn't matter. If they'd heard she was part-one-of-them, they didn't show it. A dog would have been just as welcome. She could believe they did know, or she could believe they didn't, the beat went on.

After forty-five minutes of hot singing, they seemed to tone down to singing without music; the same rhythm carried over into the preaching. The tall, thick-necked preacher in a fancy gray suit and a tie red as Jesus's blood preached with his whole body. At random, the members of the congregation got up and switched pews or wandered out the front, leaving always a body to chorus amens. What air remained in the little church was stirred with cardboard fans, the scent of musk perfume a blanket over the ponderous mass of swiveling heads and bodies.

One of the men in a tux shirt brought the hard-preaching preacher a glass of water, and he stopped cold out of a heated onslaught of biblical ejaculations and panted. "This here the Lord's water," he said slow and low. "See how cold it be fresh out of the pump." He presented the glass with vapors forming on the sides. "See," he said, setting the glass on the podium. He smiled, thick features closing in for a frown, and switched back to his lashing hellfire sermon, water forgotten.

Chanell could have gotten up and gone out, as the others were doing, as any decent person would in her position. She was there for one thing and one thing only. She wasn't there to look, she wasn't there to prove or disprove a thing. Just for revenge. And the Negro church was exactly what she'd always imagined, no better and no worse. As simple as she'd thought, as complex as she'd wished. They never looked right at her, and other than the usher placing her up front, so far they hadn't treated her as one of them or none of them.

At one point, she thought about the soot she'd worn to the basketball game and talked herself into believing they had seen her. So maybe they were mad now—they should be—their heavenward faces haughty for that reason. But even that threat didn't move her from the hard deacons' bench.

"Some of y'all's getting hungry"—the preacher lowered the volume from harsh to kind—"some of y'alls done smelling that fried chicken these good ladies bring. I's 'bout done." He downed some more water and switched back to his furious preaching.

What if this is a special Sunday? Chanell thought. Like Baptist dinner-on-the-ground. If it was she'd stay and eat, with or with-

out an invitation. She thought about the numerous contradic-
tions concerning white notions about blacks, about how most
white people she knew wouldn't think of eating with a Negro,
and yet they doted on eating out—high point of the weekend—
where the cooks were likely Negroes. At dinner-on-the-ground,
spring and fall, the Baptist Church hired two Negro women to
serve iced tea and wash pots and stand around with dish towels
draped over their arms. Two or three of Chanell's customers
even boasted of hiring Negro cooks, and that many more
boasted of ancestors having owned slaves, old mammies who
gladly veined collard greens in the kitchen while nursing the
white babies of what would go for Swanoochee County gentry.

Yes, Chanell would stay for dinner. If the Negro church
tarred and feathered her, she would stay. If the Baptist Church
came and tried to cart her off, she would stay. This would be
her last big stab at her own church, her own half people.

"Thank you, Jesus," a woman in the front row shouted.

"Amen," sang out another one.

"I hear you, brother," the preacher shouted, "I hear you,
sister. And the Lord hear you too. He see what in your heart.
He know. He know us all."

"He know us all, amen," a man in the crowd shouted,
shooting to his feet, then down.

"He got all God's children counted," the preacher said.

"He got all God's children counted," the same man dit-
toed.

"Ever' hair on yo head."

"Ever' hair on yo head."

The preacher switched to a wrapping-up tone. "All God's
children say amen."

"Amen."

"Amen."

"Amen."

"Amen, brother," the preacher said and laughed. He jigged to the edge of the platform and held out his hands so that the tawny palms shone. "The Lord say, If you love me, feed my sheep. If you love me, feed my sheep," he shouted, with his back bent, and stamped his sledlike feet. "And come unto me ye who are heavy laden. I will give you rest." He said the last part softly, then shouted, "Get up here and pra-a-ay, child of God!" He was slick with sweat, stamping like a mad daddy. "Get up here on yo knees, come to Jesus."

A crowd funneled down the aisle to the front, kneeling in double-rows at the plywood altar.

Chanell didn't know if this was the right time. She couldn't tell. Maybe there was more preaching to come. Maybe a quieter time was in the offing. Right now, prayers were being murmured, the stifling air thick with the perfume of prayers, bodies shifting, heads popping up, bowing down. A woman in rhinestone-studded glasses stood from the throng at the altar and caught the preacher's big hand; he listened hard while she whispered in his ear, then snatched her onto the platform, shouting, "Hallelujah, a soul saved." The wild chord shuttled along the altar. Hallelujah. Hallelujah. A soul saved. The woman cried, her horsey face lifted and open.

"You mayn't never git another chance, brothers and sister, come to Jesus." The preacher held both hands up again, imploring the two men and a woman with a crying baby on the back pew. One of the men got up and made straightway for the altar. The preacher still held up both hands, his waist sucked in like a boy's.

The woman stood and shifted the big-eyed crying baby to another hip and wandered toward the fretwork of adorned heads along the plain plywood altar.

Chanell got up and made her way toward the preacher at the podium, past heads and bodies and prayers like the hissing of hell. She had to reach out and touch the preacher on his scratchy coat arm to get his attention.

"I'd like to move my membership to your church," she said.

part

three

chapter thirteen

Without Bell to bring her food or pay her bills, Chanell would soon have to start thinking about what she'd eat, what she'd do. She supposed she should do what Bell had suggested—go to Valdosta and look for a job. She just hoped what she'd been hearing about job shortages didn't have to do with beauticians. But like doctors, she figured, hairdressers would always be in demand. A woman might go without food, but she wouldn't go without a bleach job if her roots were shining.

Chanell knew a few beauticians in Valdosta but only a couple well, and they would have heard the rumor. They had relatives in Swanoochee County and probably were the ones now fixing Chanell's customers' hair. She couldn't imagine any of her customers going to someone unfamiliar, to someone totally unrelated to someone they knew. Well, she'd skip those shops and try all the others—hoping they hadn't heard—maybe go by the supermarket and spend some of her remaining money on food. Picking up groceries in Valdosta also meant she'd not have to go to Walters's store and face anybody in Cornerville.

Early Monday morning, in mid-October, she dressed in her tailored navy suit and matching pumps and went out to start the car. She raised the hood and tapped the battery cables with the Coke bottle before even testing to see if the Datsun would start. She had just enough gas to get to Valdosta.

Mr. Jim was already out, hoeing in his greens patch, less than ten yards from the car shed. He didn't look up. She slammed the car hood, and still he looked down, working up the row of turned black earth toward the creek slope. The rising sun struck the naked treetops, glinting silver on the vines and his hair.

Chanell got in the car, backed out of the shed, and drove up the road toward the highway. At the church, she steered right onto 94, and at once realized she hadn't looked left, saw black and heard brakes screeching, and stopped facing the passenger door of T.P.'s pickup, so close she could see his lips parting his scraggly black beard, his expressions shifting from fear to anger and then surprise. He yanked his head high, swerved toward the courtyard sidewalk, and gunned the truck through the blinking red light at the crossroads.

Chanell's face tingled; her eyelids grew heavy, her eyes dry. Her body ached like a fevered foot. She sat, drained suddenly, staring out at the closed courthouse and post office, sinking into the fading roar of T.P.'s pickup, a reminder of how close they'd come to colliding with each other. And whether or not she would have been killed, she wished they had wrecked. Get it over with. She felt lonely and sick, sick of her purple house, sick of herself. Sick of the wind-flung trash along the sidewalk, in the churchyard, in the courtyard. She'd never hated herself before, but she did now. She didn't hate T.P. or the town anymore, only herself, so much so that she didn't even want to feed herself anymore, which meant now she wouldn't need to look for a job. Her whole body seemed to fold from the neck down, a black weakness curling over her. She put the car in reverse and backed to the house, leaving it parked in the sideyard.

Inside, she collapsed across her unmade bed, heart thudding against her ribs, and closed her eyes, not sleepy but dazed and limp, fire streaking from her stomach to her face. If the roof of the house had caved in, she would've stayed there. Silence rang in her ears. This had to be as close to death as she could come without dying. She lay, a little afraid—maybe she was having a heart attack—but not afraid enough to do anything about it. She would rest for a while; she lapped her hands on her chest, corpse-style, and listened for birds outside the window, for Miss Neida's usual bumping about in the old jail. But only a ringing silence, as if the whole town had emptied, a sucking void pulling her down, down. She let go, drifting, and conjured swirls of purple in the before-sleep dizziness of her darkened eyes. She felt as if she were allowing the purple swirls in, not making them, a simple giving in to what was already there. And it made no sense, and it didn't need to make sense now. Sinking deeper as into a feather mattress or a cloud, she let herself inside too, the tardy, reticent child Betty Jean, and then Joy Beth and Linda Gay, both laughing with their mouths open like T.P.'s at the crossing.

He wasn't laughing, Betty Jean.

Mama Sharon's voice? Go away, you betrayed me, Bell said. *I should shake my head and wake up,* somebody thought and swallowed. *Where were we? Yes, on the whirlaway at school. Why that? I don't know, for the hell of it, I guess. Purple too? Yes, purple too, and don't ask me why I love that color. You never did before. I do now; it's the color of my apartness. Not my voice—who are you? Damned if I know.*

Who are you? Your past. I don't want one. Okay, but would you like the whirlaway to go backward or forward? I'll push.

Betty Jean jumping off the whirligig and feeling her feet give in the run-around trough. Holding to the metal rung, running as though pushing, but really keeping up with the purple scarves flying from metal rungs and the smiling faces of Joy Beth and Linda Gay, whose new teeth were too big for their faces. An orgasmic thrill and yet fear of not making the whirlaway go; trying to brake and reverse the whirlaway, feet sliding in the clockwise trench of spinning gray sand. Panties wet—if she peed on herself they would laugh. Hands slipping and then spinning to the grass, floating up to the blue sky, watching Joy Beth and Linda Gay blend into the purple scarves like the tigers into melted butter in *Little Black Sambo*. Ears ringing shrilly, as if somebody was blowing a whistle into them. She opened her eyes, yanked her head up, and listened to the phone ringing in the beauty shop.

Over being dizzy, alert and rested now, she dashed for the shop. How long had she slept? How long had the phone been ringing? Surely it would stop before she got there. Did she even want to answer? She did.

"Hello?"

"Chanell, it's me, Bell."

"Bell."

"How you doing?"

"Fine. What time is it?" Chanell twisted round and looked out the window at the showering sunlight of noontime.

"About twelve. Why? I mean why would you not know?" Bell said.

"I just . . . I just got up."

"Are you over feeling sorry for yourself?"

"I'm not . . . I never was."

"Well, are you over setting around and thinking up ways to get back at people?"

Chanell didn't answer.

"Listen, honey. You ought to know me better than to think I'd just bail out on you."

Chanell sat down. "Bell, believe me, if you keep hanging around me, they'll start calling you a . . ."

"Nigger lover?"

"Yeah."

"Well, honey, I reckon I am if you're a nigger. That's my business. You can't just set there by yourself."

"No." Chanell knew she couldn't. "I miss you, Bell. I miss Mama Sharon."

"Give her time."

A cry sounded in Chanell's throat. "I keep thinking I'll wake up."

"Well, wake up then. Get up, get dressed, and get going."

"I am; I started out to look for a job this morning." Chanell looked down at the chenille lint on her skirt and began picking, and the dream tried to curl back in on her.

"Good," Bell said. "Have you got any gas in your car?"

"Yeah, and I've still got a little money."

"Don't get mad now." Bell's voice got coarse and breathy. "Don't fly off the handle again, but I put two hundred dollars in your checking account."

"Why? How?"

"I got your account number off a check you gave me for some hair stuff I picked up awhile back."

"Thank you, Bell, thank you. I'll pay you back."

"You have."

"'Bye, Bell."

"I'll be over tonight to hear about the new job. 'Bye."

At least Chanell wouldn't starve, but the last thing she wanted to do was look for a job. Now she'd have to, to pay Bell back, and she still owed her and Mama Sharon for beauty school. She went in the kitchen and opened a can of chicken noodle soup, heated and ate it. She wouldn't think; she couldn't. She rinsed her bowl and went out to the car again, got in, and backed over a sardine tin. The wind had shifted, and the trash in the churchyard had blown to the post office, her own personalized blue-and-white perm carton skittering along the sidewalk to the traffic light. Familiar as it looked, she couldn't believe the trash was hers, that she'd done that. When she stopped at the blinking red light, checking for traffic to be sure she stayed on the side of the law, her old car shimmied and puffed smoke. Oh, God, she wanted to go home and hide inside and give in to the hangover of the nonsense dream in her head.

The light changed and she drove on, letting out a breath she hadn't known she'd been holding. Crossing the river bridge, headed for Valdosta, she thought about the last time she'd ridden west up 94 with Archie Wall, and how she'd been carefree and happy and hadn't even known it. The comparison seemed overwhelming.

But as she got to the city limits of Valdosta, she felt better. At least she'd be among people who hadn't heard the rumor, and even if they had they probably wouldn't care; she could hold her head high for one afternoon, and she had money in the bank. She had Bell again. More than a lot of people had.

She started with the best and newest beauty shops on the north and west sides of town—no help needed—and worked her way down to the south and east sides, fearing she'd find something at one of the Negro parlors if she stopped. By four o'clock, she knew it was either take a job at one of those shops or nothing, and maybe not even that. She pulled off a side street between shed crepe myrtles and got out at a place called Bobbie's with a soap-smeared glass front that kept her from seeing inside. Before she got to the door, she changed her mind, got in the car again, and drove to Winn Dixie. No Negro shop would hire a white beautician, not even if she confessed that she was part-one-of-them.

It was time to accept who she was, to accept and quit interchanging tags. She considered the word "Negro," which was correct but sounded too proper, too close to "nigger," then settled for "black," which was pretty close to "colored"—what she'd always said before—because "black" felt about as comfortable as she was going to get.

On the way home, already on the outskirts of town, where the pinewoods sprawled, where houses thinned to small dwellings on large-acre farms, she began to dread going home and being alone again. Unsatisfied, because she hadn't really talked to anybody in Valdosta yet—no one she could be herself with. She tried to think of somebody she knew in Valdosta, somebody who might not have heard she was part-black yet—just to visit and be herself with somebody from her past. She wheeled the Datsun around and turned north when she got to Perimeter Road, then west on Lakeland Highway and north up Ashley Street to LaRue's Nursing Home. A few cars in the street-front parking lot of the low brick building, motel-style. Passing through the glass doors at the front, she spotted a circular nurses' station in the open lobby, where old people sat slumped in wheelchairs along the walls. Some dozing, some wringing handkerchiefs, lightless eyes turned inward, lined up in their wheelchairs as if waiting at heaven's gates.

She walked toward the nurses' station to ask which room Miss Fancy was in, then spied her standing on the other side, laughing and talking with another woman, both withered and bent and waiting, it seemed, for the nurse in a white uniform and cap behind the counter to finish writing on a chart.

"Miss Pansy," Chanell called, circling the station.

The two women kept on talking.

When Chanell got close, she reached out and tapped Miss Pansy on her bony sloped shoulder. She turned, smiling: the left side of her face tugged down, her soft brown hair had gone wiry-gray. Her once-sharp eyes were drained and set.

"Honey, you'll just have to wait in line for your paycheck," Miss Pansy said to Chanell. "I gotta get home and cook."

"Miss Pansy, it's Chanell."

"Say who, honey?" She tilted her head.

"Chanell."

"I know you," said the other woman, hugging Chanell— her body felt like bones dipped in mush. "You the one they said was coming to take us to the picture show." She turned to Miss Pansy. "Remember, Pansy, they told us to wait at the corner."

"Uh huh," said Miss Pansy and propped on the counter of the nurses' station, facing the nurse writing on a chart.

"You ladies go on back to your rooms now," said the nurse. "Almost suppertime."

"I gotta pick up my paycheck and get home to cook," said Miss Pansy.

"Yeah, honey," said the nurse, "me too," and turned away, riffling through a standing wheel of charts, more old ladies who had to get home to cook.

At home that evening, Chanell worked on wigs set atop the bald heads of faceless mannequins—shaping, trimming, maneuvering pageboys from flips, arranging bangs from straggly to full—and cried. This is for Joy Beth and this is for Linda Gay and this is for Jimmie Mae and her little girl, and this is for all the old ladies who have to get home to cook. For the factory gals with families waiting for supper. For the schoolteachers and wives of preachers, for the old maids and the young brides, for all the girls who never won a beauty contest and for those who did. Let me fix your hair, honey. Let me make you quiet inside for a while, and special. Put your feet up and here's a magazine . . . Would you like a glass of tea? Hot out, ain't it? Say he did, huh? Say he told you right for a change? Well, honey, men have it rough too: ain't it the truth, men slave eight hours a day, six days a week, for Sundays off with their families, or maybe just for a warm body in their beds at night, for a home-cooked meal once in a while. Yeah, I know, we buy things and get pretty with their money to make them proud, but still and all . . . Uh huh, I heard about that—ain't it pitiful, her dying in her prime, and her languishing in the misery of old age and can't die. House up for sale.

Chanell cried.

Bell came that night and Chanell tinted her hair. The gray was shining in one-inch bands of new growth. Fine and flat, no texture without color. Chanell told Bell about going to all the shops and not finding work. Bell said something would come up. Then they watched a movie on TV and had coffee and cake, some of Mama Sharon's Mississippi Mud brought by Bell. The marshmallowy, nutty chocolate cake was too rich for Chanell now—used to be her favorite—and she couldn't help thinking of it as snitched from Mama Sharon's kitchen and not meant for her. Bell smoked Kools and giggled during the movie, trying to act as if nothing had changed. She teased Chanell about her purple-streaked house, about an envelope with her name on it that had blown all the way to the school gym. They laughed about the time T.P. had shot one of his buddies for shitting near his deer stand. Chanell told Bell about her dream and Bell called her crazy the way she used to.

Chanell closed the beauty shop that night, trying to call up her sense of nostalgia to situate herself in the security of old times.

The weather was good and cold now, and as much as Chanell used to dread the nights, she now looked forward to the dark so she could get outside without being seen.

She would slip on her leatherlike jacket and ease out the kitchen door, around the post office and across the highway to the courtyard. Sometimes, she wandered through the breezeway of the courthouse and around the courtyard, at first keeping within the metal boundaries under cover of oaks. But after two or three trips, she started walking by the new library and the health department, up the school bus shortcut to the schoolhouse. Listening to the glisten of laughter inside the row of boxy frame houses fronting the road. TV sets limning living images on the windows, many tuned to the same station so that alien voices linked house to house. She had almost quit watching TV because she felt so sorry for celebrities hit by the tabloids. Sometimes a dog would bark and she'd go on and it would quit when she got past its known boundary. If a car or truck passed, she would step behind a tree till the taillights were snuffed by the darkness. She was quiet now, and she missed her own racket.

In the schoolyard, while a basketball game was going on at the gym, she idled about the grounds where she used to play. Once she sat on the whirlaway, tasting her dream, what it meant. She could hear feet pounding inside the gym, the ball dribbling hollow on the floor, yowls and hoots when the team scored, and knew she didn't belong there.

Stars above, nail pricks on the tin sky. She could hear children crying in the Negro quarters, south of the school, men and women shouting and laughing. She didn't belong there either.

She thought about suicide, vacillating between believing and not-believing in heaven and hell. But even during bouts of not-believing, when she felt pretty sure that a bunch of deacons had written the Holy Word, she was afraid that if she killed herself she'd never know whether she'd gotten even with the town. And death was like falling through the trap-door of life. She didn't belong there either.

On the way home one night, she took the oak-shrouded road between the courtyard and Archie Wall's house. A light was on in his living room, so she went up on the porch and knocked on the door.

He peeped around the shade of the window by the door, then let her in. "How you, Betty Jean?"

"All right. What about you, Archie Wall?"

He stepped light for such a heavy man, his white-socked feet like bunnies. "Doing a little book work."

"If I'm bothering you, I'll go," she said. "I was just out walking."

"Ain't you afraid you'll get dog caught?" He crossed to his desk and sat in the chair behind it.

She pulled up the chair on the other side. "You ever been lonesome, Archie Wall?"

He reared with his hands locked behind his head. "Can't say as I have."

Chanell wished she hadn't asked something so personal, but kept talking, not because she didn't care about his feelings, but because she needed to talk. She missed talking.

"Why didn't you ever get married?" she asked.

"Why *did* you?"

"For love."

"Love?"

"Something like that." She decided to change the subject. "Do you really go to the capitol in Atlanta, Archie Wall?"

"I'll take you sometime."

"So you do?"

He looked down.

"Then how come you didn't that day?"

"I thought maybe you'd set your cap for me 'cause I'm a lawyer."

Chanell laughed. "I'm not laughing 'cause that's crazy; I'm just laughing at you, Archie Wall. How you handle stuff."

"No different than you; we both battle trifles with trifles."

This time she switched subjects because she could— friends are like that. "How's the feud going over Miss Pansy's house?"

"I think it's done for. Linda Gay didn't get the loan."

"Who'll buy it?"

"Nobody right now."

"I wish you would."

"You want me to?" He sat up, stubby hands flat on the paper-plied desk.

She shrugged. "I could do with a friendly neighbor."

"Well, I couldn't buy it if I wanted to. No money."

"Then why'd you leave me ten dollars last time you come to the shop?"

"'Cause I know what it's like to not get paid for services rendered."

"We're a lot alike, Archie Wall. But maybe you shouldn't associate with me."

"I like being associated with you, Betty Jean." He began writing, his face green in the cast of the lampshade. "You know, gal, if you wanted to, you could do your neighbors some dirt."

"I do want to."

"Do you?"

"I don't know, but it would be funny." She folded her arms on his desk and rested her chin on them. "Like what?"

"You could dig up stuff on them—shouldn't be too hard."

"I'm just as bad as they are—stringing trash in my yard, putting dog fennels in the church, acting black." She sucked in. "I'm over fighting back, Archie Wall."

"Just don't get down," he said, leaning close. "Sometimes when the fury's gone, the fight's gone."

"Maybe."

"You know, little lady, I fully expected you to start something on your friend Joy Beth."

"Joy Beth?"

"That Frank Lewis business."

"How did you know?"

"I've always known too much," he said and leaned back again, "been in positions of seeing things. For instance, one hot summer day three little girls are out playing. One branches off and goes into the old jail. A little later, a boy goes in—the same boy she would later marry—and then he comes back out. Frank Lewis, out 'lectioneering, happens by and goes in the old jail next. Still later, the second little girl goes in and even later comes out and goes back in again with a bundle under her arm like she's spending the night. The first little girl comes out after while, dressed in blue instead of pink. Even a nosy young man, destined to be a bachelor, notices things like that."

"Most don't."

"I did." He peered down his nose till his eyes crossed. "Second girl comes out with the first, but no Frank Lewis, not till two days later when the sheriff and his deputy drag Lewis's stiff, stinking body out."

"It's not my story to tell, Archie Wall."

"Then don't; I think I've pretty much pieced it together anyhow. I just like to tie up loose ends."

"You'll have to use your imagination this time."

"You're a good person, Betty Jean; don't deserve such treatment . . ."

"No victim here, Archie Wall."

"Is that what Joy Beth would've ended up? A victim?"

"That or looked down on, one. Around here you're either pitied or damned."

"True."

Chanell got up. "Archie Wall, can I ask you a question— no, two?"

He nodded, sinking his chin on his chest.

"Is it tough being a outsider in your own hometown?"

He thought a minute. "It's tough being a insider with a outside mind," he said. "What's the other question?"

"My mama's friend, Jo Ann Davis. Was she really a whore?"

chapter fourteen

Chanell expected the KKK. Anything but what happened next.

Linda Gay showed up with three fidgeting teenage girls from her Sunday-school class.

At the front door, she hugged Chanell, and Chanell figured what was up. She stood stiff, feeling Linda Gay's soft, abundant flesh wrap her. When Chanell didn't move or speak, Linda Gay stepped away and tittered, but looked as if she'd been slapped.

The paint on the stoop still smelled fresh and was now bubbled from having been brushed on in wet weather. Linda Gay and the girls tried to ignore the purple splash, but their eyes kept drawing to it.

"Come on in." Chanell led them into the living room, hearing Linda Gay slip in on tiptoes with the three girls trailing. "Y'all set down," Chanell said.

All the windows were closed, but she left the door open for the cold to scour the overheated edges of the too-bright room. She thought about how Linda Gay had always prided herself on being a leader, on taking the first step, doing first what she felt somebody else was about to do. Something that would show her in a good light. At church business meetings, Linda Gay would hidy-hi to the floor, making a motion that the church send flowers to the sick. Send a card to what's-her-name, who just had a baby. And by the way, the carpet in the nursery needs cleaning. Will somebody second the motion, please?

Linda Gay sat in the chair by the door with her old-timey bone flats together, hands wringing on her lap. Wearing a blue shirtwaist dress with large plastic buttons, which had to have been bought from a flea market. It had been out of style that long.

The girls perched on the edge of the couch, chewing gum and staring at the wall above Chanell's recliner by the window overlooking the vacant lot.

"I thought we'd just drop by and pay a little visit," Linda Gay said and waited for Chanell to speak. Then went on, "How you been doing?"

"Fine as can be expected." Chanell could tell that Linda Gay wanted to skip the old business and get on with the new.

Linda Gay crossed her legs and sat back, trying to appear at ease. "We've been missing you at church."

"Really?" Chanell stared out the window. "I moved my membership."

The girls shifted on the couch, got still.

Linda Gay ignored Chanell's interruption of her planned speech. "We always miss our regular members, don't we, girls?"

One of the girls nodded, her blond hair haloed by the lit window behind.

"Lots of flu going round," Linda Gay said.

"Well, Linda Gay, as you can see I don't have the flu." Chanell thought about their last class reunion at the Holiday Inn in Valdosta. Linda Gay had insisted on renting and decorating the banquet room in a "Stardust" theme like their senior banquet. How she'd taken over as speaker, singing "The Lord's Prayer" in her warbling soprano while her classmates bowed their heads. When the revered and ancient superintendent came in—the one credited with felling the old smoking tree behind the school—Linda Gay had sent her little girl over to ask T.P. to put out his cigarette.

Linda Gay tugged her skirt over her fat kneecaps. Chanell could almost see her panties beyond overlapping white thighs and thought about her fanaticism for white panties, pink maybe, red never. Only whores wore black.

"Anyhow," Linda Gay said, "we hope to see you in church again soon."

"No, you don't."

Linda Gay stood, freeing the bogged belt of her shirtwaist. "Guess we'll be going, girls."

After they'd left, Chanell sat thinking about Linda Gay's visit, what it meant. Had to mean that the majority of people in Cornerville had voted Chanell in again, and Linda Gay, loving to be first, had seconded the motion and brought news of the victory. Yeah, Chanell could probably have the church back now, maybe even her old customers—she didn't know for sure—but they'd be coming out of Christian charity. The Baptist preacher had probably preached a do-unto-others sermon last Sunday. And Chanell might take them all back; she might have to.

Linda Gay called on Monday and asked for a frost job. Chanell said she'd check her appointment book, held the phone away, counted to ten, and spoke into the receiver again. Come at four on Tuesday, she told Linda Gay.

Joy Beth called next. Could Chanell trim her hair? She told her to come at two on Tuesday, she'd work her in. Didn't want to put Joy Beth and Linda Gay together, not while Chanell was still healing.

That night, Miss Lou called. Could Chanell set her hair? Chanell said she had an opening Tuesday morning. Could she come in around nine? Miss Lou didn't like to come later in the day. Eight-thirty would be better, she said, okay? Okay.

Chanell was back in business, if not in society. She felt like a child who'd been crying, shuddering and calm, almost over getting her feelings hurt. Had that same warm, mellow taste in her mouth.

Miss Lou handed Chanell her pocketbook and settled into the shampoo chair, her crepe-papery lids closing over watery blue eyes.

Chanell put her pocketbook on the drier chair and strolled to the shampoo bowl, running the sprayer to warm. The edgy old lady had already shown the latest snapshots of her grand-children—surface stuff. Not her usual chatter about her daughter's problems. It was a start. Chanell was standoffish, answering only yes or no to Miss Lou's general questions, but never her usual yes ma'am and no ma'am because then she'd feel too eager, too black. She didn't even say Miss Lou's name because she couldn't say it without feeling guilty for not say-ing Miss before Lou, the way she'd been taught. The way all children in Cornerville had been taught to speak to their elders, black or white. Chanell wouldn't give in. Like when she was a child at the river, she was staying in shallow water, not yet ready to wander to the opaque drop-offs.

She sat Miss Lou up and covered her head with a towel. "You want to switch chairs for me?"

Miss Lou peeped out from under the towel and grabbed Chanell's hand. "Bless your heart."

Chanell couldn't tell if it was real or not. She couldn't imagine what had happened to bring Miss Lou around. But Chanell wasn't buying. "Step over to the combout station."

Miss Lou withdrew her hand and ambled over, sitting cautiously. Then she began to whimper.

Chanell handed her a Kleenex. "You want it set on bobby pins?"

"Yes 'um," Miss Lou said.

Chanell started twirling the blue-gray strands on her finger, pinning them to the scalp. Her hands were shaking; her neck was stiff. Was Miss Lou afraid of her? She gazed out the window at muddy clouds crowding out blue streaks of sky. Old homebody like Miss Lou probably watched lots of TV and had seen the first woman serial killer on the news the night before; maybe she thought Chanell could be number two. Surely she'd heard about Chanell's rampages on the courthouse, the basketball game, the churches. So why was she here?

"We're living in the last days," Miss Lou sniffled.

Before she thought, Chanell said, "Yes, ma'am. But I always say when you die it's your last day anyhow."

"Mother against daughter, father against son." Miss Lou sniffled and blew her nose.

"That's the truth," Chanell said.

Miss Lou scrunched her wasted shoulders.

Chanell's eyes began to mist. Call it pity, call it weakness, but Chanell felt sorry for the old lady. She thought about the TV commercial for a certain toothpaste with a book showing underlined words, proof in print that if you used that toothpaste you'd never lose your teeth, and she wished there was such a book to go by in life, a sure and simple way to get life right without guessing or trying new things.

In a few minutes, Miss Lou really started crying, choking sobs that sounded like she was tickled. Crying even after Chanell put her under the drier. Chanell slipped outside and stood on the stoop in her old corner. She felt scalded all over, inside and out, but the sun was beginning to break through the clouds.

By the time Joy Beth came in at two, the clouds had formed to a lit-gray hull overhead with the kind of hard-driving rain that seems to have no beginning or end. Chanell had had at least a dozen calls, her appointment book was as full as it had ever been. She felt as if she were floating.

She didn't expect Miss Lou's humility from Joy Beth, and she didn't get it. Joy Beth acted as if nothing had ever happened, infuriating Chanell. She ripped the comb through Joy Beth's drab teased hair, crown down, while Joy Beth chattered away. Never flinching, just picking at her fingernails with her shoulders scrunched and her arms goosefleshed from Chanell's torture. "Are you working the 4-H booth at the Halloween carnival this year?" Joy Beth said.

"Nope," said Chanell. She combed easier, then yanked Joy Beth's head till her white neck shined in the mirror above the driers. She could smell fear on Joy Beth around her White Linen cologne.

"I reckon you been busy, huh?" She flinched as Chanell snatched a knot on the nape.

"Today I have, Joy Beth." Saying her name seemed to open them up, to stop the crap.

Joy Beth clamped her hand over the comb and stared up at Chanell. "You don't have to pull my hair out, Chanell. I'm here to say I'm sorry, to ask you back."

"Back to where?" Chanell stood aside, tuning the teeth on the comb.

"You know"—Joy Beth stared at her hands on her lap—"like we used to be."

Winter thunder rolled in the west.

"How was that, Joy Beth? I can't seem to remember."

"God, Chanell! We was raised up together."

"Can you put aside the fact that I'm black?"

Statement laced with laughter: "Chanell, you're not all that colored."

"No?"

"'Course you're not."

"If I was?"

"You're not." She reached out, grabbed Chanell by the wrist, and shook it, laughing as if it had all been some joke.

"Why'd you suddenly . . . why did all of you suddenly come back?"

"I don't know what you mean."

"You're not that stupid."

"I'm not stupid."

"Well, I guess I am. So tell me."

"Well . . . I just missed you. Me and you goes way back."

"That's a lie, Joy Beth, and you know it."

Lightning flared the glass of the windows, the lights overhead flickered, blinked off then on, and Chanell began combing out Joy Beth's hair again while she talked.

"Remember how your mama used to bring you over to play on rainy days? Remember how we'd splash in the mud puddle around my doorsteps? Me and you and Linda Gay." She got low, so low Chanell had to strain to hear her ground-down voice around the rain sluicing from the corner gutters.

Chanell combed easier, letting her talk. "Remember how

your mama used to make popcorn and put it in waxpaper
cones for us to take to the tent show on the lot behind the
café? What about the baboon staked out next to the old tent?
Remember how as long as he was tied, we were brave, feed-
ing him popcorn while he paced the dirt ring, grunting and
shining his red behind? Then when he got loose, we were all
so scared. Wouldn't go out to play till the show people caught
him in what Miss Petty called her second kitchen.

"Remember the wiry little show woman who sold fire-
crackers from her Silverstream trailer, how we made fun of
her striped socks and high heels? You called her the Firecracker Lady." Her voice got high and eager for a good one
coming up. "What about the time poor old Miss Pansy took
her Sunday-school class to the Twin Lakes Pavilion? Remember
how we swam out neck-deep in the green water and stayed
all day, bobbing to keep from drowning and flirting with the
boys? How we played like we couldn't hear Miss Pansy calling
us? We could see her waving from the sand off the ell-shaped
dock and we'd wave back." She waved her hand in the buzzy
lit air of the shop.

"I remember," Chanell said, raking the comb across her
palm.

"Remember on the ride home that night how sunburned
we were—even you for once? How our hides peeled like
sunned rubber for two weeks?"

"Yes," Chanell said and sucked in. "Remember the old
jail?"

Joy Beth stiffened. "That's dirty of you, Betty Jean."

"Dirty of me?"

"I don't aim to talk about it."

"We are talking about it."

"Don't." Joy Beth held up one vein-shot hand.

"We should have told."

"No, I've never regretted not telling." Joy Beth hung her head. "I'd never of lived it down; they would've hounded me for life."

"You *are* *they,* Joy Beth," Chanell said, combing again. "So am I."

"Did you ever know that Linda Gay had a crush on T.P.?" said Linda Gay, seemingly delivering jab for jab, but maybe only changing subjects.

"Yes," Chanell lied to keep from looking dumb. Linda Gay? "How did you know?"

"She was all over him half the time. 'Course he used her, then told all his buddies . . . practically ruined her reputation."

"Good." Chanell only half believed it. "That how come she hates me?"

"That and because you're pretty, I guess." Joy Beth got speechy, as if ready to recite some proverb. "First love leaves a big hole in your heart, don't it?"

"I wouldn't know." Chanell did know and she felt for Linda Gay.

"I know you don't know this," Joy Beth said, "so don't make like you do; but remember the night of your wedding rehearsal at church? Well, Linda Gay slipped off and slept with T.P. under the river bridge. She cried and begged him not to marry you."

"I wish he'd listened."

"Linda Gay always believed you were the reason he turned out so sorry."

Chanell laughed.

"Funny, huh!"

"She called me white trash to my face awhile back."

"That was kind!"

"I thought so."

"I've missed you, Chanell." Joy Beth placed her hand over Chanell's on the comb. "You've got magic hands, Chanell. It's a gift, a gift. I never told you, but when you brushed my hair from my face that day I pushed Frank Lewis . . ." She stopped talking, sucked in, and buried her face in her hands.

"Don't worry about Frank Lewis . . . about me telling," Chanell said calmly, screaming inside: My God, she pushed Frank Lewis, he didn't fall. I can't believe it!

"I never doubted you," Joy Beth sobbed. "I knew you wouldn't . . . won't tell."

"Listen, Joy Beth, one thing we've all got in common is waiting in the pawpaw patch at one time or another."

"The pawpaw patch?" Joy Beth peered up with smudged crying eyes.

"Yeah," Chanell said. "'Come on, boys, and let's go find her, way down yonder in the pawpaw patch.'"

"Remember us singing that in first grade?" Joy Beth said brightly. "How cute everybody said we was. How once the word got around to all the teachers, we had to sing it at ball-games and PTA? Me and you and Linda Gay."

Chanell remembered, and though she suspected there was more behind this sudden change of heart, she knew Joy Beth meant from the heart what she said. She had missed her old friend. They were coded as one forever by more than merely colors and secrets.

But not Linda Gay.

Linda Gay came in at four o'clock, bringing her dollish blond child to offset awkwardness.

Chanell worked the snug, perforated rubber cap over Linda Gay's head, snapping it on her ears. Then she took the knitting-needle device used for frost jobs and began jabbing the tip through the holes, hooking strands of hair and yanking them out. Linda Gay, who looked like a fat, pained Esther Williams, kept talking to Chanell through her little girl. "Tell Miss Chanell about you getting all A's on your report card, baby."

The little girl nodded and twisted in the drier chair, swinging her bruised legs.

Linda Gay teeheed, sucking air through her teeth. "Honey, Miss Chanell's 'bout to gouge mama's brains out."

"I'm right here, Linda Gay," Chanell said.

Linda Gay scrunched under the green plastic cape, laughing as if she thought Chanell was teasing.

"Mama's about done, sugar," Linda Gay said to the little girl later.

Chanell had been slowly poking and snatching strands of drab-blond hair through the cap for at least an hour, while Linda Gay squirmed and stared at her watch.

Still later. "Sugar plum, this drier's burning mama's ears up." Linda Gay ducked. "Reckon Miss Chanell could part with some cotton?"

The next day June Herndon called to ask if Chanell would clog with her group at the carnival Friday night. Various clogging groups would be providing entertainment on the tennis court at the recreation center.

Chanell told her she'd given up clogging.

"Well, I hope you can make it anyway," she said. "We been missing you."

Now Chanell knew something was up. And whatever it

was had nothing to do with that "do unto others" stuff they'd been teethed on. She was being drawn back into the big circle. She tried not to feel good, but even knowing more was behind it, she felt relieved. Almost healed.

Eloise Hamby, who considered herself rich because the Hambys had a family cemetery on their cattle farm, called to say she'd woke up that morning with her hair in a mess. She could come in around two if that was okay. Fine, Chanell said, wishing she could afford to say, Not on your life, you bleached hag; not after you failed to show up for the last appointment, not after you helped ruin my life by running your mouth at the Delta. But Eloise tipped five dollars every time she stepped through the door.

Bee Bradford and Cleona Keats called next, ringing back to back. A perm for Cleona and a bouffant with spit curls for Bee, who always called Chanell "Nellie-poo" or "puss." To show how dizzy she was, Bee would spin around, a truly ugly woman, built like a pulpwooder, and say, "I felt like I was gone do this number." Chanell put Bee on hold and tallied up how much she could make by doing Bee's hair—five bucks at the most—whether or not it was worth the bother, taking into account Bee's spreading the rumor about Chanell, according to Bell. "Bee, I'm awfully sorry but I'm booked solid."

Chanell was making coffee in the kitchen the next morning when she heard light scuffing on the concrete slab beyond the door. She peeped out the window over the table and saw Miss Neida toddling across the yard toward the old jail. Chanell's instinct was to look out and not merely out the window. Her heart struck up its hard and frantic rhythm. But better sense told her that the bad stuff was over. Miss Neida had probably knocked while Chanell was rattling the filter holder into its compartment on the coffeemaker. She started to let the curtain go and spied a newspaper bundle of collard greens and a bottle of cane syrup on the stoop. She felt weak all over, almost happy. Yes, it was over, at least so close to over she could believe it.

Before she got through with breakfast, the phone rang. Aunt Ruth after a wave set. Chanell put her down in her book. When she came back to the kitchen to clean up her cereal bowl, she heard more scuffing on the rear stoop, feet scraping on concrete, then a knock on the door. Probably Miss Neida back with a boxed Toni—about time for another home perm. Chanell wouldn't do it; this time she'd tell her: my perm or nothing, when I have the time.

She opened the door to Mama Sharon, standing with a painted-on smile and a red nose. All smooth and round and tan, with that sameness of manner and dress Chanell had so loved, Mama to Mama Sharon stood cradling the bundle of greens and the bottle of cane syrup.

"Somebody's left you a little present, looks like," she said and brushed her feet on the shedding hemp mat.

"A peace offering." Chanell took the greens and the syrup and unloaded onto the tabletop.

Mama Sharon stepped inside and shut the door and blew her nose. "I've come down with a old cold."

"They say flu's going round." Chanell sat at the table. "Have a seat." Just as with Miss Lou, Chanell felt funny not adding Mama to Mama Sharon's name. Mama Sharon. Miss Sharon. What would Chanell call her now? Judas?

Mama Sharon pulled out a chair and sat, lacing her big work hands on the table before the newspaper-wrapped greens. "I been meaning to drop by. . . ."

"Since everybody else decided to." Chanell was mad now.

"That's not what I went to say, honey."

"Honey?"

"Don't take it so hard. Don't make it so hard on me, sugar."

"Don't make it so hard on you?" Chanell rose and leaned against the refrigerator, her back chilling all the way to her heart.

"I know what you been going through," Mama Sharon said.

"You don't."

Mama Sharon blew her nose. "You don't leave a body much room to say I'm sorry."

"No, Mama Sha . . . no I don't aim to make it easy."

"I didn't expect you would." She stared out the window, her big, round bun aimed at Chanell.

"Make your point." Chanell thought she might cry. Of all people to turn their backs on her, Mama Sharon!

"I don't have a point." Mama Sharon's padded shoulders shook. "I just ask your forgiveness."

"Well, I don't forgive any of y'all." Saying y'all instead of you seemed a little kinder. "Someday I might."

"That's all I could ask, you know?" Mama Sharon's head turned, they snagged eyes.

"Do you love me, Mama Sharon?" Chanell started to cry. "Do you love me even with black blood?"

"I do, I always have." Mama Sharon cried hard, quaking from her bun to her brown dress loafers. "Hush now." She took her glasses off and wiped them on her skirttail. "Hush, honey."

Chanell pressed her head to the refrigerator, crying louder, a scream inside with the buzzing of the motor. "I'm scared, Mama Sharon."

"You don't have to be, honey. I'm here. Hear me, I'm

here." She got up, stepping off blocks of white-speckled tiles to the refrigerator, reached for Chanell, and wrapped her in strong, fleshy arms, rocking while they both cried, while Mama Sharon shushed, while both sets of feet lifted and lowered on the screaking floor.

Chanell buried her face in Mama Sharon's soft, sweet neck.

"What you scared of, sugar?" Mama Sharon crooned.

"I'm scared of my ownself."

Mama Sharon caught her chin and stared into her bawling face. "Of yourself, sugar?"

"I'm scared I'd of done the same thing."

Chanell hadn't gone to Wednesday-night prayer meeting in years—usually she worked late and, since there was no singing, the service bored her—but she decided to go now. She had to know why; she had to know. Not why this sudden change of behavior, but whether her nightmare was really over. Would the church take her back? Could she go if she wanted to and be treated white?

Going back to her own church would be as hard as going to the black church for the first time—that's how it would feel—but she had to go, she had to know. If she waited till Sunday for a bigger crowd, a truer measure of how she would truly measure up, she might not go at all. Wednesday-night church would be her breaking-in place.

When she finally got up the courage to go, trekking numb through the cool dusk, when she finally mustered the courage to tip through the lit pine vestibule, her shoes seemed to hammer on the polished floor, up the aisle with her eyes on her same third pew—don't look too bold, don't look too meek—then scanning the scattered elderly couples, all watching, all smiling, all welcoming her with just the right degree

of lip stretch, and Chanell sitting, hearing shoes scraping
ahead and behind, deacons flocking to shake her hand—not
too bold, not too meek. A tired but tried Wednesday crowd.
No Bell to offset the sameness, to make Chanell feel safe.
Maybe she should have waited till Sunday, till Bell . . .

Her tongue felt like wet wool, her eyes began to draw, and
then she realized she was more relieved than afraid. She
couldn't be sure yet, but she suspected she could come back
now—that she'd have the guts, for one thing—if she wanted
to come back. That's what she kept thinking while the preacher
led Bible study, while he prayed for the sick—no mention of
Miss Pansy—and closed with prayer. One whole hour that felt
like five minutes, and she was standing and walking down the
aisle instead of up, almost at the door, waiting behind two
warped elderly women to shake with the preacher. Almost out
the door. Then he stopped her, saying would she wait please—
he needed to speak to her. She stepped to the side and leaned
against the wall, her face a wrung-white she could see, while
he finished good-night partings with his feeble congregation.

When he and Chanell were alone, he stepped over and
stood before her. "Chanell"—he spoke low as if somebody
might hear, a reverent whisper, each word coming clean and
apart without unction. "I got the request for your membership letter from across the creek." He shook his fair head.
"You don't mean it . . . you don't want that."

Chanell felt herself getting taller, fuller. "I don't?"

"Of course not." He scratched his shiny, freckled ear.

"I do." Chanell didn't. She didn't want to make the blacks
more miserable, didn't want to involve them in her predicament. Later, maybe.

"You're just hurt," he said, so close in her face she could
smell his purified Listerine breath.

"You should be hurt," Chanell said.

"Me?"

"For me, for all of us." She started to walk out. "Feed my sheep."

By Friday, she had talked herself into believing that everything was back to normal. The more they came—and all her customers had come or were booked to come—the easier it got. She was rolling in dough. Well, not exactly, but that's how it felt. And the excitement of the Halloween Carnival coming up that night was making her happy again, high on what it would be like: hot dogs skewered and revolving over a steaming rack; high-priced Cokes in waxed-paper cups; candied apples and popcorn; Rice Crispies and divinity candy and chocolate cupcakes with candy-corn eyes; the smell of hay and dust kicked up by chasing children; lots of racket, music and squeals and laughter, big people acting like kids. The lazy evening curving to night, the ripeness of autumn about to turn winter, something coming and something gone, rest when it all would be over, when the great harvest moon began to wither. Of course, Chanell knew it wouldn't turn out that way, that the moon was in half-phase, milky and underblown.

She called Bell and told her she'd be clogging that night. Bell said she couldn't wait, that they'd even try to round up a male clogging partner for her.

Chanell said, "Don't go to no trouble."

"Honey, finding men to clog with is always trouble. Men are hard to come by."

"T.P.?"

"Honey, you know better?"

"I didn't mean would he be my clogging partner; I meant has he come around like everybody else?"

"Don't ask me."

He'd slept with a part-black—forget the fractions—unforgivable! "I didn't think he would," Chanell said.

"His ass!"

Bell had offered to pick Chanell up that evening, but she insisted on walking. She wanted to test the people along the sidewalk in front of the school, as she'd been testing her customers all week. Still, she hadn't gone to the Delta or Walters's store—there were so many places to go for what seemed the first time. Even going to the post office and the courthouse would seem like walking in fresh, because now she was somebody else. Not Betty Jean, not Chanell, but whoever the town had made her this time, at this phase of their game. But the new Chanell felt some undisturbed center inside, or a place maybe once disturbed but now calm like water under a riffled surface, where it was all right no matter what. Because she'd been passed through fire and come out alive.

She set out walking in her red gingham clogging dress, the prissy short skirt shifting above a buoy of whispery crinolines, in black patent shoes with satin ribbon bows. No less foolish than in the soot face worn on her last trip along that sidewalk. She wouldn't clog anymore after tonight. Kicking aside a June copy of *Hairdos*, she thought that maybe tomorrow she'd pick up her trash all over town, maybe go to Valdosta and get more paint to cover the purple, but she would leave the pink flamingo in memory of George, that gaudy bird.

The last time she walked here, she kept thinking, same as she had after her mama had died, thinking back to how it had been then. She was walking past the schoolhouse, toward the gym. The last time she walked here, same as when she had driven the highway into town, looking for a job. And she made up her mind to be done with backtracking, and if her

243

hair looked good today, she'd enjoy it, rather than worry whether it would look good tomorrow, how long the do would last.

She was well past Joy Beth's and Linda Gay's houses, walking in front of the gym, about to turn off on Mama Sharon's road to the recreation center. Cars and trucks were slowing, turning in, and suddenly Chanell felt afraid again and wished she was back at home. Home was safe, and church was safe compared to being shunned by the whole county. How did she know everybody wouldn't turn on her again? Did she expect everybody to accept her as Mama Sharon had? Mama Sharon loved her; the others, at best, might only like her, might use her for sport tonight. Maybe they had to have somebody to look down on in order to feel tall, or maybe it was as simple and nonsensical as picking up pawpaws, something to do, something mindless like that.

chapter fifteen

Cars and trucks were wedged into every available space along the road, from Bell's mobile home on one end, to Mama Sharon's house on the other, even the yard of the Church of God, adjacent to the recreation center with its crop of carnival canopies.

Children in Halloween costumes popped up from between parked cars—miniature Hulks and Raggedy Anns, a devil in a dimestore mask with an evil sneer but snappy bright child eyes. Rock music blasted from the main building, the old warehousey Sampson commissary. A half-moon hung high in the dimming blue sky like a broken mother-of-pearl button. Scents of hot dogs and popcorn wafted from the canopied booths set between hay bales in the cordoned carnival ring behind the building.

Chanell edged through the crowd at the gate, dodging a gang of children, a Robin Hood and a Mickey Mouse and a Frankenstein, and then north toward the tennis court, where the cloggers were gathering. So far, nobody had even eyed her.

Lottie Simpson, president of the PTA, was hustling between booths with a cigar box of change. She was wearing tight jeans, the pressure of her heavy thighs punishing the denim. Meeting Chanell, head on, she smiled and spoke, "Hey, girl, I haven't seen you in a coon's age." Chanell kept walking, relieved that somebody had spoken, but aggrieved that most of them hadn't. Lottie was not one of Chanell's regular customers, but every six months or so Chanell would get stuck with the task of trying to tame her wild brown hair with hot oil treatments.

A portable record player had been set up on the gate end of the tennis court. Bell was placing a record on the turntable while talking to June Herndon. Other cloggers in tan stockings and red-checked dresses, like Chanell's, were gabbing and idling about the green concrete square. Already an audience was dragging up webbed lawn chairs to the chainlink fence. Mama Sharon in her brown dress loafers among a gathering of women. Chanell didn't want to clog; she wanted to go home. The fried Spam she'd eaten for supper set high in her stomach, threatening to float up and choke her.

"Hey, Chanell," Bell shouted, and suddenly the whole carnival seemed to stop, only the music of the hootchy-cootchy show at the old commissary rocking on. Faces blurred, the children's masks among them—the teenagers at the dunking booth, the kids at the fish pond, the cakewalkers along the baseball fence. Everybody standing in line at the homemade candy stand seemed to twist around to see Hey Chanell. The cloggers in masks of makeup stared, faces stark in the artificial lights coming on as the sun went down.

Chanell questioned why she had ever wanted to be different. Why she had changed her name. Somehow, Betty Jean, that name, seemed to stand a better chance of not sticking out. She didn't know how long she had stood there, but Bell's hand seemed to poise forever over the record-player arm, about to let the needle down on the black spinning disk, and when she finally let the arm go, Chanell walked on through the gate of the tennis court. Everybody outside began talking and moving in the leftover daylight, the skin masks of adults more scary than the plastic masks of children. Chanell swallowed hard, swallowing back her fear with the fried Spam.

"We couldn't get no men," Bell called and laughed, then minced out on the court to the rhythm of the clogging music, while the other cloggers formed lines and paired off. "Chanell, you be my partner," said Bell.

Chanell wondered if Bell was offering up front to offset the awkwardness of the others possibly refusing to partner her. She had a feeling that the two men who usually clogged with June Herndon's group were absent tonight for the same reason.

Outsized and silly in her little-girl dress, Joy Beth tapped her shoes on the concrete, hands hooked on her waist. "Come on, slowdy-poke," she called to Chanell and pranced over to her partner, touching white net crinolines. The others began giggling and motioning for Chanell to hurry, as friendly as they'd ever been unfriendly.

Chanell felt really foolish, but no longer self-conscious. Just eager to get done so she could wander around the carnival with the others. To see how many would speak, not how many would snub her, and try to figure out why. What in the world had come over everybody?

First number, "Rocky Top," the fiddle music fuzzy against the backdrop of squeals and laughter, security lights overwhelming the lapsing dusk and the paltry glow of the moon. Then "Old Timey Rock & Roll," faces tilted up as if call-stepping to voices in their heads. Rock, step, rock, step, turn; rock, step, rock, step, turn; tapping to the drumbeats, no movement from the shoulders up. Chanell whirled Bell, Bell whirled Chanell, and as Chanell made the round of Bell's swishing skirt, she spied T.P. standing behind Mama Sharon's chair. He watched the clogging for a few minutes, then strutted off toward the carnival ring, fingers shoved into his tight jeans pockets. Would he speak this time? Had he changed along with everybody else? She didn't care. If this rumor served no other purpose than to get rid of T.P., it was almost worth it.

After the first set, the audience clapped, then scattered out toward the carnival games and food booths in the baseball park.

"Let's go get a Coke," Bell said, yanking Chanell's arm.

Joy Beth, dabbing her dark, dewy makeup with a Kleenex, tagged behind. "I'm 'bout to burn up," she said.

While they waited in line at the hot dog and Coke stand, four women made it a point to come over and speak to Chanell. Touching her arm and talking in her face. It was impossible to tell what they were thinking, but they tried too hard, the way they might with somebody rumored to have cancer.

Joy Beth started picking on June Herndon's choice of clogging music; they hadn't practiced "Rocky Top" in months. "Did y'all see me over there messing up?" she said.

"Shut up, Joy Beth," Bell said. "I'm the one picked that song."

"Oh," Joy Beth said and shut up.

Chanell felt sure that Bell had picked "Rocky Top" because she knew Chanell was familiar with the steps; she also felt sure that Joy Beth now knew she'd messed up again. T.P. was in line for a hot dog and Coke, six people ahead of Chanell and friends, with three of his buddies. After he got served, he'd have to walk back by Chanell, either to the left along the cakewalk or to the right, where another line formed to the popcorn booth. Would he speak?

She watched as he got his Coke and hot dog, paid, and stuffed his change in his jeans pocket. Doubling back along the cakewalk, he chomped on the hot dog, washing it down with Coke. "How y'all?" he said when he reached Chanell, Bell, and Joy Beth, then strolled on toward the circle of game booths on the baseball field. His three buddies paraded after him with hot dogs and Cokes, and Alex stopped to give Joy Beth a sip of his drink.

"Hey, Alex," Chanell said, sidling closer—she had to know. "Can I have a sip too?"

"Yeah, yeah. Shore." He passed the Coke to Chanell. "Y'all take it; I'll get another one afterwhile."

Chanell passed the paper cup back. He shook his head, biting into his hot dog. She kept pushing it at him. "Huh uh," she said, "you keep it. You'll have to get in line again if you don't."

He took it and walked off.

Chanell watched him pass through the gate to the baseball field; she watched him drop the Coke into the trash barrel and keep walking.

Okay, all the women were speaking, friendly as they'd ever been, but the men—no, boys old enough to be men—were still cold and standoffish. The same men who'd tried to go with her behind T.P.'s back. And T.P. . . . Her blood boiled. She'd always believed that men were quicker than women to warm up after a fight, to forgive and sincerely forget. But this was crazy. Whatever was going on, whatever had caused this sudden forgiving and forgetting in the women hadn't affected the men at all.

Linda Gay, taking orders and making change at the Coke booth, beamed at Chanell. Eyes shining in her bright, stupid face framed by the week-old hairdo. She was so stupid she couldn't even comb her own hair, but she was smart enough to look up other people's backgrounds. If somebody as narrow-minded as Linda Gay could gush so, why not those men with cocks like water witches' sticks? Chanell had decided long ago that none of the men she knew was worth a cuss, but why the split now?

She got her Coke and wandered through the park gate with Bell to get some divinity from the fourth-grade candy booth. Joy Beth still tagging behind. Chanell's eyes were periscoping for T.P.; her ears were perked for the men strolling with the women—all of the women spoke—to speak to her. But not one man, not a damned one!

Finally, she singled out T.P., across the grounds near the front fence, at the dunking booth. A mob of boys were taking turns tossing softballs at a red-ringed target behind the pudgy basketball coach, who perched loose-armed on a plank above a livestock watering trough of shaky lit water. Not a wet spot yet on the patchy grass surrounding the ribbed metal tub.

Kr-rak, bap, kr-rak, bap, kr-rak, bap! Ha, ha, ha! Balls bounced from the backboard, rapid fire, and rolled to the wire fence. The water shimmered in the lights overhead, calm as a wait-ing bath. The boy at the head of the line, having missed all three chances to spring the trap and dunk the coach—"Hot amighty damn!"—loped off to the card table at the end of the line to buy more tickets and try again. Next boy up, gangly with a straight body, wound up and tossed the ball with one knee hiked, stood flat and baffled as the ball smacked the backboard above the red target. The coach hooted; T.P. let out a whoop.

While Bell was waiting for change at the candy stand, Chanell slipped away through the crowd, keeping her eyes on T.P. He was like a snake act drawing her. At the hay-bale boundary of the dunking booth, she squeezed between him and another man. The swag-bellied man glanced at Chanell and wandered away, resetting his Bass Buster cap. Still facing ahead, T.P.'s eyes rolled left, as if he'd been expecting Chanell—By God, this time you won't surprise me!—had been waiting for his ex-wife to disgrace him in public by showing up, when any decent woman in such straits would have had the decency to lie down and die or at least leave town.

"How long you gone keep after me?" he said, brown eyes locking on the dunking booth, even laughing as the next boy missed the target and stalked away.

"I'm not following you, T.P." Chanell still stood there, not to embarrass him, this time, but because she had nothing to hide, nothing to hide from. And it felt good.

"Then why don't you get lost?" T.P. nodded behind him where the children fished in a fake pond, where the women and girls walked for cakes, then stared ahead where the boys lined up for the thrill of dunking one of their own.

"Because I need to know what's going on," Chanell said.

"Hold it down, will you!" His voice was muffled by his beard.

"I'm gone say it louder if you don't answer me." She had said it louder.

"What the hell you think's wrong?"

"I don't know, I'm asking."

He spoke louder too, as if mad was an excuse any fool would understand. "Here I been living with a you-know-what all this time and everbody low-rating me. That's not bad enough, huh uh! Now I find out ever last one of my buddies is been getting it from you all them years."

Chanell stood looking about the grounds for the buddies who'd been "getting it" all those years. She located Alex and Bo-Bo Quick in line for the hootchy-cootchy show, a kind of musical dance revue, where the high school boys dressed up as floozies with balloon breasts and painted bow lips.

"Oh Lord," Chanell said and laughed out. "I forgot. I forgot all about the old black-whore jokes."

"Shut your mouth!" T.P. said, facing her. "You got everbody looking."

"Well, did you or didn't you used to brag about going to the quarters to get a piece?"

"I said shut up." T.P. was towering over her as if to block the impact of her voice, which was calm compared to his.

"Liars, you're all a bunch of liars and users," she stated flatly. She had nothing to fight for, nothing to lose, but could well understand the desperation of somebody who did. She took no pity.

He stalked off, a ball tripped the coach's perch, and he dropped into the water, splashing the mob of boys. They skirled away, whooping and laughing.

Chanell caught up with T.P. and grabbed his arm, double-stepping to keep time. "Think about it, T.P. You're mad 'cause you married a half black, and at the same time all of y'all have boasted about going with black whores."

He snatched away and stomped off toward the park gate.

She followed, walking fast, calling through the crowd, "So, it's okay to screw a black woman; just don't marry one. Right?"

Everybody parading past, crisscrossing between Chanell and T.P., turned to take in the fight.

"I'm warning you, Chanell," he yelled behind, walking through the wall of boys in line for the hootchy-cootchy show.

"And I hear you, T.P.; I've been hearing you." She stopped, watching his rangy body part the crowd.

"T.P.?" she hollered.

He wheeled with his fists balled.

"T.P., I'm sorry," she said. "You were right, you were dead right about me going with all these fellows"—she made a wide sweep with her arms, locking eyes with a dozen stricken men, their wives' faces cracking like eggs. "They wouldn't let me alone, and you know how hot I am. They'd come begging and I was putting out, said their wives was dull as case knives."

Now the carnival did stop—no illusion this time. The men looked as if they'd swallowed hunks of ice; the women went limp, a riot of silence. The children behind masks of Hulk and Raggedy Ann and Frankenstein stood gazing. The grownups started talking and milling, smiling as if they were getting their pictures took. And all the faces looked more like masks than the masks themselves. Chanell pictured her own face too, her old mask, and knew she'd been just as ignorant and just as bigoted and just as hypocritical as the best and the worst of them. And if not for finding out she was French Creole she would still be.

Bell drove Chanell home, both shivering in short dresses while the car heater chuffed around their feet. Chanell could tell that

Bell expected her to begin crying any minute, but she didn't even feel like it.

"I guess I started everything all over again, didn't I?" Chanell laid her head back on the cold plush car seat and closed her eyes.

"I've got to think a minute." Bell stopped in front of the gym and punched the cigarette lighter in, stuck a Kool between her teeth, and waited for the lighter to heat up and pop out. She stuck the red coils of the lighter to the tip of her cigarette, took a long lip-puckering draw, and drove on, one hand on the wheel. Then she started laughing.

"Bell, wait a minute." Chanell sat up. "I didn't mean that I'd been with Pete, you know that. I ain't never been with none of 'um."

"Crazy!" Bell slapped Chanell's arm and turned in at the Baptist Church.

At Chanell's house, they got out, Bell snorting and stumbling up the stoop like a drunk. Chanell laughed too, though she couldn't think of a thing funny. She'd started another rumor, for sure, and now she might have to move, and she no longer wanted to.

Inside, Chanell lit the gas heater in the living room and sat on the couch, the green vinyl cold on the backs of her legs. Bell, still laughing with her eyes squinted, warmed before the purring level blue flames, her dress standing out on her tan-stockinged legs. The long black hairs under her nylons looked laminated.

"I feel like a fool," Chanell said. "Okay, what's so funny?" She was glad Bell wasn't mad, apparently didn't believe any of it.

Bell wiped her eyes on her puffy dress sleeve. "Well, just imagine what everbody's thinking."

"I tell you what, Bell, I hope they fuss and fight for a year. I oughta done worse. I oughta named names." Chanell laughed. It was all funny now.

"Yeah, what if you'd said, 'Linda Gay, hey, you and Joy Beth, I been sleeping with your men since . . .'" Bell couldn't finish for laughing. "And to top it off, here they got to worry about . . ." Chanell couldn't make out a word of what Bell was saying in that squeezed-tight voice. Bell wiped her eyes on her skirt with her mouth wide and moaning.

Chanell got up and crossed to the heater. "Bell, what's going on? Why'd all my customers come back? How come the women to suddenly turn friendly? What's going on?"

Bell reached down and scratched her panty hose, tried to talk but sounded as if she was choking. Sobering, she held up one hand to check her nails, her rings. Satisfied. "The truth?"

"Truth." Chanell held her breath.

"Another rumor's going round."

"Oh, no!"

"No, sugar." She caught Chanell's shoulder, speaking in her face. "Not about you."

"Well, what? Just tell me."

"It's going round that they's a bunch more in Cornerville that's got a little bad blood."

"Black blood?"

"Yes!"

"No!" Chanell walked to the couch and plopped, slapping her knees. "Who?"

"I don't know; they don't know. Could be me."

"You?"

"I don't care." Bell waved her hand down.

"But they do, right?"

"Yep."

"Bell, you old goat, you started that rumor, didn't you?"

"Nope," she said, laughing and swaying in her silly short dress. "Wish I had, though; wish I had sense enough to come up with something like that, 'stead of trying to whip asses all over Cornerville."

Sense, sense, Chanell thought. Archie Wall.

Chanell watched from the stoop as Bell left, the taillights of her Buick barely out of sight before Chanell took off inside and jerked on a pair of jeans and a sweatshirt and headed for Archie Wall's.

The sky was clear and star sharp, like air off ice, with a winy chill that sealed off the sour smells of summer. The kind of cold that opens up your head like an inhaler. A rooty smell of cooling earth.

Around the seams of the shades on Archie Wall's living-room windows, Chanell could see that same dim desk light burning green. Obviously, he seldom slept. Most people in Cornerville who didn't go anywhere watched TV and went to bed early.

"Archie Wall?" she called out from the porch.

His pot-bellied silhouette floated behind the drawn window shades, like Alfred Hitchcock's on the old TV mystery show. This time, he didn't peep out, he just opened the door. But as always, he brushed his hand across his waxen scalp.

Now that she was there, she didn't know where to start, and she felt ridiculous for calling out with such urgency, ridiculous for acting so familiar. Still, she hardly knew him.

"Betty Jean?" he said.

"I need to get the straight of a little matter, Archie Wall," she said.

"What's that, Betty Jean?" He walked to the desk, and she

followed, taking the chair that was beginning to feel like her own.

"Archie Wall, I heard about the new rumor."

He laughed—at least she thought he laughed—maybe he groaned. He reared in his chair. "Go on."

"No, you go on." She fingered a stack of papers before her. Ruled paper with small, level script in pencil. "Tell me the story of what you said—I know you did it—how come it all to work."

He held up one hand. "Hold on, Betty Jean. I ain't owned up to nothing." He smiled—she knew for sure that he smiled—a break in his smooth bland face.

"It had to be you, Archie Wall. Nobody but you could come up with something like that. Nobody else ain't got the sense."

"A bunch of folks wouldn't agree with you on that." He tried to hide a proud look, but his pupils tilted.

"They don't know you, Archie Wall, they really don't." She sat up, staring into his steadying eyes. She talked on, easier than she'd ever, ever talked to anyone, preacher or daddy or lover. "I see how part of it works, I do. I see how they all might get to wondering about their own blood and families. But why wouldn't they go check it out at Folks-Huxford? Just like Linda Gay checked on me."

He grunted. "And risk running into each other? Looking guilty?"

"Yeah, but . . ."

He did laugh then, right out loud, stretched lips that didn't belong on that reticent face.

"Talk to me, Archie Wall, talk to me. Tell what-all you think."

"Listen, Betty Jean." He sat forward. "They're all scared to look, scared of what they'll find. A sort of Golden Rule by their standards. They ain't for certain how they'd act in your shoes."

"You mean maybe they'd paint their houses purple?"

"They're afraid of what might come out. They don't know. In my experiences with them, though, they don't think all that much; they pretty much feel their way around. Mostly go by their senses." He stared off in a deep study, that jowly face losing its new glee.

"But Linda Gay? Archie Wall, Linda Gay's not scared of having bad blood. You know she's checked her own family out, maybe when she checked mine."

"Yeah, but maybe she's worried everybody'll think the rumor's true. Even if she can dispute it." He got loud, then low, as though arguing some case before a jury. "She knows the sin in the South is not having been born well. She knows how rumors spread—true or false—how rumor could ruin her."

"Like me."

"Yeah, like you." He stared right at Chanell with that turned-in gaze that made him appear to be staring at the tip of his nose. Then he went on talking about what he called research. Said he'd done a little book research at Folks-Huxford in Homerville, then some more on-the-spot research in Cornerville. How he'd gone to several old family and church cemeteries and the town cemetery near the river. Got to poking around family plots. "Betty Jean, you ever noticed that row of graves just inside the Simpson plot? The sunk-in ones right at the feet of Old Man Simpson and his wife?" He didn't wait for an answer, though Chanell was nodding her head. "Well, them wood markers and crosses is the Simpson slave graves. Old Man Simpson give 'um the same names and all."

"Yessir, so . . . ?"

Archie Wall was off by himself, sanding the desk with a sheet of writing paper. "Anyhow, I got to thinking about what-all went on away back, stuff I'd heard about slave masters having, you know, things to do with the slave women. Some of it I got from books; some of it from rumor. Run up with a old man over a hundred years old that owed me a favor, and he give me the facts about a bunch of well-known family men right here in Cornerville whose grandpappies messed with slave women."

"And he didn't think nothing of it, did he, Archie Wall?"

"Didn't make like it, no."

"But marrying a black woman would've been a whole nother matter, wouldn't it?"

"Is this my trial or theirs?"

"Ain't nobody's, Archie Wall, I'm just trying to get a handle on things, trying to figger how men work. And you're a man."

"Don't sound to me like no compliment."

"It ain't, in my estimation. You get it, though, don't you?"

"The contradiction?"

"Yeah."

"Don't forget, I'm an outsider." He drew his elbows back on the chair arms, then shimmed his stubby fingers over his paunch. "Anyhow, back to that genealogy business—call it history. A bunch of families around here is older than they think, got more history. I found a couple with more Negro blood than you. See, they know enough . . . they remember just enough history," he said, "to know it could be true, it could be them with Negro blood in their veins. They can't risk it."

"Did you threaten them, Archie Wall?"

"I did." He stared square at Chanell. "I did before and I'll do it again. And if this don't work, if they keep on shunning you, treating you like they've done, I'll tell which one's boot-legging, which one's evading taxes. Who killed the revenuers and who blew up the dip vats. Who bribed which judge, when and where. More bad blood than Negro blood."

"You'd do that for me, Archie Wall?" Chanell's body felt like ice melting. She thought she might cry, and thought Archie Wall might too—his face was slack, hands spread flat on the desk.

"All I'd have to do, Betty Jean, is let the word out—they know that. It'd spread by itself from mouth to blabbing mouth."

He went into another deep study, and Chanell knew if he ever did spread the word, it would be as much for himself as for her. For every wronged stranger to step foot in that little closed world of Cornerville. A place where you either become one of them or none of them, black blood or not.

"Makes you wonder, don't it, Archie Wall?"

He seemed to remember she was there, that they'd been talking, so used was he to talking only to himself. "About what?" he said.

Chanell hadn't meant anything when she said that, so to keep him from thinking she was loose-lipped like the rest, she said, "About life, what it is."

"It's what you find as you go, what you find where you're at. How you hold up under the weight of what comes down on you."

"Like that redheaded Cato fellow under the tractor?"

"Like Chanell Foster."

She laughed. "You mean Betty Jean, don't you, Archie Wall?"

"Six of one, half dozen of another."

JANICE DAUGHARTY is the author of *Earl in the Yellow Shirt*, *Necessary Lies*, *Dark of the Moon*, and a short-story collection, *Going Through the Change*. She is writer-in-residence at Valdosta State University near her home in south Georgia.